FIRST LIGHT

ISABEL JOLIE

CHAPTER 1

ali

Nym's angular ears faced forward. His lips curled over sharp white teeth, amplifying the guttural growl.

"At ease." The formidable warning halted. I ran my fingers through his fur, and his tail wagged. The knock on my solid wood front door persisted. Light streamed in through windows, and behind me, the swells of the ocean reflected the setting sun.

Wanting him near, I instructed, "Sit." After all, I didn't know these people well.

With quick steps, I hastened down the entrance hall. I glanced back once, double-checking Nym obeyed, before opening the front door to greet Poppy, the zealous, blonde extrovert who lived a few doors down. She used to be a bartender at the restaurant on the marina, and from what I could tell, she knew every single inhabitant on Haven Island, as well as many returning vacationers. Soon, she'd be opening her own restaurant. Her southern accent was stronger than most of the North Carolinians I'd met here, and she explained she had been born in Louisiana.

For the longest time, she and I had barely qualified as acquaintances. She'd wave if our paths crossed, and I'd wave back. People out here sometimes waved to total strangers, so the action did not constitute friendship. I thought of it as merely southern hospitality. Then I moved in a couple of houses down from her and her fiancé, Gabriel. She latched on to me like a pet project. In a different situation, I wouldn't think twice. I was sure we would've been fast friends.

"Hi." I greeted my neighbor with a wide smile, hoping it appeared genuine.

"Are you ready? I've got the cooler loaded." Poppy pointed a well-manicured nail at her red wagon with oversized rubber wheels.

"I am. I picked up some chicken tenders and made some brownies." I left her standing at the front door and hurried to the kitchen to gather my contributions.

"Oh, my word. Hello, doggie. Can I pet her? She's a German shepherd, right?"

Nym sat at attention, lips down, no growl. He wouldn't attack unless commanded.

"He's safe," I said as I pulled the cooler strap over my shoulder and lifted my water bottle off the counter.

Poppy bent down on her knees and rubbed all over him. His tail wagged and his tongue lolled out to the side, deceptively detached.

"What's her name? Or did you say he?"

"Nym. He's a boy."

"Such a gorgeous doggie. Where'd you get him?"

"My brother gave him to me." I shuffled toward the front door.

"Gabe has been talking about getting a dog. Is he good about keeping pace with you when you run?"

"The best." I held the door, waiting. She bowed before Nym, in no apparent hurry. "Do you run?"

"Good god, no. But Gabe does. He's been training for Iron Man. So he's always running. Or doing something. A dog might be good to help occupy his time. Do you know where your brother got him?"

"Nowhere close by. My brother lives in California. Ready?"

Poppy stopped scratching behind Nym's ears, and he held a single paw up, his sign that he wanted her to continue. I clucked my tongue, and his paw hit the floor.

"Oh, lordy. He did that because you clucked." Her long sundress swayed with her movement as she joined me at the door. Nym remained in position. Poppy cooed. "What a good little doggie."

"German shepherds are intelligent dogs. He's a great pet." Out of habit, I comforted said dog by promising, "I'll be home soon," before pulling the heavy door closed. "Where's Gabe?"

"He's already down there setting up the table."

Poppy shifted her cooler, making room for mine in the narrow wagon, and I glanced back at my house, mentally running through my departure checklist.

"Wait. I need to lock up."

"You lock your door?" Poppy asked with a mix of mockery and disdain. I understood. This island didn't allow cars. The speed around here was markedly slower, and a sense of safety shrouded the slower pace. People left bikes on racks without locks, and almost every golf cart had a key in its ignition, no matter where it was parked. Still, I needed to lock my door.

"One minute." I ran back up the four steps, opened the door, and punched in a code. The alarm didn't connect to the police station, but it would send out a shrill sound that I could hear from the beach. I twisted the lock and dropped the heavy key into my pants pocket. The outline shone through the thin cotton material of the capris.

Poppy gave me an inquisitive glance but lifted the wagon handle and tugged while rattling on about the weather and the chili recipe she found. On the path to the beach, she visibly strained as the oversized wheels settled into the sand.

"Here, let me help." I gripped the metal handle and put my weight into it.

Each month, on the night of the full moon, residents and vacationers gathered on East Beach for dinner in the sand. I'd watched for the last two months from my deck. Yesterday, when Poppy cornered me in the market, I'd been too tired and slow to think of an excuse.

Before us, a crowd of people congregated on the beach for Howl at the Moon. The sun set low to the west, over the island horizon. The intense heat of the summer day had drifted away, replaced by a warm summer night with a mild ocean breeze. Seagulls and pelicans flew nearby, and the occasional squawk pierced the hum of the crowd. Poppy frantically waved her arm in the air. Her fiancé, Gabe, smiled.

He stood near a circle of foldable chairs with a low collapsible table in the center. Standing with him were Luna, Tate, and Jasmine, a family I knew well. My edginess eased. I wouldn't count Luna or Tate as personal friends, but I'd been tutoring their adopted daughter Jasmine for well over a year, and we'd grown close. Luna worked as a scientist at the conservation center, and Tate was a lobbyist for an environmental group out of D.C. Tate adopted Jasmine, and when she arrived here, she had an extremely limited command of English. That was when he hired me.

Poppy headed over to Gabe and the others. The wheels sank further into the sand, and I tugged harder. A tall, attractive, bearded man approached, presumably to help me with the cart. He smiled and reached for the handle. Sunglasses blocked my view of his eyes.

"Here, let me help you."

None of the others paid us any mind. Poppy hugged Luna. Jasmine read a book while sitting in a chair, oblivious to any of the surrounding adults.

His warm hand covered mine, and I snapped it back, sending the handle down onto the sandy beach with a low thud.

"Sorry. I didn't mean to startle you."

"You didn't. I'm sorry, it's just, do you know these guys? I can't let you walk away with the food unless I get confirmation of identity," I joked. We were on a beach surrounded by dozens of families. The potluck dinner offered up twenty yards away was free. The man seemed harmless enough in his shorts and flip flops, but still, I didn't recognize him.

"Sorry. I thought you knew me. I've seen you around the island so often."

"You have?" I studied him more closely. He had broad shoulders. He wore an ironed button-down shirt that hung out over his shorts, untucked. A thick black watch with a face that could be used for SCUBA wrapped around a thick wrist, and he had a resident's tan.

"Wow. Way to maim a man's ego. I'm Logan." He thrust a hand out. "And yes, I'm friends with these guys. I'm glad you finally made it out for a good old-fashioned Howl at the Moon."

I accepted his offered hand. He shook mine with a firm grip, warm and friendly. A tingling sensation radiated from my palm, to my fingers, and along my forearm. I found it hard to raise my gaze, not that it mattered, because the sun reflected gold against those Wayfarer lenses.

"Poppy's been trying to get me to come all summer." It felt like an admission.

"It's a fun night." He let go of my hand and lifted the handle from the sand.

All around us families gathered in groups. A long set of narrow, eight-foot folding tables with navy plastic tablecloths held a mix of Crock-Pots and platters of food. Several kegs and coolers filled with ice and beverages circled the ends of the food tables. A line extended about fifteen feet back as people waited to sample the different kinds of chili and the random mix of casseroles, sides, and dips.

Poppy, as a soon-to-be restaurant owner, donated some food for promotional purposes, but she had told me that Gabe liked to have his own dinner set up in his own group. She'd laughed and said he didn't do well with lines. Plus, one time his favorite chili had been all eaten before he made his way through the line, and he'd had to eat a dried-out egg salad sandwich. He'd declared never again. She'd told me the story while I waited in line at the market to buy my groceries, and the cashier had laughed and asked her to tell Gabe hello.

Logan effortlessly pulled the wagon over the remaining stretch of sand, and I followed along. Luna wrapped me in a hug, then Tate and Gabe followed suit. After getting all the cordial niceties out of the way, I plopped into the chair next to Jasmine and tapped her leg. She looked up, and the dazzling white of her teeth shone bright.

"Cali. You came."

"What book are you reading?"

She lifted it up so I could see.

"Jane Austen? That's pretty advanced." When I first met Jasmine, she had a Level 1, borderline Level 2 English comprehension. She astounded me with how quickly she'd picked up English. If I were so inclined, I could write a case study illuminating the effects of language immersion based on her advances over the prior year.

"I watched the movie last weekend. It's on the summer reading list." The idea of her entering ninth grade made my throat tighten ever so slightly. I hoped I'd done the right thing by recommending she enter the US school system at that level. I didn't actually have a degree in education. Most of my work involved translations. I'd responded to Tate's job post on a whim. I didn't have the exact experience outlined in the job post, and when he hired me after a phone interview, I'd suspected I was the only applicant for the position.

"Are we still on for tomorrow? Did you get through the word problems?" I expected math would be her biggest challenge. We'd been working all summer. I planned on continuing to work with her each day after school. She could do the work, but I enjoyed seeing her. Our relationship had grown beyond that of student-teacher into friends. She checked the time on her wrist and closed her book.

"Nine o'clock. I'll see you then." Jasmine stood and picked up her bag.

"Where are you going?"

"Oh, I'm babysitting this evening. It's a vacationing family. I don't know them." She shrugged, like it was nothing. Like she didn't realize she was abandoning me.

"Do you need a refill?" Logan stood high above me, next to my chair.

"Nope, I'm good. Thanks." To my dismay, he sat down in the chair Jasmine vacated. I watched as she made her way over to her parents, presumably to say goodnight.

"What're you drinking?" Logan asked. I eyed him suspiciously, reluctant to dive into a conversation. He chuckled.

"Is it a secret?" he asked.

"It's water." I held up the solid metal bottle, offering proof I spoke the truth, even though he couldn't see inside.

"Well, there's plenty of bottled water in the cooler if you need more. Poppy said you live near her, but I see you down in the inner island. Do you work down there?"

"You see me?" I studied him again, puzzled because normally I thought of myself as good with faces.

"Yeah, riding around." He shrugged like it was completely normal to be observant. He had a commanding air, which contrasted with his friendly, easygoing smile and the leather flip flops. As I studied him, it hit me. He'd ironed all of his clothes, including his cargo shorts, loaning a bit of formality to an otherwise relaxed outfit. His hair clipped close around his head. Not in a buzz cut, but short.

"Wait." I snapped my fingers. "Is that beard new?"

He scratched his jaw, raised his sunglasses on his head, and grinned. "Yeah. I decided to grow it in. What do ya think?"

"That's why I didn't recognize you. You're the police chief on the island." On the island, they called it Public Safety, or at least that was what the vehicles combing the island were labeled, but it was just a different name for police.

"That's me." I'd received two photographs of him with background information. He'd graduated from West Point, and he'd been Special Forces. Then he'd spent nine years working in an Illinois police department. *Steer clear of him.* Erik didn't mince words.

"And you're Jasmine's tutor, right?" I nodded. I suspected every resident on the island knew me as Jasmine's tutor. "And you live three houses down from Gabe and Poppy? The green wooden house?"

"Yeah." My stomach swirled as he revealed, drop by drop, how much he knew about me.

"They said you're divorced."

"Yes." Across the circle of chairs, Poppy tilted her head back and laughed loudly, the sound barely rising above the hum of conversations and the crash of the surf. Several people I recognized as waitstaff surrounded her. I scanned the crowd for Tate and Luna. The sun had set, and while the bright moon lit the beach, the dark shadows made it difficult to see past the clusters of people congregating around us.

"I'm divorced too." He took a long swallow of his beer.

"Oh." I shifted. I hadn't known that about him. "Did you move here after your divorce?"

"Yeah. About two years ago. I've lived here longer than any of your crew." *My crew. Ha.*

"Where did Tate and Luna go?" I straightened my spine, hands on my lap, carefully scanning the scene. He pointed toward the public food table.

"Looks like they're surrounded by the interns."

Sure enough, several of the college-aged kids out on the beach every day during my walks circled them.

"You've got a great dog. I've seen you out running." The man did know a lot about me.

"Thanks."

"So, you moved here a year ago. From Seattle, right?" *How does he know this?* "University of Washington? I have some buddies who went there. How're you liking the East Coast?"

I gestured to my dry and itchy throat. "I'm not feeling well. I'm going to head home. Would you mind letting the others know?"

"Let me walk you back. Here, I'll get your cart."

"No." His stunned expression told me I must have responded too strongly, maybe shouted. "It's Poppy's cart. I need—" I stood and ran my hand across my forehead. It felt damp. I didn't have any business being here. I needed to go. "Thank you. Nice to meet you, Logan. See you around."

As my feet sank in the thick sand leading up to the dunes, away from the crowd, my brother's words haunted me. *For god's sake, Cali, don't get close to anyone out there. The less anyone knows about you, the better.*

CHAPTER 2

ogan

I WATCHED HER PASS THROUGH THE CROWD. SHE KEPT HER HEAD down and avoided eye contact, her arms folded across her front, shoulders hunched. *Fear?*

I scanned the surroundings. Kids played in groups, some running along and splashing the surf. One plump toddler fell, and her father scooped to pick her up, and she subsequently laid her head on his shoulder and sucked on her thumb. Chords of laughter punctuated the low hum of conversation. No one looked out of place.

She arrived by the public boardwalk entrance with Poppy, but she chose to go home along the beach, close to the dunes. No one followed her.

"Hey, you want another beer?" Gabe offered a cold, dark brown glass bottle with water droplets running down the side. He glanced down the beach, following my gaze, then smirked. "See something you like?"

"What's her story?" I took the beer from him and murmured a thanks.

"She's Poppy's friend. Prefers to be a loner, but Poppy won't have it. She's always dropping by, trying to spend time with her." My friend didn't look pleased.

I swallowed the cold ale, welcome on the warm summer night, while considering the now-empty stretch of beach toward her home. She cut off our conversation as if something had bothered her. I scratched my jaw, a new habit as I adjusted to the recent growth on my face.

"She's divorced. That's about all I know." Everyone knew that. People theorized that was how she could afford her beachfront home on a tutor's salary. Maybe. I didn't particularly care about her finances. But a divorce could explain her reclusive tendencies. After mine, I hadn't been in a communal mood.

"Where's her ex live?"

"No idea." Gabe turned his attention to watch his fiancée. She stood in the center of a circle of the crew that worked at the shops and restaurants. A young surfing instructor stood by her, gripping his side, laughing at something she'd said.

"How long ago did she get divorced?"

"I'm not sure. She's been a tutor for Tate and Luna for over a year, so at least that long. You thinking about asking her out?"

His question unsettled me. I hadn't considered asking her for a date. I hadn't considered dating anyone since arriving on the island two years ago, wounds fresh. If she arrived here in the same condition, then I understood her reclusive tendencies.

"If you want, Poppy and I could invite you both over for dinner. No guarantee she'd come. She's turned us down far more than accepted."

"What reasons does she give when she turns you down?"

"Oh, let's see…" He ran a hand through his hair as he considered the answer. I suspected he hadn't cared enough to listen to or remember the reasons Poppy provided. "Migraine. Busy with work."

"Tutoring?"

"Nah, she does more than that. She's a linguist. She speaks five languages. Even Arabic. According to Tate. Luna isn't really close to her. They've kind of remained distant. But Tate has a lot of respect for her. And Jasmine… those two are close."

I knew all about Jasmine. Heard about the adoption a few times when sitting at the bar at Jules. Unbeknownst to Tate and Luna, I'd even pulled Jasmine over one time for driving a golf cart underage. I didn't write her up. The other kids on the cart were laughing hysterically, and I would've written them all up. But Jasmine's silent tears were too much for me. She'd clearly been coerced into driving. And it wasn't like driving a golf cart at fourteen was a path to drug addiction or other felonies.

I searched the crowd for Tate.

"I doubt she'll be coming back," Gabe commented.

"Do you know where Tate is?"

"Nah, but knowing those guys, they probably headed back to the conservation center. I heard Luna say they were fully booked for the turtle watch. Tate usually goes with her."

"Hmm." I took another swallow of my beer, and Gabe pivoted to better watch Poppy. "How is she for a neighbor?"

Yes, my questions bordered on interrogation, but the dark-haired, timid woman piqued my curiosity.

"She's fine. The garbage guy seems to like her more than me."

"Say that again?"

"The garbage guy. Have I not told you about him?"

"No."

"The guy refuses to put my garbage can back in that little garbage shed we have. It's crazy. I've written notes. I paid the guy. Twenty dollars with one note. Thanking him for putting it back in the shed. Do you know what he did?"

I shook my head, mildly amused, pretty sure I'd heard the story before.

"Took my twenty. Left the can out in the driveway. No one else. Every other person on our entire street, he does it for them. Puts it back in the little house. Drives me fucking nuts. One day I was in my office, on the phone, and he looked up into the window and waved. He fucking waved. If I hadn't been on a call, I would have run off after him. That guy is my nemesis."

"So, he handles Cali's garbage can correctly?" I asked, steering us back to the topic of interest.

"Yeah. Everyone else on our street." He took a swallow of his beer, then angled the long glass neck toward Poppy. "You think that guy realizes she's taken, right?"

Having had a wife who cheated, I took his question seriously and observed. The guy who hovered near her was one of the surfers who sometimes lined up with us in the surf. He was a bit of an ass, often ignored right of way. Young, though, twenty-one. I'd checked his ID once when I found him and some friends out on the beach with a cooler of beer. He might be the kind of guy who would actually go after someone else's girl—for fun. But Poppy barely acknowledged him. Her attention was mostly directed at the waitstaff. She wiggled her fingers and directed a flirty smile at Gabe during a break in conversation. We might have been twenty feet away, but she was as aware of Gabe as he was of her.

"I don't think you have anything to worry about." I patted him on the back. His gaze remained glued on Poppy. "But as for Cali. Do you know what her schedule's like?"

"You do want to ask her out." His smirk annoyed me.

"I'm curious." Depended on where she was, post-divorce, but if she was still digging herself out of an emotional abyss, then dating wouldn't appeal to her. "I've seen her running before. Does she have a typical schedule? Early morning riser?"

"You planning on casually bumping into her?" Friendships had sparked under more unusual circumstances. Knocking on her door and asking her out on a date felt awkward.

"She looks like she does yoga. Does she go to the spa for their yoga classes?" I'd seen some of those classes on the beach before, too.

He gave an exaggerated sigh, signaling I'd met my Cali question quota. "I wouldn't know. Neither Poppy nor I take those classes. But I rarely see her out when I meet up with Tate for early morning surfing. It's not like I pay close attention. When we're out on the deck at night, though, her lights are usually off. Poppy's asked me before if I thought she might be out of town."

Interesting. I sat outside sharing beers in the evening in the two more popular areas on the island, and I never saw her. This town defined small. Technically, it was a village. Too small to qualify as a town. Admittedly, in my job, I needed to be more observant than anyone else here, but she stood out simply by being absent. She'd piqued my curiosity for a while.

"Hey, you want to go parachuting this Thursday? I booked a plane."

"Let me check my schedule. If I can work it out, sure." Gabe stayed busy, and he liked to push himself with high adrenaline activities. The guy spoke to my adrenaline-junkie soul. If it weren't for my knee injury, I'd still be Special Forces, with a very different life.

Poppy walked up and slid her arm around Gabe's waist. He kissed her forehead. A beat of jealousy tore through me. Once upon a time, I'd had that. I chugged back the rest of my beer, ready to call it a night.

"Logan here is interested in our neighbor." It took all of three seconds before Poppy connected the dots.

"Cali? Oh, my god. That would be awesome. I really like her. She's quiet. I think…" She paused long enough to convey hesitation, but in a split second she transitioned back to eagerness. "She's great. Do you want us to invite you both over to dinner?"

"Your man already offered. Thanks, but I think I'd rather go about it a little more independently. Any tips you got for me?"

"You know… I don't know her well. I try."

Gabe added, "She does."

"She's an introvert. She has a dated laptop she carries around."

"Since when do you know anything about computers?" Gabe asked.

"It's just thick. Like, the new ones are thin, you know? Her dog is beautiful."

I agreed. A gorgeous specimen of a German shepherd.

"My gut says she had a nasty divorce." I raised an eyebrow. "She doesn't talk about it. And I've tried. She changes the subject. It's sad. I mean, I could be reading into it, but I just wonder if maybe she really wanted kids and there's something there, you know. Maybe her marriage wasn't what she hoped, and now she's in her early thirties, and he feels like she won't be able to have kids. Or who knows, maybe she can't have kids, and that's why they got divorced, and she's completely heartbroken, and that's why she won't talk about it. When it comes to divorce, there are just so many options, you know? But I'm pretty sure whatever the case is, she's heartbroken."

Gabe and I both stared at her.

"But I don't know anything. That's all just me speculating. I was a bartender for years. I've heard all the worst divorce stories."

You haven't heard mine.

Gabe chuckled and affectionately pressed her up against his side. "She's got an imagination."

At the conclusion of the event, as the full moon lit the sky and the crowd applauded and howled, I went home the long way. All the lights were off in Cali's cottage as I drove past. Potted plants lined the edge of the stairs to her front door. A motion sensitive light came on as I crossed the edge of the pavers on her driveway, and I pressed the pedal forward.

Poppy had some amusing theories. Made me wonder what she'd assumed about me when I first arrived here. I hadn't been too social my first year or so, either.

Regardless, divorce was something she and I shared. And we also happened to be single in a ridiculously small town. A date didn't have to mean anything. In a worst-case scenario, both of us could benefit from gaining a friend. The trick would be dusting off my dating skill set. I'd been told it was like riding a bicycle. Something that came back naturally.

A date might be good for both of us. Sometimes a date was just a date, time spent between two people with a potential connection, and in this case, potentially similar history.

CHAPTER 3

ogan

"Jim Stenson called me yesterday." Chad, our village mayor, crowded my tiny office, towering over the single guest chair. His unusually stern demeanor set me on edge, as if a military superior had entered the room.

"Who?" I asked. The name was familiar…

"The governor."

"Is everything okay?" Chad had never mentioned the governor's name to me before.

"No. Not really." Chad stared at the wall, his lips a flat line, jaw flexed.

"Sit down and tell me about it." As Public Safety Director, it wasn't that unusual for me to hear about squabbles between landowners. I failed to see what the governor could possibly have to do with me. Maybe he'd require heightened security on an upcoming visit? Maybe he asked for a favor Chad didn't like? A Sunday phone call would likely be a favor. I wheeled my desk chair away from my laptop to the center of my desk so I could give Chad direct attention.

An older man, probably in his seventies, Chad had once been a business titan. I'd always suspected he ran for mayor because he didn't really know how to retire. He'd once told me it was essentially a volunteer position, and his only power lay in the ability to declare a pothole should be fixed, but I knew he took the job seriously.

He sat down, put his elbow on the thin armrest, and chewed on a thumbnail. His eyes narrowed, and I had the distinct impression he debated how to broach a topic with me.

"Just spit it out."

"We have to justify our existence."

"What?"

A look of disbelief crossed his facial features. "Have you heard of The Responsible Expenditure group?"

"No." It sounded like a committee, but we didn't really have many of those out here.

"Me neither. But Jim says they've got a lot of clout. Or they're getting attention. Even on a national level. Lots of Facebook shares. It's like a government watchdog kind of group. Anyway, they're sharing reports with claims that more is spent on safety in wealthy areas than poor areas, and I guess Haven was picked as an example. He said it's getting a lot of steam. He wants us to provide a full report of the kinds of things we do, justify our staff."

"Wouldn't that be in the yearly report we do for the community?"

"No. We're coming up on an election year. Jim needs more. It's bogus. Most of our budget is funded by the county. But if the state pulled everything…" He rested his thumb and index finger on the bridge of his nose and closed his eyes. "It feels like we're preparing for a hostile board meeting." He opened his eyes. "How much experience do you have in hostile meetings?"

"Hostile how?" I'd faced heat in Chicago, but this time my actions weren't on the line. And he couldn't be talking about the same thing.

"As in they want your entire department removed."

"They want to get rid of Public Safety?"

"Crazy, right? I don't know. I'm never on the Facebook. Hardly watch the news these days. The *Journal* is about all I skim, and that's out of habit. I don't know if Jim is… I don't know, but I'm going to help you with the report he needs, okay?"

"Okay."

"I'm going to put together a bullet list of the kinds of information I want. You send it to me, and we'll work through it. I think it's best if we get this to go away. I don't want Haven highlighted as some resort area for the white elite."

Years of military experience prevented me from rolling my eyes at that. This island had a lot of strengths, and the year-rounders were good people, but diversity hardly ranked as a strength. Still, the village had a streamlined team. As far as town budgets went, we weren't excessive. I didn't know how we ranked in the state.

I stood when he did and reassured him, "I'll be on the lookout for your email. Will get the data to you as quickly as possible."

I followed him out into the narrow hall. "You know, I

thought you were coming in to tell me about some teenagers doing something dangerous, like speeding on golf carts." Given the speed limit on the island maxed out at eighteen miles an hour, and most golf carts didn't possess a speedometer, much of what qualified as speeding remained subjective.

"Why would you think that?"

"Because those are the complaints I usually receive."

He grimaced. "Pull out your emergency preparedness deck. Also, see if you can get in with Julie and get her IT expense. Cybersecurity. That's a part of everybody's budget these days, important given some of the high-net-worth people who spend time out here. Think about justification of VIP protection. But also theft prevention. You get where I'm going? Think along those lines. I'll send that email in a bit."

He pulled out his phone and tapped away on it as he shuffled out the door. The sunlight coming through the window shone brightly on his scalp and the surrounding brown age spots.

As I watched him exit the building, I couldn't help but wonder how serious of a threat this was. Most likely, this so-called heat posed the most danger to his golfing pal's reelection than to anything here on the island.

I returned to my office and placed a call.

"Matt. It's Logan. Do you have a minute?" Matt worked for the NSA and had been in my class at West Point. We'd gone into the army together. Our career paths diverged, but we'd always stayed in touch. We hadn't lived in the same state in over a decade, but he was like a brother to me. And given his role in D.C., and his role in finding me this position when I needed time to decompress—his words, not mine—I owed him the update.

"A brief one. About to enter a meeting."

"The governor called our mayor this past weekend. There's apparently public pressure to control town budgets. Lower them. I suppose also to ensure an even allocation of tax dollars across all communities."

"Groups always fight over money."

"I've been tasked with defending Public Safety's existence on the island."

"That's illogical. Each county has their own budget based on tax revenue."

"But the state, I guess the focus is on distribution of state funds?" I hated politics.

"It's probably election-year bullshit. The need for you on that island has never been greater."

"Why?"

"I can't say more on an unsecure line. I've gotta run."

As I checked the phone to confirm he disconnected the call, a text came through.

Risk of rip tides elevated.

I sent out a quick notice to the team.

Raise red flags. Rip tide risk. Shift to heavy beach patrol.

Twenty-four hours a day we had between three to six officers on duty, but it wasn't enough to be everywhere. We also didn't offer lifeguard service on the beach. But we stepped in to warn people of unexpected dangers, like rip tides or sharks. The biggest danger lay in tourists who weren't familiar with the ocean and didn't know what conditions to be wary of. I made a mental note that I'd have to put beach safety in Jim's report—and mitigation of legal risk. The US was nothing if not a litigious society.

I hopped on the public safety ATV and headed out to East Beach to check conditions. It was high tide, and the ocean narrowed the stretch of sand. I lumbered along, keeping a careful eye out for sand shovels and buckets, towels or anything else the big rubber tires might trounce over. I focused primarily on the shoreline, the direction of the waves and the swimmers, but I took a second glance at the green beach cottage, nestled back beyond the dunes. I could see only the shingled roof and the top floor of the home from the sandy shoreline.

The swirl of the sea foam told the tale of strong current. Most parents had called their kids in close, recognizing the powerful undertow. One father stood two feet in, yelling at a child jumping wake that the current was too strong and to come closer in. The surf school sat around in foldable chairs, munching on sandwiches.

Farther down the beach, an attractive, fit woman with a white sports bra jogged at a steady clip with her long-haired dog keeping pace directly at her side. Her white top set off a deep tan, and her straight black ponytail swung from side to side. As she drew closer, I prickled with recognition. *Cali.*

The noon sun, high above, beat down directly overhead. My thumb slipped off the ATV gas, and I slowed to a stop.

She dropped to a walk as she entered the more crowded section of East Beach, checked her wrist, and wiped sweat from her brow. Her chest heaved as she sucked in air. Her jog bra cupped perfectly proportioned breasts. My gaze fell to her trim waist, flat belly, and ridiculously short jogging shorts, then down those lean, long legs. She leaned over one leg, stretching her calf and thigh muscles. I sped up, seeing my chance.

"Nice day for a run," I shouted over the hum of the motor engine and the crash of waves.

She placed her hand on her forehead, sheltering her deep brown eyes from the overhead sun, and a slow smile spread as recognition dawned. The upward curve of her lips struck me as a good sign.

"Not too hot. You out checking conditions? I saw they raised the red flag."

I nodded and set the brake on my ATV. I hopped off and walked up to her, bending down to greet her dog, who eyed me warily. I held out a hand for him. His dark eyes tracked my movement. I glanced up at Cali, questioning.

She reached down and scratched between the dog's ears and muttered something to him. The tip of his nose pressed into my palm. I scratched behind his ears, like she had, and his tail wagged.

"He likes you."

"Are you surprised?" She sounded surprised. The bright sun impeded my upward view of her facial expression.

"No. But he is a good judge of character. If he growls at someone, I listen."

"Do you run every day?" Beads of sweat ran down her chest, and I imagined it ran between her breasts. I forced my gaze up to her face and to her shiny, thick black ponytail.

"I jog at lunch to get Nym out of the house and give him some exercise. I've got to get back. Nice to see you."

"I should get back to my rounds." I glanced at my ATV, swallowed, pushed down some unruly nerves, and asked, "Hey,

I was going to ask you. Would you like to go out sometime? For dinner?"

"Oh. Ah, thank you, but now isn't a good time."

"I didn't mean right now." She fidgeted and angled her body toward the green house on the hill. "I mean if you're not—"

"I'm sorry." Her gaze remained downward as she added, "It was nice to meet you."

She rushed up the beach, and I called out to her retreating back, "Cali." She stopped, once again shielding her eyes from the sun as she spun to hear me. "We can hang as friends. Us single divorcees need to stand by each other."

Her plump lips curled ever so slightly, and I thought I saw a tilt of her chin, maybe a tiny nod. "Sure. I'll see you around." She spun back toward her house with Nym at her side.

Shot down on my first attempt at a date, post-divorce. I could hear my platoon in the back of my head howling with laughter. The thing was, I wasn't hitting on a random girl in a bar. The island was tiny, and off season lurked in our future. I'd see her around.

I completed my beach patrol, watching the waters, with my thoughts on the dark-haired mystery. Divorce was an ugly thing. I lived it and bore the scars. I wasn't blowing smoke when I offered her my friendship. She might simply need to find her way out of the pain. I knew something about that.

CHAPTER 4

ali

THE WHIMPER CUT THROUGH THE MARSH SYMPHONY, AND I stopped short, searching for Nym.

"Nym. Here."

Another whimper cut through the air. A chill swept over me as I circled, searching the low-lying ferns, past the grasses lining the marsh water. Crickets and frogs chattered continuously, immune to my presence. My breathing quickened.

The tips of his ears shone above the grasses. I exhaled loudly, relief pouring out.

"Nym! Here."

His head bowed down, out of sight, then up, then out of sight, then up. He held his right paw suspended in the air, never allowing it to touch the ground.

"Oh, Nym. What did you do, baby?" I rushed over to him and felt down his leg. I snapped my hand back as something cut into it. "Ow."

He stood, obedient as ever, but instinctively jerked as I returned to his leg and his paw. Visible sand spurs dotted his left leg.

"Oh, baby," I groaned. "You're eaten up in them." I sat down, trying to get a closer look at his paw so he wouldn't have to limp home. I couldn't see through the thick black fur, but I could feel. Several thorny pieces were bound down into the curves of his paw. With care, I dug my thumb against one. A sharp sting punctured my finger.

"Ow." A droplet of blood oozed off the pad of my thumb. I needed light and scissors to dig the burrs out. The evening dusk had set over the marsh, and nestled in the woods, I couldn't see the culprits to effectively work at them.

"Okay, boy. This is what we're going to do. I'm going to carry you."

He weighed in at sixty-five pounds. I wrapped my arms around his waist and lifted. My back ached, and I couldn't right myself. He squirmed, and I gave up, gently setting him back down on the ground.

"So, that didn't work. All right, let's see how you do limping. I'm so sorry, boy. We've got such a long walk back."

Nym bobbed along behind me on the narrow path, and I flinched every time he whimpered. At this slower pace, I estimated we had about a forty-five-minute walk in front of us once we made it onto the paved road. A sense of helplessness weighed down. I had a phone in my bag. But I didn't feel close enough to anyone to call and ask to come out and help. Luna, Tate, and Jasmine had gone into Wilmington for shopping and then dinner. And because of my stupid brother, I'd kept everyone else at arm's length.

Nym's whimper hurt. Me maybe more than him. I knelt down to my baby boy and scratched below his ever-alert ear.

"It's okay. We're going to get through this. I promise you. We're survivors. It's gonna be tough. We've got a long walk in front of us. But we're going to make it home."

His brown eyes conveyed trust. I patted his head and got an idea. I bent down and picked up his front half, like I sometimes did when I jokingly tried to get him to dance with me at home. Only once or twice had I done it. He wasn't the type of dog who played around.

"Let's see if I hold your front half, if it seems easier to walk on your back legs."

He took a step forward and faltered. I bent over to lower his front body to give him a more natural position. From behind me, the faint sound of wheels on pavement alerted me to a golf cart approaching. I edged us over a bit, although any cart had room to pass without me doing so.

"Do you need help?" I instantly recognized the deep, husky voice. The same voice I'd heard in my head over and over for the last however many days since he asked me to dinner and I gave the world's most dimwitted response. I gently lowered Nym to his one good front paw and straightened my back, swiping back the hair that fell across my face.

"Hi," I breathed. In the dim light of the woods, he wore no sunglasses, and the creases between his eyebrows relayed his silent question. "He got wrapped up in sand burrs. Some are in his paw."

"Those things are vicious." He grimaced. He got off the cart and came over to look for himself. Nym eyed him suspiciously.

"I don't think he'll hurt you, but he's in pain. I wouldn't recommend grabbing his paw right now." Nym qualified as beyond well-trained. He'd had eighteen months of training in Germany. But still. If he got angry, I'd always worried the switch could flip. Erik selected him.

Logan's hand moved forward, inches from Nym's paw when a low growl reverberated from deep within his rib cage. Logan withdrew and straightened.

"Maybe we should get him home. Then see what we need to do. Hopefully, we can get those burrs out. The vet only works from the island one day a week, I think on Thursday. If he needs to, though, we can always bring him over to Southport." He scratched his beard thoughtfully. "Do you think you can get him onto the back seat?"

"Let's try it." I liked that idea a lot more than the alternative of Nym whimpering.

Nym hopped up as directed. He sat on his haunches, paw in the air. I put my arm around him and stroked his soft fur. Logan drove slowly. We talked about the weather and the waves. Typical island conversation.

When he stopped the cart in my driveway, Nym jumped off the cart before either of us could assist. I followed him up the steps and keyed in the code to turn off the house alarm, then pulled the key out of the wristlet I carried with me on walks and unlocked the deadbolt, then unlocked the doorknob.

I glanced up long enough to observe the quizzical expression on Logan's face. My security system stood out as unusual, but I couldn't exactly hide it with him standing right beside me.

I opened the door wide for Nym and Logan to enter. Our

motion automatically turned on the entry and overhead den lights.

Blood from Nym's paw dripped onto the light pine floor.

"He's bleeding." *Shit.* I rushed to the kitchen and snatched some paper towels. Logan entered as I ran the paper bundle under the tap.

"Do you have scissors?"

"Yes." I slid open a narrow kitchen drawer and handed them over.

"Do you think we can get him near a light? A lamp light? Or can you hold your phone's light over him while I try to get the burrs out?"

"At the kitchen table." I pointed at the empty set of four chairs as I dashed into the den and yanked at a lamp's cord, unplugging it from the wall with one swift tug. I set it on the edge of the kitchen table and plugged it in. The overhead kitchen light lit the entire room well, so it didn't feel necessary to me, but if he wanted to take the lead on removing the sharp objects, I planned to let him.

He lifted the lamp and set it on the ground, then called Nym. Ever obedient, he limped to him.

"I may need you to hold his side, comfort him, calm him down. Say whatever you need to say to set him at ease."

"Okay."

He lifted the lampshade and held it over the paw. I couldn't see what he did, but in less than sixty seconds he held up the offenders coated in black fur.

"I think that's the worst of it," he continued, combing over Nym's fur, periodically slicing chunks of fur to remove more of the additional sharp objects. I held up one long, sharp point, almost an inch long.

"These are no joke."

"No kidding. One reason you don't walk through tall grasses barefoot." His hands stroked all along Nym's fur, and I stifled my shock when Nym licked his hand.

"I think that's his way of saying thank you."

Logan grinned but remained focused, searching throughout his fur for any more offenders. Satisfied he'd gotten them all, he stood and set about cleaning up after himself.

"You don't need to clean. I've got it. Thank you. I really appreciate it. You were great. I…"

My phone vibrated on the counter. The noise grabbed my attention—and Logan's. I tugged at my hair, setting it behind my ears. My cheeks warmed at the awkwardness in the room. Social situations always set me off. Should I offer him a drink? Did I escort him to the door? What would be expected?

I unzipped the tiny bag and pulled out my phone.

"You use a BlackBerry? I haven't seen one of those in ages."

"Yeah," I commented as I read the text, letting his dig slide. BlackBerry smartphones were the most secure, and my brother insisted I use one. Although I had an iPhone, mostly for apps and playing around. I always kept my BlackBerry on in case my brother needed to reach me.

24.22.0.24.26.9.22.21.6.15

My brother and his codes. Knowing I'd have to decipher his code later, I dropped the phone down on the counter, and it clattered against the tile.

"Is there a problem?"

"No. It's just work." Logan stepped closer to the counter, and I flipped the phone over, screen down. "I'm sorry. I would invite you to have a drink or something, to thank you."

"Hey, I understand. No problem. So, you work, in addition to the tutoring you do?" He leaned against the counter and crossed his corded and tanned arms.

Logan's casual pose and his sexy smile didn't convey interrogation. Getting to know someone required asking questions. I ran my fingers along my scalp, hating my brother for being right, because these little benign bits of information were what he didn't want me sharing. But, then again, Logan was a good guy. He cut lethal sand burrs from my dog's fur. *Be smart with what you share.*

"I do some contract work. Plus, I take on translation projects. Mostly for books."

I sensed he wanted to ask more questions, and while I trusted him, I didn't want to risk upsetting Erik. My brother had enough on his plate. He worried too much about me as it was. I stepped toward the front door, willing Logan forward.

"I understand you've got work to do, but I'd like to take a rain check on that drink. If you were serious." I swung the door open, avoiding his gaze, hoping he didn't perceive me as rude.

"No pressure. I'm divorced, too. I get it. You're not ready to date yet. But I seriously think you, me, and an old lady who lives on the marsh are the three single people on the island. And I don't mean single like that means we need to get together. But... friends can be helpful when you're coming out of the pain of a divorce. Trust me."

"You're a nice guy, but..." I said it more to myself, but he shoved his hands in his pockets, and his shoulders sloped, lending a bashfulness to his stance. My insides twisted and pulsed as his hesitant eyes sought my direct gaze. He anticipated my no, but he faced it head on. I planned to politely decline, but instead, what came out was, "Sure, you're on for the drink."

As he walked out the door, his chocolate brown eyes once again sought direct contact. "I'm going to hold you to it."

"Just let me know when." I forced myself to look him in the eye as I said it, even though uncertainty that I'd do any such thing prevailed.

"Hey, wait…" He held out his iPhone to me. "Enter your number in." I stared at the device. "So I can reach you. So we can coordinate that drink."

Right. I accepted the phone and tapped away, entering the number for my iPhone and only my first name, Cali. When I was in grad school, I had many friends. Even attractive male friends. A drink didn't have to mean anything at all. *I can be careful.* I'd never do anything that would endanger my brother.

As I closed the front door and clicked the two locks, a low rendition of Bob Marley's "Three Little Birds" played. I smiled. Mom. I'd picked that ring tone for her because she used to dance with me to that song. I opened the drawer and pulled out my iPhone, and the beat got louder until I slid the bar to answer.

"Cali, did you get my photos?" Mom sent photos and memes and all kinds of fun things to my iPhone. She, of course, didn't know about my BlackBerry. She could never know all of Erik's safety precautions. If I followed all of his precautions, I wouldn't keep the phone on. He believed it was best to keep trackable devices off unless in use.

"I haven't checked yet. I'll check once I hang up. Unless, do I need to check now?"

"Oh, no. But do look. I got the best photo of a hummingbird eating from the feeder I hung over by the peony bushes."

"With your phone?"

"Yes. You won't believe it. And to think I lugged that heavy camera around for all those years."

"You're a photographer. It's hard for me to imagine you being satisfied with photos on a phone."

"Right? But this phone does incredible things." Mom recently upgraded her phone to the modern era. It had been a joyride. "I'm preparing for the future. You know, when I need to photograph those grandbabies." *Right.* "Have you heard from your brother?"

"I have." Very recently. His most recent request stared back at me.

"We saw him last night."

What? "He was in Seattle?"

"No, he's so busy these days. We met up with him for dinner in Portland. He had these circles under his eyes. He's working too hard. I can tell. When you talk to him, how does he sound to you?" *Like a little shit.*

"Like Erik. He doesn't say much." *Once I rip into him, he won't be saying much at all.*

"Your dad is so proud of him."

"Uh-huh." *If only he knew the truth about his perfect son.*

"Did you say something?"

"I just agreed."

"He's proud of you too. You know that, don't you?"

"Of course, Mom."

"You're amazing. I could never learn all those languages. And now you've taken on so many clients. I saw that book you translated on a shelf in Barnes & Noble last weekend. I forgot to tell you."

"*The Joys of Baker Holly?* In French?"

"Oh, no. It was in English. But it's the book you translated into French, right?"

"Yep. That's the book. Cool. So, tell me about that pottery class you're taking."

After hanging up, with me promising once again I'd come to visit soon, I powered up my laptop to read my perfect brother's request. If Mom and Dad knew how in over his head he'd gotten, they wouldn't be gushing. But they didn't know, because I'd helped him keep his secrets. That shit owed me an explanation. He'd told me it wasn't safe for me to visit Mom and Dad…yet he did it? If he wasn't a Jujitsu master, I'd strangle him the next time I saw him. I read through the little turd's text from an unidentified number. Most likely another burner phone. I replied with a snarky, not completely in code response…

BITE ME.

SINCE I NEEDED MORE PROCESSING SPEED THAN I HAD HERE, I SET Nym up on his bed with a kiss to the top of his head, gathered my laptop, turned my phone off, locked up the house, and under the cover of night, slipped out the basement door.

CHAPTER 5

ogan

"Okay. I think we're in a good place. I had Patrice retrieve the annual budget numbers. I like this IT bit you put in the deck. Cybercrime. Nice touch." Prepared for Chad to drone on, I relaxed back in my chair and tapped my index finger on the desk. The time count on my phone showed twenty-seven minutes. "All right. I think it's good. I drive to Raleigh this afternoon, and then I'm playing the back nine with Jim tomorrow afternoon."

"Are you planning to leave the deck with him?"

"Yeah. I'll talk him through it on the course. Get a feel for how serious this matter is. How much pressure he's getting. You know, he's got so many advisors right now as he preps for the election. They're all warning him about different interest groups. It's got to be hard as hell to know who to listen to, who has good data."

"Have they started polling yet for the election?" The election was over a year away. I didn't follow politics. I preferred the bipartisan stance of the military. We had a mission—to protect and serve. If you focused on the mission, the rest became noise.

"I'm sure they have. This country is so divided. Every election is like a bloodbath these days."

"Well, let me know if you need anything else. And Chad?"

"Yeah?"

"For god's sake, don't beat him tomorrow."

"You don't really think he expects to beat me, do you? I play golf every damn day."

"If you win, don't talk smack."

"I would never."

"Bye, Chad."

I hung up and scanned my to-do list. Returning Matt's call was the last indoor thing I needed to do. Items on my list fell into one of two columns, indoor or outdoor. Back in Chicago, it wasn't like this. The open office space with desks back-to-back didn't feel claustrophobic. In homicide, we spent too much time out of the office. Here on Haven Island, my windowless office could suck the life force out of someone. But outside, the breeze blew and the waves crested. I dialed Matt's number, and he picked up after one ring.

"Hi. Thanks for calling me back." Background noises filtered through. A distant siren, rustling, heavy breathing.

"Are you exercising?"

"Ha. No. I'm headed into the Pentagon. I parked in an overflow parking lot."

"So that's you walking?"

"Shut it. We can't all take a cushy island job and spend hours a day outside."

"You know you took an oath to maintain top physical condition. Getting winded while walking from a parking lot—"

"I only have a second to talk. Have you noticed anything strange out there?"

"Like what?"

"Anything suspicious? Internet going out for no reason?"

"Spotty Wi-Fi is our normal."

"I need to pay you a visit. I want to pick your brain. Is next week okay?"

"Any time, Matt. It's not like I'm going anywhere."

"I'm going to have my assistant coordinate. He'll be in touch. Senator Gardner—" Then the line fell silent as he disconnected our call, clearly to address the senator in front of him. Our days couldn't be more different.

I checked my watch. By my estimate, Cali would be on her daily run. I didn't want to be a stalker. I figured a casual run-in, a simple wave, would be a good way to keep the lines of communication open. My phone vibrated.

Shark attack. South Beach. Close to Shoals Club. Ambulance dispatched.

Shark. I broke out into a run, and my pulse raced as if I'd been running for thirty minutes, not seconds. The fire engine siren fired off at an ear-deafening decibel. I climbed into the Public Safety pickup, flipped the sirens on, and slammed down on the accelerator. In two years' time, we'd never had an attack. A couple of sightings, but never an attack.

Near the public beach access, a crowd gathered around. I

arrived as the EMTs raced across the wooden plank to the beach. One slower-moving EMT carried the gurney, and I ran up behind him, lifting the end. He glanced back, and I shouted, "Go!"

The onlookers broke apart at the sight of the EMTs, and several waved frantically in the air. They backed away, and I hunted for the victim. A young pre-teen male lay on the sand with bright red blood gushing from his leg. Eyes wide, in clear pain, his skin color remained strong. It didn't look like he'd lost too much blood. Yet. The EMTs bent over his leg for a careful examination, and I stepped past the spectators, scanning the ocean.

An older man I recognized as a year-rounder stood nearby, and I asked, "Did you see it?"

He shook his head but pointed out across the waves. "It went that way. Tom saw it. Said it wasn't that big, but bigger than what we normally see." He raised his eyebrows with a glance back at the boy. "Clearly."

About forty yards out, a narrow fin rose above the dark water. I called Jay, an officer on my team. "Bring out megaphones. We're clearing the beach for the rest of the day."

"I didn't think we could legally tell people to get out of the water." Jay didn't mean to be argumentative. He simply relayed his understanding of our state's law.

"No one here knows that."

"But—"

"Jay, bring the megaphones. If anyone complains, we'll tell them we're strongly encouraging people to stay out of the ocean for the rest of the day."

"You got it, boss."

Directly in front of us, no swimmers braved the waters. But

farther down the beach, I could see two kids jumping waves. I charged toward them, waving my arms at the kids and the parents. The parents lounged in chairs, and the woman had a baseball cap pulled over her forehead.

"Come on out of the water, kids," I shouted. They came on out, the youngest pulling a Boogie Board behind him.

"What's the chance of two shark attacks in one day?" The man remained seating in his chair, legs sprawled out, feet buried in the sand.

"Given there's a shark swimming about forty yards out right now, while I can't give you a percentage, I'd say it's possible. But if you don't mind if your kids lose a limb, by all means, let them stay in the water."

His wife shifted in her chair and raised her ball cap.

"There was a shark attack?"

"Yes, ma'am. Right up the beach."

The flashing lights could be seen farther back, over the dunes, but the sirens had been turned off. Her kids approached.

"Someone got bit?"

"Yes. I recommend you remain out of the water. At least for a while. We saw a fin moments ago, not too far away."

The boys dropped the board and ran up the beach to the crowd, no doubt hoping for a view of blood.

As I continued down the beach, scanning for swimmers, I picked up my cell and spoke to Siri, sending out a command to the entire Safety Patrol team.

"All officers to report to South Beach, east end. Beach patrol until sundown. We are closing the beaches. I repeat, swimmers not allowed for the rest of the day."

A distant mechanical whir sounded, and I searched the sky. A navy blue helicopter rose above the tree line.

The rest of my day passed in a whir of shouting directions and answering phone calls. Every news station on the East Coast and some as far away as California called with inquiries about the shark attack. The communications director wrote up a press release detailing the limited information we had available, and that helped, but it didn't slow the calls. Especially since that blasted news helicopter located two sharks off the coast and hovered over, presumably tracking and filming the animals.

Ever since sharks had taken to mating off the coast of North Carolina, we'd known our day would come. Mostly, we saw harmless sand sharks. Small ones that couldn't do much more than tissue damage. At a nearby beach, a couple of years ago, a swimmer lost a limb.

As the sun set and the risk of people swimming lowered, we wrapped up beach patrol, and I returned to my desk. The stream of email in my inbox approached insanity. Beside my keyboard, a yellow notepad filled with our communication director's scribble listed out all the people awaiting a return phone call. Mostly media who wanted to get a quote. Chad's name topped the list, and she'd circled his name and put three stars by it.

Hours later, I powered down my desktop computer. My neck ached from craning over the keyboard, and a tight pull pinched when I turned my head right or left. A dull headache pulsed below my brow. I popped two aspirin and called it a day.

I climbed into my personal cart, eager to head home and crack open a cold beer. The white of the moon shone through the winding tree branches of the inner island. Silvery Spanish moss hung in clusters. The song of the crickets filled the salty night air. The headlights on a lone cart approached. Out of habit, I checked out the passenger as we crossed the divided road.

Cali's black hair, tied up on top of her head, came into view. Her tan skin boasted an effervescent glow in the moonlight. I floored my cart to the next crossover and whipped around. The faint red of her brake lights illuminated the dark and turned onto an unmarked road.

I floored it, then slowed, searching for cart lights. I scanned Market Alley, but all the shops were dark. I turned and drove down the adjacent Purveyor's Alley. Then out of curiosity drove down Edward Teach Wind and hunted for her along a few of the small office buildings. No headlights, no brake lights anywhere. She must have been flying. I grinned. So, she's a little speed demon. Of course, a speed demon on a golf cart is a different thing than in a car. Still, she had to be nearby. So, I texted.

Hey, you just passed me. Where'd you go? Want to meet up for that drink?

CHAPTER 6

ali

T HE HEAVY DOOR ROUNDED THE TRACK WITH A DULL, LOW rumble, gathering speed as it descended to the ground. The plastic bumper hit the concrete floor with a thud. Zero light penetrated the walls. I sucked in my breath and reached an arm out, feeling blindly for the switch. Logically, I knew I was in here alone. This building was safe. But one too many horror movies had me half-expecting a masked man with an unwieldy machete.

My fingers rubbed the plastic lever, and bright lights lit the narrow stairs. The light confirmed my solitude. A dirty shovel hung on the far wall, along with some rakes and buckets I'd purchased from the hardware store per Erik's direction to make this look like a storage shed, should any curiosity seekers decide to check it out. My golf cart filled the middle of the concrete floor.

Erik purchased this metal-sided building shortly after I accepted the tutoring position. Utilities and water, garbage disposal, all the services that keep a town running were situated on this strip. There were also a few small businesses located on parallel streets, the kinds of businesses that required an office space.

At the time of purchase, there had been one window on the top floor, but Erik had had his team seal the window. The upstairs housed servers and they needed a temperature-controlled environment. And that was how I came to spend hours of my life in a windowless room surrounded by hardware cages.

I climbed the stairs, and as the upstairs floor came into view, I scanned for feet. *Cali, if someone broke in, you would've been alerted. Get a grip.*

I wiped my sweaty palm on my thigh. Back in Seattle, I hadn't been so jumpy. I hated the nervous worrier I'd morphed into, looking over my shoulder, envisioning a gun or ski mask–wearing villain at every turn.

All the servers hummed along, a series of lights on machines underneath black wired cages. The machines took up one wall of the room. The opposite wall featured a small kitchenette with a microwave, sink and a counter. I added water to a pot and set the plate to boil. My desk, a kitchen table, a foldout sofa, and a beanbag completed the rest of the space.

As I waited for the water for my tea, I entered my login on my computer, and a wall of monitors came to life. I set my BlackBerry on my desk and clicked back to my brother's text.

24.22.0.24.26.9.22.21.6.15

I stared at the number and rapped my nails against the desk, waiting for my tea. If it weren't for my brother, I wouldn't be here. I'd be back home, with my friends. Living a happy, carefree life in a small craftsman rental. My runs would be along the waterfront. But no, my twin pulled me into his mad world. Tiny bubbles ascended in the glass pot. As I waited for the green light, I thought back to the first day it became apparent Mom wasn't just being overly concerned.

"HEY, WONDER TWIN, GUESS WHAT?"

Erik barely shifted, his back hunched over as his fingers flew over the keyboard, his head forward like a turtle. I tugged a chunk of hair.

"Ew. When was the last time you showered? Grease isn't a good look for black hair." He swatted my hand away and resumed typing. I plopped down in a nearby beanbag. "I came by to give you a heads up. Mom and Dad are getting serious about kicking you out of the house."

The flurry of fingers on keys continued.

"Erik? Did you hear me?"

"They'd never. And you know it." Given they'd prefer we remained home until we married, he had a point. Which was why it was so extraordinary they'd consider this step.

"I dunno. I also never thought the day would come they'd see me as the good kid." He continued to type, and I crawled forward on my hands and knees to get a better look at his screen, expecting to see an interactive game. A machine gun and explosions. Zeitgeist Battle or Overwatch. Instead, the black screen held code blocks. I sat my butt on the floor, closer to Erik, at an angle where I could see both his profile and screen.

"What're you working on?"

"Cecilia. Fucking stop. Get out."

"Ouch. Full name usage. Pissy, pissy." He kept typing. "So, you're okay if they kick you out?" If Mom was right, and he didn't come out of his room except to eat... they might not have a choice. I'd assumed Mom had been overly concerned about her precious son, but the whole lack-of-hygiene situation unnerved me.

Erik pointed to the door without looking at it. "Out."

I stared at him, then back at the indecipherable screen. He'd never ordered me from his room. Hell, for ages, we shared a room.

As I descended the stairs, Mom stood at the base, concern etched around the corners of her light blue eyes.

"Anything?" she asked.

"No. Do you know what he's working on?"

She shook her head as she sucked in on her bottom lip. "He didn't talk to you?"

"No. Something's off. He's not playing games."

"I told you. Besides, if it was games, you'd be playing with him, right?"

"I haven't played games in years, Mom. But no, he's coding. Maybe it's a project for school? Maybe he has a deadline coming up? Or a term paper kind of project?" I kept my tone light. Her eyes became glassy, as if she might cry. I squeezed her hand.

"He's no longer in school."

"What?"

"Your father and I are going down to meet with the dean to find out more. He violated the student code. But he's over twenty-one, and he's been paying his own tuition, so I don't know if they'll tell us anything." My parents believed Erik would be the next Jack Ma, the founder of something enormously successful like Alibaba, or the next

Jeff Bezos of Amazon fame. To my parents, Erik was brilliant and successful in all things.

"Why didn't you tell me?"

"I didn't want to tell you something like this over the phone."

A lone tear fell down her cheek. I'd never seen my mother cry before. The construct of my world shifted. Nothing would again be as it should.

THE GREEN LIGHT FLASHED, THEN CHANGED TO RED. I POURED the steaming water into my ceramic mug, dropped a black tea bag in, added a drop of honey, and returned to my desk to call that pesky brother of mine.

"You summoned?" I asked when his deep voice growled through the line.

The sound of fingers clicking on a keyboard rang through. Some things hadn't changed.

"Is that my sweatshirt you're wearing?"

I waved at the glass globe in the room's corner and smiled. I'd stolen it from him in undergrad, and he'd only asked me a thousand times if I had it. It now had a hole near the armpit. These days, I rarely wore it and had considered donating it a few times when spring cleaning. A surge of glee that wearing it pissed him off lightened the annoyance eating at me.

"Yep. You can come and get it when you want it." I grinned up at the corner and pushed my chest out so he could see the faded Washington letters.

"Bitch."

"Asswipe," I retorted, glaring up at the circular glass.

"Whatever. Can you create those profiles for me?"

"If you explain to me exactly how it's safe for you to be in Portland." *And not me.*

"You spoke to Mom?"

"Yes. Was she not supposed to tell me?" A wind tunnel sound vibrated through the phone line, as if he let out a long exhale. *Is he actually annoyed at me for asking?*

"No. It wasn't a secret. We've been over this before. I travel incognito. I had them meet me in Portland. I took precautions."

"And you can't set me up with the same precautions?"

"No. Well, maybe. Give me time."

"Time? Erik, it's been a year. A year of this bullshit. You told me you'd get this under control. This wasn't supposed to be permanent."

"I know. I know. It's complicated."

"You don't know how to get out, do you?"

"I am out. I told you. But while I'm working to stop Kane, I need to keep you safe. He's proven how vindictive he can be. You know this." I did. His hired goons trashed my apartment. And according to Erik, he'd done far worse to a colleague's girlfriend. Hence the reason Erik squirreled me away where I couldn't be found. Apparently, Kane held a deep respect for older generations, so Erik believed he wouldn't harm Mom or Dad.

"Can't you go to the FBI? Or I can—"

"Jesus, Cali. Is that what you want? For me to spend the rest of my life behind bars?"

"No. That would kill Mom and Dad."

"Gee. Thanks, Cal."

"Erik. Of course I don't want that for you. But you are the one who got yourself into this." At this point, I was a broken record. There was no point in rehashing a tired argument without a good resolution.

"I'm fixing it." He'd said this before.

"Well, fix it faster."

"Cali, I swear. I'm doing everything I can."

Except turning yourself in and getting help from the authorities. The words were on the tip of my tongue, but I held them back. Because he wouldn't do it. And I didn't really want him to. Yeah, he pissed me off, but I loved him.

"Look. Heat is on right now." *Tell me something new.*

"Heat's always on."

"No. Not like this. Someone anonymously posted info on a board about us. Russia, China, Venezuela, Cuba…you name a country, they want us. Those are a lot of unscrupulous countries searching for us."

"But they'd never figure out who you are. And you're not even with that group now."

"You think there's an active employee directory? And the post mentioned a splinter group. Which makes us even bigger targets. And don't forget, Kane knows I have a twin. He knows what you look like. AI recognition will pick you up in an airport."

"You can't keep me here forever." The trouble with my brilliant brother was he saw too many possibilities—too many ways for a plan to play out. The ability made him an amazing game player, but it bred paranoia. I found it difficult to believe this guy living in Asia was actively monitoring feeds from airports.

"Cali, I need more time. I promise, I'm doing my best." An awkward pause filled the line as disappointment crushed around me. I don't know what I expected or hoped, but nothing changed. Nothing ever changed. "And you'll get me those profiles?"

"Yeah, sure."

"Thanks. I don't have the time to do it myself." My brother's ex-partner, or boss might be apropos, scared him. Terrified him. He'd never said those exact words, but the extent to which he'd gone to protect me spoke volumes. Whenever my anger surged, I needed to remind myself of this. "I promise you. My plan is coming together. I need you to stay out of the way. Please?"

"I just want to go home for a visit."

"Soon. Any more Howl at the Moon events planned?"

"No."

"Well, if you want to hang out with your neighbor, Poppy, I think she's fine. I've done a background check. And the guy she lives with, he's clear too. But I expect the feds are watching him, for other reasons, so be aware when you're in his home it could be bugged."

"You know, I truly believe you have become insanely paranoid. Like, I know you'd never ever see a therapist, but—"

"I'm not saying for sure, but it's possible. The guy's being investigated by the Justice Department and the SEC."

"They dropped the investigation."

"Don't huff."

"Why? You huff."

"Cali, just… what else?"

"I was asked out on a date." A smile broke out on my face. It wasn't so much the prospect of a date that had me smiling up at that black globe as it was that I liked rubbing my asshat brother the wrong way.

"By who?"

"The head of Public Safety. I met him at Howl at the Moon."

"The cop? But you didn't tell me?"

"I'm telling you now."

"I researched him back when he first came to the island. I told you, he's former military."

"Was." Sometimes I couldn't help but question if Erik was truly worried about my safety or if he worried more about the prospect of me unwittingly giving away information that could lead to him getting caught. A prolonged silence filled the line, and I flicked the mouse, bringing my screen to life.

"You know, he's probably just a washed-up cop. In the last year, he's left you alone. To prove to you I'm not overly paranoid, if you want to go out with him, go ahead. Be careful. Don't do anything to make him suspicious."

"You're giving me permission?" The idea kind of pissed me off. But at the same time, it excited me. I could go out for that drink without a nagging conscience.

"Jesus, Cali. I can't win with you. Look, my goal isn't to make your life miserable. It's keeping you safe. This'll all be over soon."

I nodded.

"Cali, look at the camera."

I gritted my teeth and faced the glass globe.

"It'll all be over soon."

ali

*Hey, you just passed me. Where'd you go? Want to meet up for
that drink?*

I'D CARRIED MY IPHONE WITH ME SO I COULD EASILY CHECK OUT
the photos Mom shared, and therefore, I received Logan's text.

The Image Creator Icon whirled, indicating the software
processed the commands, or as I preferred to think of it, spun
magic. I sipped my tea, waiting. Re-reading the text. I now had
my brother's quote-unquote permission. But I'd still have to be
careful.

In uniform, Logan possessed a commanding air. And, when
I first moved here, he'd been clean-shaven, his dark hair cut
close to the scalp. Out of uniform, that night on the beach, in
shorts and flip-flops, with his shirttail out, he came across like

any of the other guys on vacation. Hints of gray peppered his beard, giving him an older, more distinguished vibe. He didn't have any hints of gray in his thick hair that I'd noticed, but in that beard, he did. His shirt hung loosely on his waist, a trim waist I imagined flaunted a six-pack, given the way he looked in uniform with a thick leather belt and gun holster.

I envisioned him in one of my study groups, attempting to blend in with my band of nerds. He'd overwhelm the frame of a wooden library chair. I could also see myself straddling his lap in said chair… I shook the vision away. Spending time with him could be fun. And I could easily play the divorce card if he seemed too inquisitive.

Fully loaded, my in-progress profile came to life with a flicker of bright light. Photos of images I'd found of real people, online, filled squares on my screen, the friends of a San Bernardino Valley resident and the spouse of a congressman. I got the formula now. She was the kind of woman who knew so many people, she wouldn't think twice about accepting a friend who looked vaguely familiar. She and her husband also wanted a large friend group to shout out their messages to, so they probably accepted every single friend request. And she had politically involved friends. I didn't select the profile targets for Erik, but it didn't take a rocket scientist to understand the logic.

I pulled the eyebrows from one photo, the lips from another, the brow and hair from a middle-aged woman. I gathered all the elements and hit the merge button. A circular button appeared as the software performed its magic. The low hum of the fans and machines irked me. I pressed play, and the Chainsmokers filled the room with a pulsing beat.

Despite my desire to blare the music, the volume remained low—always low. Privacy. No need to raise questions. I'd love to have one enormous window on the back wall. But the black machines in cages with all their blinking lights required a steady, controlled temperature. My job with the machines was limited to light dusting and checking temperatures. Although an alert would sound if the temperature rose too high.

It was funny. Back when I led a normal life, I was an introvert, but I still had friends and a life. It was a little scary how easily I settled into a life of seclusion. Jasmine, my pupil extraordinaire, saved me this past year. Spending my days studying with her gave me a semblance of my old life. Once school started, I'd miss her. *No need to be sad. You'll see her in the afternoons.*

Bleep. Bleep. Bleep.

An image downloaded on screen. A bizarre Frankenstein-like creation. I searched the subject's feed and found a different photo for hair, pulled up PhotoShop, and altered it a bit, lengthening it. Replaced the hair and studied the unfinished facial image.

"Erik, I hope you know what you're doing." No one responded. I chewed on my nails. Not enough to bite them off. My grandmother rid me of that habit when I was in elementary school. But enough to soothe.

I picked up my iPhone and typed in a response.

Working tonight. What are you up to?

Then I deleted the text without sending it. After completing a round of profiles and sending them off into the ether, I closed up and went home. The profiles would be used as part of Erik's efforts to fight the ongoing disinformation campaigns. Fake profiles to counter other fake profiles. When Facebook originally created their algorithms, they simply wanted the most entertaining posts to rise to the top, so college students would see funny drunk posts over the boring I-Ran-Three-Miles posts. And they'd keep coming back for the entertainment. I seriously doubted anyone ever had the foresight to realize how a seemingly benign algorithm could be used to foster propaganda.

I didn't mind helping my brother with this task because I knew for every fake account that successfully distributed accurate information, there were other fake accounts spewing lies. All the accounts posted and followed, hoping one person would like or share, and another person would see a trusted friend shared, thus adding an additional layer to a web of lies.

Once home, I dropped my bag. The darkness bothered me. The walls closed in. I called Nym and headed back outside. The wheels crunched the asphalt. As I turned right, then left, winding my way through the back streets of the newly constructed Cape Fear Station neighborhood, I found myself in front of Logan's cottage. Way back when I first responded to Tate's ad and subsequently discovered the island, Erik had called.

"*That sounds like the understatement of the year,*" *I said.*

"*Cali. I thought we were through this.*"

"*Through it? I had to move to the East Coast. I feel like I'm in hiding.*"

"*Cali, I promise. It's only for a few months.*"

"*Why are you calling me?*"

"*I did a background check on everyone working on Haven.*"

"And?"

"The Public Safety Director is former military intelligence. He also worked for Chicago PD. The house he bought is new construction, so it's not showing on Google Earth yet. Can you swing by?"

"What exactly am I looking for?"

"I want you to check out his roof. Look for anything he might use to extend his Wi-Fi."

"Send me the address."

I PULLED UP OUTSIDE OF THE COTTAGE I'D SCOPED OUT BACK then. A nice covered porch graced the front with three windows set on the second story. One Adirondack chair sat off to the side of the porch. Warm light flowed through the large downstairs windows, highlighting the wide panes in the modern farmhouse style. Well-manicured green grass filled the small patch of land between the porch and lane, and a narrow path with gray stone pavers led up to the front door. The cart inched forward. Floodlights lit the darkness from the side of the driveway. Motion-controlled lights—not surprising.

Few of the houses installed them. Heck, most people in this town didn't even bother locking doors. That was one aspect Erik didn't think through. He forced top-of-the-line security on me, not realizing that for all his efforts to not attract attention, that security did exactly that. With Nym around, it wasn't like I needed the locks...theoretically.

All the houses on Writer's Way, Logan's short street, were dark. A low hum of crickets filled the air, and if one listened hard, the indistinct sound of crashing waves cut through the tree line. I pressed the gas, easing away from the peaceful setting.

The solid wood front door, painted black, opened, letting out a flood of yellow light onto the middle of the covered porch.

"Cali?"

Shit. "Hey. I was riding by…" I floundered for words. His street was hardly a major thoroughfare. He stepped across the porch and down two steps. "I couldn't sleep and was just out riding around."

"No worries. I spend most of my nights riding around."

"You do?"

The corners of his lips turned up into a slight smile, and he continued down the path, closer to me. "Insomniac. Right here." His thumb angled at his chest. "Nice to meet another one."

"It's late. I wasn't really…" I held my hand up over my forehead. Talking to Nym was easier.

"My bedroom's right there." He pointed to the large windows overlooking the front porch. "I saw you pull up. I wasn't sure it was you until the floodlight came on. Come sit."

"It's after eleven."

"I won't be sleeping. It's a gorgeous night." He pointed up at the sky filled with stars, bright specks of light dotting the dark canvas.

I twisted the key and followed him. My nerves rebelled. My insides jumbled. Uncertainty twirled. I wiped my palms. *Ridiculous. There's no reason to be nervous.*

He sat down on the third step of his porch, to one side of the railing. I joined him, my back to the far-facing railing.

"I like your home."

"Do you want to look inside?"

"No, thanks. That's okay."

"Want anything to drink?"

"No. I should probably—"

"Sit. Talk. The offer for that drink stands. But hang out."

The quiet filled the night air, and I looked through his wide windows. They opened into a living area, and stairs were off to the side.

"Aren't you worried about bugs?"

"Screens. I leave the windows open most of the time. Unless the heat gets too oppressive."

"I guess that means you believe the island is pretty safe, huh?" My question earned a chuckle.

"We don't have a lot of crime. Besides, the most valuable thing I have is a TV. How is anyone going to get that off the island without raising eyebrows?"

"What about your computer?"

"I access everything of importance on a VPN. If someone did nab my ancient laptop, they wouldn't get much. I suppose if someone stole it, I'd see it as a blessing. Excuse for an upgrade."

Well, that answered that. Erik would appreciate the confirmation Logan didn't represent any kind of risk to his operation.

"That's a good dog. My old dog would have never in a million stayed like that." Nym's ears perked forward.

"He's the best."

"Can I call him over?"

"Here," I commanded. Nym leaped off the seat, tail wagging, and trotted straight to me. "Sit."

Logan crouched down before Nym, scratching near his ears and all around his head.

"You said old dog." I halted, realizing nothing good came from the question I mindlessly headed down.

"The ex-wife got the dog."

"Oh."

"Yeah, that's our common ground."

"What?"

"We're both divorced." He shrugged, like what else could I possibly be thinking. And for the first time since telling it, discomfort rose around that portion of my cover story. And I couldn't even be mad at Erik. That bit had been my moment of brilliance, creating a reason for a single woman to hibernate on an island. A reason that would mean no one wondered how a tutor had money to live in an oceanfront home.

"Do you miss your dog?"

"Yeah, I do. More than the wife." His smile fell, and I suspected that wasn't an entirely truthful answer. "What about you? I see you got the dog?"

"Oh. No. Nym is mine." He tilted his head in a way that asked for me to say more. To continue talking. "I don't like talking about that time in my life." Another clever angle of my cover story—no one questioned a divorced woman not wanting to share. I expected most would welcome a closed-lipped divorced woman.

"I get that. My divorce was two years ago. Well… it became final less than a year ago. The process takes a while, obviously. Is your divorce final?"

I bent over my legs, stretching out my lower back, and zoned in on the gray-painted step beneath my feet. "Yeah. It's final. What kind of dog did you have?"

"A lab. Great dog."

"They are good dogs. My neighbor had one when I was a kid."

"Have you always had shepherds?"

"No. Nym is a gift from my brother. He didn't like me living on my own. Growing up, we always had cats." My mom loved cats. So did Erik. It'd surprised me when he purchased two dogs for us, but he didn't see them as pets. To him, they extended our security system. And I didn't want to answer further questions about my security. I looked back to his wide-open front door. "This is new construction, right? Did you recently move in?"

"About a year ago. I'm slowly decorating. It's not high on my list of priorities, but Luna put me in touch with her favorite decorator. She keeps showing up with suggestions. She found some art for the walls, which was good." He stretched out a muscular leg. A scar ran up the side, barely visible in the moonlight and beneath the dark, curly leg hair. His shorts had risen to mid-thigh. He massaged his knee as he spoke. "You never know what a big difference art on a wall makes until you live for months with white walls. I think she said her next project is my porch, but I told her to wait for spring."

"I think you'd be safe getting furniture over the winter. It's not like it gets that cold here."

"You're probably right. I've still got the Chicago mindset. It's fine. I'm not in a rush."

"Do you miss Chicago?"

"No, not really. Do you miss Seattle?"

"I do. I lived in a little craftsman near downtown, and I could walk to get coffee in the morning. I loved going for a run along the pier. On the weekends, I'd go out to the San Juan Islands sometimes. I mean, it's nice here too, but it's different there. The trees are larger. It's a vibrant city, but it's also peaceful. I mean, my neighborhood." I rubbed my forehead, cognizant I wasn't making any sense. It wasn't like Haven Island wasn't peaceful. "Have you ever been out there?"

"A couple of times."

"Did you know that there's phosphorus in the water, and at night, when a school of jellyfish floats by, the glow, it's like a thousand stars lurking in the depths."

"I'd heard about that, never seen it."

"My favorite thing used to be going to Harbour Island and camping out near the beach. They have a public campground right on the beach." Nostalgia swept over me in a wave, and I yearned for those days, before Erik went down his rabbit hole and pulled me along. I'd spend the weekend camping, alone, studying. Playing language tapes over and over and speaking back into the void.

"Well, you can camp out here any time you want. The stars aren't in the water, but they're definitely in the sky. And I'd bet our summer nights are warmer."

I breathed in a low laugh. "You can't beat a southern summer night. So, are you planning on staying out here? You sound… contented." The resort island seemed to be more of a place for someone to either come and retire or to stop off temporarily. Our mutual friends Luna and Tate were planning to move away within the next year.

"It's not my forever place. But it's serving a purpose. What about you?" He shifted again on the wood step, grimacing as his joints cracked.

"Do you hear your joints?"

"Feel 'em too." He grimaced, but the low chuckle set me at ease. I liked the sound.

"It looks painful."

"It's not pleasant. But they've taken a beating."

"Have you tried yoga?"

He pulled on his shoulder, and his jaw muscles flexed. He needed a massage. For someone to knead those tight muscles that he no doubt never stretched. His stretched-out leg brushed mine, and a flurry of sensations skittered across my skin. Goosebumps sprouted along my arms, and I rubbed them down.

"I'm not a yoga kind of guy." My belly flopped. It was his smile. Friendly and warm. I squirmed, and the rotation of my wrist lit up my watch face.

"Oh, my word. It's after midnight." I stood and brushed off my butt. The skin tingled as blood returned after my extended stay on his stoop.

"Glad you stopped by." His dark eyes gazed into mine, and my breathing slowed. As if floating, suspended in time, he inched closer. I breathed in hints of cedar. The lines of his throat shifted as he swallowed. The shrill cry of an owl broke my trance.

I mumbled nonsense, stepping to my cart, waving my hand into the night air.

"Cali?" I stopped and turned. "Let's hang out again."

Hang out? I could hang out. Thanks to Erik, a relationship with law enforcement wasn't exactly a part of my future, but hanging out, or even a casual date, if he asked again, that I could do.

CHAPTER 8

$\mathscr{L}$ogan

"YOU WEREN'T JOKING. THIS STUFF IS GOOD." MATT TILTED THE
paper cup, inspecting the sugary frozen concoction we on
Haven Island favored above all else.

"Mike's Ice. It's the stuff of legends." The small hut across
from the original lighthouse foundation housed Mike's Ice and
served as a cheap lunch stop with items such as pre-made
sandwiches and hot dogs. But the Italian ice drove the man's
business. In the summer, kids and adults alike lined up in front
of the narrow service window.

"It's good. Really good. I used to live in New York. This is
the good stuff." He dipped his plastic spoon back into the cup
and scraped for remnants.

"I've been telling you to come out and visit. You know, it hit me the other day…we're pushing twenty years since our training days. Two decades. Unreal."

He barely acknowledged my realization as he continued to scarf down the scoops. He'd put on pressed khaki shorts for his visit to the beach, black dress socks pulled straight up, and a short sleeve button-down with heavy starch. He reminded me of a senior military officer who had been told he had to dress down and no longer had any clothes in his closet that fit the bill. Nothing about him resembled my buddy from those training days. But something was off. I couldn't put my finger on it. And it had to do with him, not his clothes.

"So, how're Tiffany and the kids?"

"Good. She's…" He trailed off and sucked on his spoon.

"What?"

"Nothing. The kids are good. Zoe started kindergarten last week."

"Really? Wow."

He opened his phone to a photo of a little girl with pigtails, a backpack about as wide as she was tall, and an enormous grin standing in front of a standard-issue yellow school bus. "She was so proud. I tell you, it was hard watching her climb those bus steps."

"I bet." I swallowed some of my ice. The limbs on a nearby palm tree swayed in the breeze, and the voices of the Mike's Ice patrons a few feet away drifted by.

"You know, we could use you back in D.C." His gaze remained inside the cup in his hand. At a glance, you might have thought he was focused on weeding out one of the three flavored scoops, but…

"What's going on, Matt?"

"I just want you to know that I can easily get you a position in D.C. Or probably almost any other city. Are you happy here? Is this what you want to be doing?"

His fascination with the inside of the paper cup confirmed to me he wasn't coming clean about something.

"Matt. What the hell? Did you find something out about our budgets?"

"No. How would I have access to North Carolina budgets? My focus is on activity outside the US, remember? Nah, I wouldn't worry about your job security. At the end of the day, no matter how riled up people get about budget expenditure, you live on what is basically a resort island filled with rich residents and tourists. Budgets will probably get cut, but they aren't ever going to completely remove Public Safety. But you came here to regroup. I figured you might want to get back to something more. That's all. And right now, with the state of the cyber world, we could use you. If you're bored. Or need more..." He trailed off.

If I was bored...I understood where he was coming from. But... "You said you needed to come down and talk to me. And NSA doesn't monitor the domestic arena. What did you need to talk to me about?"

"There's chatter. You know, on the boards."

"What are they saying?"

"There's a pod of servers in the southeast. Being used by one of the more powerful international crime syndicates."

"Wouldn't they have servers all over the world?"

"Yes. And I'd been hearing you talk about this island, and I had it in my head it would be an ideal place. But now that I'm here, I see it's not."

"No. I told you. Connection here is too iffy. If you'd told me that was what you were thinking, I could have warned you off. The southeast isn't exactly a small stretch of land."

"No. It's not. But, for various reasons, we're thinking it's North Carolina."

"Maybe Wilmington? It's a college town. I'd think you'd want mainland."

"I agree."

"You couldn't talk to me about this on the phone?"

"We have reason to believe we're being monitored. Or we've got a leak."

"Shit. That sucks."

"It does. But, ever since Solar Winds, you know, we've got to be careful. Always. Anyway, FBI is working with us. I wanted to see you. Used checking this area out as an excuse."

He crumpled the empty cup and set it on the table.

"You wanted to see me. You didn't come to vacation." He stretched out his fingers then balled up his fist. His knuckles cracked. "If the wife and kids are good, none of this job stuff sounds urgent… I'm running out of ideas. What's going on?" He frowned and stared down at his balled-up fist. "Spit it out."

"Bethany's pregnant."

The words hit like a punch to the gut. A shield formed, jamming all emotion.

"That's good. She'll be happy about that." I said it, but it didn't mean I was actually happy for my ex. No, the recoil inside my chest could not be described as happy.

"I didn't know if I should tell you. But I didn't want you to return to Chicago and see her without knowing."

"It's good. I'm happy for her."

I felt him examining me. I reached for his crumpled cup and used spoon, picked them up, and threw them away in the garbage along with my barely eaten ice. The tart lemon flavor didn't hit the spot.

"You're taking this well."

"Was a matter of time, right?" No need to get worked up about it. Bethany had always been clear about what she wanted. What did he expect? For me to fly off the handle? Punch something?

I drove Matt back to the office so he could brief me in a secure location on things to look out for, just in case. I don't remember any of the ride back to the office. As he spoke, I kept telling myself to pay attention. I kept telling myself to listen. He had important things to share. Things he didn't want to share over email or on the phone. Nothing he said caught my attention. I kept drifting as he shared rumors gleaned from intel sources. It sounded like any other day monitoring whispers. Those whispers could be from folks on the street, from highly coveted sources, or I supposed the vast DarkNet. Didn't matter which world, physical or virtual. Virtual meant a whole lot more whispers and a billion more false leads.

"Does anything jump out at you?" he asked.

"No." I emphasized that the chatter about a server cluster in the general vicinity was meaningless. The Outer Banks and barrier islands encompassed a sizeable swatch of land. As it was, our internet signal was so weak, I couldn't see any hacker worth his salt choosing this island or any barrier island.

He left behind some reports for me to read. He hadn't shared anything groundbreaking. Without a doubt, he came down to tell me face to face about my ex-wife. He'd worried about my reaction. If I'd break down like before.

I drove him to the ferry in silence. He patted my shoulder before he left, an expression of pity on his face, and it required a substantial amount of willpower to stand and take it. I didn't want his pity. His news didn't deserve pity. But I hated he created some bullshit reason to come down and tell me. I wasn't angry at him, per se, but yeah, a good deal of anger lurked and stewed, enough I couldn't stomach returning to Public Safety.

I parked in one of the public parking spaces, took off my shoes and socks, rolled up my slacks, and found myself on the beach. The cool sand between my toes placated me. I walked aimlessly along, breathing in the salt air.

"Logan, you're being stubborn. Just go get tested."

"A twenty-three-year-old woman was brutally murdered today. Excuse me for letting a murder derail my doctor's visit."

"Did you go to the center today?"

"No. There was a drive-by shooting on Milwaukee Avenue. Rumors are there's about to be a gang war."

"Did you by chance visit—"

"Do you have any idea what my average day is like? It's not easy to just walk out in the middle of the day."

The distant fights in my head drowned out the crash of the waves. She dropped it. Stopped mentioning the fertility center. I thought she'd become engrossed in a case defending one of my colleagues. I missed the signs.

A fishing boat drove along the coast, off in the distance. Long lines extended from the back. The boat journeyed closer to shore, and I strained to see the fishermen, curious. A sharp pain punctured my foot.

"Fuck." I held it up for inspection. The corner of a shell sliced the skin below my big toe. I stuck the injury into the edge of the salt water and closed my eyes, absorbing the sting. I breathed out and admitted to the air what I'd probably known all along. "She was right. I was the problem."

A soft touch on my shoulder intensified into firm pressure.

"Logan? Are you okay?"

A dog's nose neared mine, inches away. He panted, mouth open, and the pink tongue rested along bright white teeth. The dog's dark eyes evaluated me, and I scratched the soft hair on his neck. I blinked my way out of the fog. Night sky, a moon partially covered by clouds, and the whites of crashing waves encircled me. Cali's brow crinkled, and her dark eyebrows drew close together. With a loud exhale, I stood, my knees crunching as I rose.

"Hey," I said. I brushed the sand from the bottom of my shorts and discovered damp fabric.

"I came out here to check on you. You've been sitting here for quite a while. Is everything okay?"

"You saw me?" My extended stupor impacted me like a deep nap, and I struggled to piece together how day became night.

"My deck's a few houses down." She pointed at her green

cottage, barely visible above the dunes. "Come up and let me get you a glass of water."

"I'm okay."

"I spend my days with only Nym to talk to. You'd be doing me a favor." I suspected that was bullshit, but I didn't have a reason to fight her. She clutched my elbow as if she worried I might pass out or break down. *Christ, I must have been sitting for hours.* My throat felt dry and raw.

"Water sounds good. Thank you."

I followed her through the narrow path in the dunes that led to her cottage. Nym tracked close to my side. I wasn't sure if the dog shared her concern for me, or he simply didn't plan to let me stray with his owner nearby.

"Sit here. I'll be right back." She clutched my elbow, guiding me to a chair on her deck, not letting go until I was safely seated. Nym sat on his haunches at my feet, his pointed ears erect and alert.

"Hey, buddy. It's okay. I'm not going to hurt her." Nym gave no acknowledgement he understood. If I were to translate his immobile response, he said, "I am watching you."

She handed me a water. The thin plastic crinkled in my hand, and condensation covered the bottle. The cold water hit the spot, and I downed about half of it in one long gulp.

"If you need more, I can get another." Cali hovered over me, standing near my knees, observing all too closely.

"Sit. I'm fine. Where's yours?"

"I'm not thirsty." She sat down in the chair to my side, and we both faced the ocean, our view barred only by the thick top wooden rail on her deck. "Do you ever study the stars?"

A layer of clouds muted the skies, but a few bright lights cut through as pinpricks in the gloom. "Special Forces. In training, we learned how to navigate. Are you an astronomer?"

"No. But I used to be friends with someone who had one of those expensive telescopes. You know, the ones that cost a crazy amount of money but can see planets?"

"Did you see the planets?"

"Yeah. Sometimes. But… I'm from Seattle, and clear nights aren't guaranteed."

"Clear nights aren't guaranteed anywhere. That's why you have to have alternate options."

I downed the rest of the water and fisted the bottle, crumbling it into a wad.

"Do you want more?"

"No. Do you mind if I use your restroom?"

"Oh. Ah." She looked to the sliding glass doors in a way that I turned, expecting to see a person.

"Is someone else here?" I'd heard she lived alone.

"No. No. It's… of course you can use the restroom." Her hand flew up to her hair, and she brushed it back from her face. "Here…" Something was off. Maybe I looked worse than I realized. Maybe she worried I was close to a breakdown. Just like Matt had worried. Maybe I did have a breakdown and that was how I lost hours. She opened her sliding glass door for me and then followed me inside.

She decorated her living area with the standard beach decor. Off to the side, a bright white kitchen and an oval table overlooked the ocean. Like the time I'd been here before, nothing appeared out of place. The two dog beds, one in the kitchen, and one in the living area, were the only two items that made the place feel lived in. She and I both liked things sparse.

"It's right here." She slid a pocket door back into the wall. As

I relieved myself, the shadow beneath the crack below the door told me she hovered nearby, and the toilet splash echoed abnormally loudly in the tiny bathroom. I took extra care to leave the room in pristine condition, toilet seat down. I washed my hands and dried them on my shorts, as she didn't have a guest towel.

As expected, when I opened the door, she stood in the hall, waiting. She'd pulled her dark, black hair up on her head, and it highlighted her high cheekbones. A light pink dusting coated her otherwise smooth, olive skin. Pronounced black eyebrows shaped her dark eyes, eyes so dark they were more ebony than brown. Wordlessly, I followed her back out onto the deck. Her formfitting white shorts curved around the shape of her toned ass and offset her long, shapely legs. Her thin, light sweater draped her breasts. The crisp, white outfit and the way she held her lithe frame boasted of a refinement, both elegant and graceful. I yearned to touch her, to let my fingers roam her smooth skin, the silky soft cloth, the curve of her waist, her hip bone, her ass. Above the sweater, then below it, and those shapely legs wrapping around me.

"Logan?" Her soft question startled me. *Get it together.*

"Were you a dancer?"

"Ballet." The corners of her lips turned up ever so slightly. "When I was younger. Much younger. It didn't take long to realize I wouldn't make the top schools. I loved it, but I didn't have what it takes."

"So, you picked a different sport?"

"I'm a violinist. Or, well, the orchestra was my thing in high school, if that's what you mean. My parents wanted us to find something we could excel at for college."

"And you run?"

Her smile widened. "Yes, I run. Which led me to yoga. And reminds me, you could benefit from yoga."

"Told you. I'm not a yogi."

"They have yoga for jocks. And you don't have to call it yoga. You can call it stretching." She pointedly looked at my loud knees. The white scar from the surgery glowed in the barely-there moonlight.

"I've been told I should stretch." I meant to get better about stretching. But it fucking hurt. And I kept forgetting.

"I'm going to work on you." Her fingers lightly tapped the end of her armrest, and silence filled the space between us. With a sigh, she asked, "Did something happen today?"

I closed my eyes and rested my head against the smooth wood of the Adirondack chair.

"If you don't want to talk about it—"

"It's fine. My ex-wife is pregnant. With my friend's baby. It's… there's no point in wading through the bullshit. Classic story. Guy works his ass off. Wife gets lonely. Screws his friend. And, now I guess, she's got her happily ever after. They'll have kids… loads of kids. Like she always wanted."

"So that's why you moved here? From Chicago?"

"Yeah. I guess guilt led her to give me a decent divorce settlement. She made more than me. We didn't have kids. But, yeah." I linked my fingers together, flipped them over, and stretched out my arms. "I want to hate her." I said it more to myself. I supposed I hoped as a fellow divorcee Cali would understand.

"But you can't?"

Her light, warm touch fell over my icy hand. I became conscious of the grip I held on the end of the armrest. An electric current traveled up my arm. Touch—it was one of those life puzzles. Sometimes the lightest of touches hit more deeply than a powerful punch. My chest ached, and I lifted my hand, the one she didn't clasp, and rubbed my sternum with the base of my palm.

"What about you?" I asked. "Do you hate him? Your ex?"

"Hate is a toxic emotion. You're so much better off not carrying it. It weighs you down and destroys you. It's a good thing you can't hate her. That's yourself in preservation mode. Keeping you whole. Healthy. I… they say that infidelity isn't what breaks apart a marriage, but a sign that the marriage had issues. Maybe hate not only isn't the answer, but it's not justified."

"So, you're saying it's my fault she cheated on me? With my friend?" It took a lot of nerve to make a statement like that without knowing jack shit.

"No. Not at all. I'm just… I don't know. I'm spouting off what I've read in magazine articles." Yeah, that was what they all said. The articles, that was. New-age theories. Her expression as she watched me held no anger, but there was a hint of understanding.

"Did he cheat on you?"

"No."

"Then you don't know what you're talking about."

"No. I don't."

The lulling sounds of the waves crashing on the beach and salt air wafted over us, discharging the tension that crested. I breathed out a lot of the crap inside in a long, loud exhale. I scratched my beard and scalp. Everything itched.

"Ignore me. I get angry. Too angry sometimes. I'm working on it. Our marriage did have problems. Some of them, I could have fixed. Some I couldn't. And a part of me is happy she's

getting her dream. I wasn't the man who could do that for her."
I opened my eyes and focused on one golden light on the
horizon. A ship far off in the distance. "And this is probably a
whole level of shit you didn't want dumped on your deck." I
braced my hands on my knees and pushed up, needing to get
away.

"Logan?"

I brushed absolutely nothing off my shorts. She didn't go on,
so I prompted, "Yeah?"

"You're a good guy. A failed marriage doesn't mean you
aren't." I avoided her gaze. "Are you going to Jasmine's party
tomorrow?"

"No. Wasn't invited." I knew Tate, the girl's father, well. He,
Gabe, and I surfed together. Parasailed. We'd even parachuted
once together for fun. I liked Tate, and Luna seemed pretty nice
too, but it wasn't like we were all so close I expected an
invitation to his teenage daughter's party.

"Well, come as my guest. It's a sort of a 'best of luck at
school' party. She doesn't have many friends her age, and Luna
has this idea that gathering a crowd of supportive people
around her will remind her how many people she has in her
corner."

"Not a bad idea. It's good to have people in your corner." She
followed me down the steps on her deck.

"So, I'll see you tomorrow?" She sounded perky. I wouldn't
go so far as to say flirty, but definitely hopeful.

"Cali, are you putting yourself in my corner?" I raised an
eyebrow, teasing her.

"Consider yourself lucky." She smiled, and I watched as she
disappeared back into her home. She played with the handle
and lifted a block to set behind the glass door. She saw me, still

standing and watching, and flexed her fingers in a slow wave, barely visible behind the glass.

I smiled into the night air. Yeah, I felt lucky. And intrigued. If she was going to put me in her corner, I'd definitely return the favor. As I walked home, I thought about Cali and her timid ways. She wasn't going through exactly what I was going through, but she got my divorce head, or seemed to. At the very least, she hadn't gone running when she heard the top line vanilla summary of my bullshit. She'd even asked me on a date. She might not be thinking of it as a date, and maybe I shouldn't...but why not? Bethany had moved on—clearly. Why not me?

ali

"We just got back from the dermatologist. Your father has gone to lie down." Mom's voice sounded as far away as she actually was, on the opposite side of the country.

"Is everything okay?" *For five minutes you've been talking about the weather?*

"She found some cancer spots. Burned them off. I've been telling him to go get them checked out for years. But you know your father, he can be so stubborn."

"What kind of cancer?"

"Nothing to worry about. That's what she said. But I've been worried about your father. He's slowing down. Doesn't go out fishing as much as he used to."

"Isn't that because the guy he goes fishing with all the time hasn't been well?"

"He has colon cancer. He's been going through chemo."

"Well, I'm sure that's why Dad hasn't been doing as much fishing. I think fishing was his way to hang with his friend as much as anything."

"He's tired a lot. He naps every day."

"You know, Mom, when I talk to Dad, he has a list of worries about you, but he says he's absolutely fine."

"Well, he has no reason to worry about me. I'm doing fine."

"He said your ankles have been swelling?"

"Your father has no business telling you anything like that. I am doing fine. These days he seems to notice all my body changes. It's quite frustrating sometimes. It's normal. I'm old. My breasts sag, and I've got wrinkles. The ankles were bound to go too. But your father…"

I pressed my knees up to my chest and squeezed, hugging myself the best way I knew how as she continued about how he didn't even want to go with her to the grocery store yesterday. I longed for my parents' home and my mom's chicken dumplings. I wanted to inhale the flowery incense my mom lit in the guest bath. More than anything, I wanted to see them with my own eyes and decide which of their ongoing list of concerns merited worry.

After the call with Mom, I signaled to Nym and took off for my mid-day run. Blue skies and white fluffy clouds awaited. My lungs burned as I stretched my legs, pushing myself faster. Far up ahead, toward the point, a blue and white ATV entered the beach. *Public Safety.*

The dark-haired driver wore reflective sunglasses and a uniform of ironed shorts and the standard collared shirt. As our paths crossed, we waved. He turned his head as I passed, and I lifted my shoulders, pumping my arms, putting my all into each stride with a smile. A wide smile. I liked seeing him turn his head as I passed, maybe a little too much.

Once home, I kicked off my sandy shoes on the deck and grabbed a bottle of water from the fridge. My iPhone lay on the kitchen counter, and on a whim, I picked it up. A thrill coursed through me when I saw the awaiting text.

I'll pick you up for Jasmine's party. Six p.m.?

While I loved the chivalry, I remembered the camera over my front door. Yes, Erik cleared him and approved of a date, but all the same…

I'll pick you up. It's on the way.

Giddiness and excitement swirled. Yes, a juvenile reaction, but the uncommon vibes were energizing. *He's cute. We can have fun. I can have fun.* I typed one more text.

Looking forward to it.

WHEN I EASED TO A SLOW STOP IN FRONT OF LOGAN'S IDYLLIC clapboard cottage, he greeted me with a sexy smile, and pinprick sensations scurried along my arms. In dark gray chinos, a crewneck black shirt, and wayfarer sunglasses, he reminded me of Jamie Dornan with a beard, a few years after *Fifty Shades.* Not quite Jamie, since he had chocolate brown eyes. And I expected he was taller, and had more breadth, than the actor. Or at least, as compared to a photograph.

A large bundle of white roses wrapped in pink paper lay on the gray wooden porch floor. Logan lifted the wrapped flowers as he stood, resting them in the crook of his arm.

My insides, which had been whirling about for the past hour as I got ready for this barbecue with friends, completely ignored my calm-down memo. I'd tried on three different outfits. And those outfit changes had nothing to do with impressing Jasmine.

Logan slid onto the seat and held the flowers out, at least two dozen.

"Those flowers are beautiful." *For me?*

"I thought I should bring something for Jasmine. I wasn't sure what to bring her. White, I thought, would be good? At the very least, Luna can use them for decoration."

"That's so thoughtful." And a gift for Jasmine made so much more sense. I had a small wrapped present for her on the back seat, although my present screamed "teacher." I'd ordered her some of my favorite books. Most kids would roll their eyes, but Jasmine was one of the most dedicated students I'd ever met. I hoped high school and an abundance of teenage friends wouldn't change that. But if it did, it was her life to lead.

Logan's tall frame filled the golf cart, and his head nearly brushed the top. He held up a second, smaller bouquet, a mixture of white and soft pink roses. "I got these for you. I know you probably won't want to bring them into the party. But I wanted to buy my date for the night flowers. So I did. Should I keep them inside my house until later?"

The smaller rose bouquet included sprigs of greenery and baby's breath. I recognized both of the wrapped bouquets from the flowers set out at the entrance to the market each day. I lifted the one with a mix of color and inhaled the soft floral fragrance.

"So thoughtful. Thank you." Through the reflection in his sunglasses, I saw myself, and surprise filtered through at my relaxed and happy image. The silky petals brushed the tip of my nose, and I considered them. "It's only Luna and Tate. I'll ask Luna for a small glass to put the flowers in until I can take them home."

With the flowers set between us, we lurched forward.

"So, how many people are they expecting tonight?"

"According to Jasmine, it'll be Poppy and Gabe, and her favorite person on the island, Alice, and then I think that's it? She invited a girl she'd become close friends with over the summer, but they left to return home recently."

"It's got to be tough to be a teenager on this island. There aren't many of them."

"Not year-round, no. I think public school is going to be good for her." Her English, while heavily accented, was quite good. "I'm hoping all the kids will see her as exotic, you know, with her accent, and they'll be nice."

"Were kids nice to you in high school?" He twisted in the seat, positioning himself so he could better see me.

"Yeah, I mean, I wasn't a big nerd, if that's what you're getting at. But I was quiet and studious."

"You? Quiet? Would never have guessed." His tone left no doubt; he mocked me.

I opened my mouth through my grin, then closed it, then opened it, unsure how to respond. He chuckled.

"You never come around for Sunday night bingo. Or for happy hour at Will-o'-the-Wisp. All summer long I've met up with Tate and Gabe, and sometimes Luna and Poppy, but never you."

The unspoken question hung between us. He'd noticed I remained distant.

"It wasn't until I moved down the street from Poppy that I really got to know them. Back when I lived off the island, I showed up for work. I didn't socialize over here at all."

"You moved here last spring, though, right? We've been getting together for happy hour all summer." If he knew how scared Erik had made me for my safety, he'd understand. But time had passed, and no one had showed in the dark of night. None of Erik's nightmare scenarios had come true.

"For a long time, Luna and I were more of casual acquaintances. Really, I was an employee." I struggled to explain. Even if I hadn't been cautious when I first arrived, I hadn't gotten warm vibes from Luna initially. "It was awkward with us at first. I met Jasmine right after Tate had adopted her. And Luna and Tate hadn't been dating long. For a long time, my conversations with Tate were all about Jasmine's progress. Luna and I…we just didn't…"

"Connect?"

"I guess? Anyway, Poppy's the one who really has brought me into their friend circle." No matter how many times I declined her invitation, she knocked at my door. Sometimes with an offer of an experimental recipe. Others she'd wave across at me from her deck, inviting me to join them for an evening cocktail.

"And Alice? You're talking about Alice Santera? The older woman who lives on the marsh?"

"Yes. She's somewhat of a grandmother figure for Jasmine, I think."

I parked beside Gabe's golf cart in front of Tate and Luna's cottage. A placard hung by the front door of the light blue cottage that read "Nana's Retreat." Tate bent down in front of his grill, fumbling with the gas.

"Hey. Everything okay?" Logan asked Tate.

"Yeah. Everyone's inside, probably on the porch. Walk on in." Tate ran his hand over the grill, frowned, then bent down again.

"Something not working?" Logan asked. I gave a slight wave of my hand to show I'd head inside, and he nodded to me. "I'll be right in." The last thing I heard as the screen door creaked open was Logan asking Tate, "Is the gas not working?"

"Oh! Look at those flowers," Poppy gushed.

"Logan bought flowers for Jasmine."

"Isn't he the sweetest?"

Gabe gave an exaggerated, "Hey," with his fingers aimed at himself, and I laughed. Then he raised a brow and asked, "Where's Logan? Is he outside with Tate?"

I barely nodded once before he was out the door.

"Where's Jasmine and Luna?"

"They went out on the beach. Some shell or jellyfish or who knows what washed up on the sand. Shocker. Alice is out there with them. Wow. That's a lot of flowers."

"Well, this bouquet is for Jasmine. He has a card on it for her, so I'll set this aside until she's back." I laid down the flowers and my wrapped gift on the kitchen island. "And these just need some water on the ends. I'll leave it wrapped."

"Did someone else get flowers?"

I tried my best to wipe the smile off my face, but my lips didn't cooperate. "Can you help me find a glass that can hold this? Or a pitcher?"

Poppy sidestepped around me, opened one high cabinet, and pulled out a clear plastic pitcher. As she filled it with water, she didn't let it drop. "That Logan is scrumptious. And he's a good friend of Gabe's."

"He is a nice guy." There was no point in denying the obvious truth.

"So, are you two dating?"

"No. It's not like that. He just…" I tried to remember exactly how he came to be my guest. "I thought they would've invited him, and I mentioned it to him. I don't think Luna and Tate mind?"

"Oh, no. Not at all. They like Logan. The guys hang out quite a bit."

"How long until the restaurant opening?"

"Lord. I'm so peeved we aren't going to catch the summer season. I'm hoping Labor Day weekend. Still waiting on permits. If I knew who to bribe, I would. Say, do you think Logan knows?"

"He doesn't have anything to do with permits, does he?" I had never tried to open a business, but I remembered with some renovations on my beach home I'd had to get a permit. My contractor handled it, but I didn't recall the police department, or Public Safety, as they called them here, getting involved.

"I'm going to go ask him. He may know someone. I bet he knows everyone."

I set my pink and white flowers out of the way, near the back wall on the kitchen counter, as voices traveled through the open windows. Jasmine, Luna, and Alice all surrounded the outdoor shower, spraying the sand off their feet.

The screen door creaked, and Jasmine's excited expression warmed me from deep inside.

"Are you ready?" I asked, beaming a smile back at her. "Can you believe Monday's the big day?"

"Do you want to come upstairs to see the outfit I picked out?"

"I'd love to."

I waved to Luna and Alice before being tugged away by Jasmine. Upstairs in Jasmine's bedroom, laid out neatly, were three different outfits.

"Which would you have worn? When you were in high school?"

"Well, that was what… twelve, fifteen… I don't want to think about how long ago that was. But I had a uniform." My grandparents had insisted I attend a private school.

Jasmine's selected outfits included a long yellow sundress with a pair of sandals, jeans and a loose flowing orange top and a pair of Converse tennis shoes, and pressed white shorts with a red cotton top and wedge sandals. I fingered the hem of the white shorts.

"It's supposed to be hot on Monday. Like around ninety-five degrees. I don't know what the AC is like in your school, but maybe not jeans on the first day?"

She nodded.

"Are you good at walking around in these wedges?"

"I've never worn them. All of this is new. It's all part of my back-to-school shopping trip."

"Well, I vote for the sundress. It's beautiful and still casual. It'll be comfortable. Those sandals look comfortable. I think the temps cool down after this last heat wave, and then you can bring out the jeans. If I hadn't had to wear a uniform, I would've lived in jeans. And actually, in college, I did live in jeans."

"What was your uniform like?"

"Navy skirt, a white or red polo shirt." Her eyes scrunched, a reaction to not recognizing a word. "Here, give me your phone."

We sat on her bed, at first searching for standard private school uniforms and polos. Thanks to weak Wi-Fi, the search took longer than it should. I downloaded the Pinterest app for her and showed her how you could search for outfits. Her eyes grew wide as ideas sprouted.

"Dinner's ready," someone shouted.

Downstairs, the hustle and bustle contrasted with the quiet of my current existence. I paused on the bottom stair, absorbing the commotion and energy. I'd so easily fallen into seclusion. But I missed this. And all I had to do to have more of this was start saying yes to these friends. And Erik agreed I could do so safely. Sure, life wasn't perfect. Erik had more to do. I wanted to visit my parents. But this right here… it was what they called a good life. All I had to do was partake.

"Hey, Jasmine, can you grab the tray I set up over there?" Luna pointed from the kitchen counter over to the kitchen table. "If you can carry the napkins and utensils, I think we've got everything."

The door slammed against the wall, and Tate entered, holding out a platter stacked high with grilled vegetables. Alice carried a white ceramic bowl filled with a tossed salad of thinly sliced strawberries and spinach. Luna stirred charred chopped bell peppers into a grain dish in another large bowl.

"Head on out, guys. I'll be right behind you."

A couple of salad dressing bottles remained on the counter, and I scooped them up and followed everyone along the boardwalk to the beach. They had set up a long table and secured the tablecloth to the legs to minimize the flapping in the wind. Folding chairs lined both sides of the table.

On the south side of the island, you could see where the Atlantic merged with the Cape Fear off in the distance. I pointed to the horizon, far out over the choppy water where the land line emerged.

"I bet you have a beautiful view of the sunset here."

Logan pulled a chair out for me, his hand on the back of the white plastic, waiting for me to sit. "They do."

"I love eating out here," Jasmine said.

"We'd do it more often, but it's a lot of work to carry everything out, then bring it back in," Luna responded.

"If you wanted to eat on the beach tonight, we could have had you on our deck," Gabe offered.

Poppy patted his hand and said, "But they have a better view of the sunset over here. It's gorgeous. I like it right here."

"Do you want to move over here? To this side?" Gabe appeared mystified.

Poppy rolled her eyes, exasperated. "No. I'm only saying it's nice here. Jasmine, tell us what classes you're going to be taking."

Logan leaned over and asked, "Can I get you wine? They opened a cab and chardonnay. Or beer is in the cooler."

"I can get it." I moved to get up, and he reached for my hand.

"What'll it be?"

"Chardonnay. Thank you."

We passed the dishes around family style, and before digging in, Tate toasted Jasmine. "To life changes, the big ones and the small ones. And the ones that seem so big, but in reflection, aren't that big at all." Quizzical and amused expressions circled the table. "What I mean is, Jasmine, I'm sure you have a world of emotions before starting your new school in your newly adopted country, but I suspect that within a week, it won't feel daunting at all. Some steps in life feel enormous, but when you actually take them, you realize it's just one step."

Over the course of dinner, the sky transitioned to a haze of pinks and oranges. Island dwellers gathered along the coastline in small groups, many with drinks in hand, to observe the sunset. Pinks and oranges mixed across the horizon as the slim, bright glow of the sun slipped behind the trees bordering the horizon and day gave way to night.

Gabe, Poppy, Logan, and I said our goodnights at the same time with a chorus of "Good luck, Jasmine."

As I hugged her goodbye, I tipped her chin up and told her, "As soon as you get back on Monday, come find me. I want to hear all about it."

"That was nice," Logan said as we drove away. "Thanks for inviting me."

"It's a good group," I said. "Being there tonight made me miss my family. Or, I suppose, just people."

"I do. I think that was one of my biggest adjustments after, you know. Getting used to living alone. Being the only one in the house. Do you have a big family?"

"No. But, growing up, my grandparents on both sides came over a lot. And then, college. People are always around. I had roommates. I miss it." As I said the words, I realized how much I missed my old life. But, living here, I didn't have to be isolated. To an extent, I had done that to myself. I could have been a part of this group of friends for a long time. They had been open; I had been the closed one.

I pulled to a stop in front of his house and turned to say goodnight.

"Thanks for coming."

His arm rested on the ledge of the seat cushion. He bent his head. In the moonlight, his chocolate-colored eyes shone black. The pounding of my heart intensified, and I wondered if he could hear it. In slow motion, his lips brushed across mine with the slightest pressure. A tingling sensation lit my skin, from the tips of my fingers, along my throat, to the ends of my toes.

Then he backed out of the golf cart. The air, crisp and fresh, filled my lungs. He rested his hands on the top of the golf cart and peered down at me. In the dark, I couldn't see his eyes, but I felt his gaze in my bones. He opened his mouth. I could swear he was going to speak, but after a pause, he straightened and walked along the path to his front door.

The kiss boggled my mind. I pressed the accelerator. So quickly, it might have been a figment of my imagination, except my breath came out in short, quick bursts. I slowed as I approached the turn off his street and glanced back to his front yard, to the scene of the kiss. He remained on the path, both hands in his pockets, watching me drive away.

All the giddiness returned in waves. *What a good date. We had a really good date.*

Nym trotted up when I returned home, and like a buffoon, I told him all about it. "Hey, boy. So, guess what? Your mommy had a good time. A really good time. Yes. I know. So hard to believe. With the good-looking man. The one you like. Yes." Nym's tail flapped back and forth. "And he kissed me. Yes. I know. He did." I squealed, because why not? Nym wouldn't tell anyone.

After locking the front door, I returned to the kitchen to

freshen Nym's water bowl for the night and to give him a treat for being such a good boy. My BlackBerry vibrated on the counter. An unknown number. *Erik.*

"Hey, there."

"Mom told me about Dad's skin cancer. I checked out his medical records. It's nothing to worry about."

"What do you mean—"

"I got onto the hospital network. It's nothing. Mom's assessment is correct."

I closed my eyes and grimaced as a familiar pain surfaced. "I don't think it's worth breaking federal laws. If you ask Mom and Dad questions, they'll just tell you the answer."

"It's easy, so why not?"

"You're addicted, Erik. Seriously. It's like an addiction."

"Cali. It's nothing. I knew you'd be worried. So was I. He's fine." That wasn't the point, but I didn't have it in me to attempt once more to convey right versus wrong to my brother.

"Anyway, did you go out on that date with that cop?"

"Logan? Yes, tonight, actually." *Funny you should bring it up.*

"Cali, NSA came out to the island a couple of days ago. I just found out about it. And they met with Logan. In his office. I don't think it's a good idea for you to spend time with him."

"What? You cleared him."

"I know. But, Cali, something's not right. That guy came down from D.C. Do you know how inconvenient that is? And he was there for a few hours. Some dipshits are theorizing locations for our servers. I think he came down to brief Logan. Cali, spending time with that guy isn't smart. It's risky."

"Erik." The whine in my response sounded childlike. *This is ridiculous. And what does it matter? I can be friends with someone without them learning about you.*

"Cali, you let him in your home. Think about it for a minute. What he can notice. What he might see."

"What would he possibly see? There's nothing here." Everything that might incriminate Erik was out at the office. Erik built a safe room for me, just in case, but even if he discovered that, it would look odd. That was it. I could say the previous owner built it.

"You let him in to go to the bathroom. Then you go on a date. Then there will be another. Before you know it, he's over all the time. He'll see a text, or something will pique his interest. If he spends enough time around you, he will get suspicious." Suspicious…the word rattled around in my head.

"How did— Oh. My. God. You watch my camera feeds. You told me those were for security."

"They are. And the security team let me know he entered the back door."

"I thought you only had cameras over the front door?"

"Cali, we've been over this. Why did he stop by and need to use the bathroom?"

"How did you know he went to the bathroom? Wait. You have cameras inside my home? And a team of people watch them?"

"Cali, you've got to think through this. It's a downward slope into unnecessary risk."

"I want those cameras turned off."

"No."

"No? I'll go around and disengage them. I'll put tape over the lens or pull them out of the wall. I'm serious. I don't like the idea of a random room of people watching me. That's creepy. And reporting to you! Over a door is one thing. No. Just no."

"How did you think those cameras worked?"

"I thought if the alarm was triggered, the security company looked at footage of the outside of the house to see what triggered the alarm. I never thought at any random hour they were watching, especially inside my home."

"Cali, that's how every security system works."

"No. That can't be." I crossed my arms. A camera in the office, over his precious servers. Fine. I got that. One over the front door—totally normal. You could buy a similar device in Target and put it over your front door. *Cameras inside my home? Forget it. No.*

"This guy has a military intelligence background. He's going to pick up on things. You have to be careful—"

"Erik." I circled my den, gritting my teeth, while scanning the room for cameras.

"You know what it would do to Mom and Dad if we're caught… if I'm caught. It would devastate them."

Yes, if their golden son went to jail, it would most definitely devastate them. On that, we agreed.

"Remember, we don't live in a binary world. There's no such thing as a good or bad side. He works for the other side, and you can't trust him. Spending time with him isn't smart."

I rolled my eyes but held my tongue. There was no point in arguing. I'd debated him down the conspiracy rabbit's hole too many times in the past.

"You said it was fine." That was the most important point here. He said I could go out with Logan.

"That was before NSA made a special trip out to meet with him. For like an hour. What could he have possibly had to say that he couldn't risk being overheard? Tell me that." I couldn't think of answers for him. Irritation and frustration and other nasty emotions threatened to boil.

"You promised me. This was supposed to be temporary."

"Cali, Jesus, you sound like you're going to cry."

"I'm not crying." *I want to punch something. There's a difference.*

"If you want to date him, fine. I can't stop you. Just be wary. Be smart. It's so fucking easy to slip up." A deep male voice resonated, and I waited, listening to the muffled exchange between Erik and the stranger. "I gotta run. Love you, sis. It'll all be over soon. Trust me."

 ogan

Thanks again for last night. Are you available for a date?

I stared at the text. Pressed the delete key repeatedly.

Thanks again for last night. Would you like to go out on a date with me?

Jesus. I never did like dating. Every text I wrote looked awkward. Back in the day, I had game. What the hell happened?

Thanks again for last night. Any chance I can repay you? Dinner tonight at my place?

I set my phone down on my desk. I didn't press send. *Dinner tonight at my place? Does that sound slimy?* The winds were optimal today for windsurfing. I could offer to take her out, although that could be frustrating if she's never done it before. My phone on my desk rang at the same time Colin, one of the men on my team, rapped his knuckle against my office doorframe. If she wanted a poet, or some super creative date, it wasn't going to work out. I pressed send.

At 10:36, in the middle of a communications status meeting, she responded.

Sure. What can I bring?

"Good news?"

Tamara, our communications director, wore an annoying grin on her face. Chad set his iPad down.

"What?" he asked, confusion evident as he glanced around the table to each of us. As mayor, he loved attending our weekly status. I suspected his monthly email to the island was his favorite monthly activity. He injected quite a bit of opinion and personal flair to the lengthy emails. But when in meetings, he generally lost interest.

"Was that smile over something in my website data?" Tamara asked.

"What?" Chad looked as lost as I felt.

"Never mind. Sorry." She continued grinning.

"Please continue with your summary. I'm listening." I tapped out a quick *just yourself* response and returned to the business at hand.

~

I left the office an hour early, stopped by the market, and picked up baked potatoes, Brussel sprouts, and two filets. Once home, I jumped in the shower, ironed a loose-fitting button-down shirt, and debated between slacks or jeans. The slacks won out.

Yes, it'd been years since I'd been in the dating game, but I hadn't forgotten the steps. I had forgotten the nerves. I couldn't recall actually being nervous with Bethany. When we'd started dating, it happened naturally. I'd been new to Chicago, and she was a junior DA. A very junior, overworked assistant to the assistant DA, but one of her cases had been one of mine. We'd celebrated a win out at the bar with the crew, hooked up, and she took charge. Everything fell into place.

No need thinking about the past. Going down memory lane wasn't the way to kick off a new relationship. Relationship—damn if I wasn't getting ahead of myself. A date. That was all. And it was about damn time I re-entered the dating world. Divorce and scandal didn't mean my life had to end. Bethany's life sure hadn't.

With the flat side of my chef's knife, I flattened the garlic cloves, then chopped them into fine slivers, perfect for working into the sides of a filet. Cali's smile came to mind as she ran by on the beach earlier today. She must've been running behind today, because I normally crossed paths at the end of her run, when she was checking her watch and counting her pulse rate. She never broke pace, but she'd smiled and waved. If she'd stopped, I would've told her to bring Nym. I considered texting her but figured it was too much.

"Alexa, play a dinner playlist."

Music filled the downstairs. After a careful inspection of the limited contents of my wine refrigerator, I pulled out a solid

Cabernet option that would go well with the filet and a Chardonnay that could also suffice. If she preferred white, as I knew some women did, I had it covered.

Thirty minutes later, the potatoes were on the stove boiling, my Brussels sprouts were in the oven roasting, and the table was set. I'd even found a small round candle in a clear glass jar. I swept the floor and wiped the counters. I circled the open downstairs and then double-checked everything in my room was neat. Not that I expected we'd make it into my room, but I had time to spare.

Did I ever put this much effort into a date with Bethany? Of course, we'd lived in Chicago. Getting a reservation at an excellent restaurant, having the foresight to request a good table, those were the ways to exhibit dating game in the city. And I hadn't even had to expend any effort on that front. Bethany made the reservations at the restaurants she chose.

A low, barely audible knock sounded against the door. The sharp chime of my front doorbell followed. I wiped my palms against my slacks, double-checked my breath against my palm, and swung the door open.

"Hi." Cali held up a bottle of Quilt Cabernet in a nervous offering, the exact wine I'd selected for us to drink.

"Hi. You didn't need to bring anything."

She shrugged and lifted her nose higher into the air. "Wow. Something smells good."

"Roasting Brussels sprouts. You're smelling the garlic. Can I get you something to drink?"

"Sure. I'll have whatever you're drinking."

"Here. I'll open this. Which happens to be the same bottle I picked out for us tonight."

"Oh, really? That's funny. I guess it goes to show there's a limited selection of wine at the market, huh?"

"It's not that limited. You picked one of my favorites." The market on the island left a lot of room for growth, but the wine section could compete with most of the grocery stores I'd frequented back in Chicago. I liked to think the odds were small we'd select the same bottle, and therefore it was a good omen. I offered her a glass and paused, at a loss for a toast. She saved me.

"To good things." Our gaze met over the rim of her glass. She wore loose black silk slacks that highlighted a narrow waist and the curve of a well-defined derriere. The fabric draped her legs like a skirt. A single gold necklace with a white quartz pendant hovered above the V of her white silk tank, leading the eye to the soft slope of her breasts. Her silky black hair hung loose and glimmered in the overhead lights. Cali struck me as both natural and elegant and probably a notch out of my league.

I pulled out a stool for her that would allow her to watch while I finished preparing our meal. "Sit."

"What are you making?"

"Well, for you, I'm pulling out all the stops." I gave her the brief rundown.

"I'm impressed you cook."

"I enjoy cooking. But I have a limited repertoire. And I'm making you my best tonight, so, fair warning for the future."

The corner of her front tooth pressed into her lower lip as she grinned. She ran her fingers through her glossy strands, lifting them higher, only to fall gracefully back in place the moment she removed her fingers. I wanted to reach out and touch those silky strands, but I busied myself with our dinner.

"I really like your kitchen. Did you design it?"

"They already had the plans when I bought it. I approved some recommended finishes. Baird, the builder, does a good job."

"Yeah, I've been into some of his open houses on spec homes he's built. He does beautiful work."

She lived in a beautiful home on the beach, but I didn't want to ask about her house. "So, you never really said before. What lured you here from Seattle?"

"I just wanted… something different. I found it online. What about you?"

I swirled my wine, buying time to derive an answer. "The same."

I busied myself completing dinner. This beautiful, reclusive woman moved across the country, all by herself. She taught one student. She probably answered me as truthfully as I answered her.

"You said you're a language translator. What languages?"

She fidgeted with the stem on her glass. "Mostly Arabic."

"Really?"

"You expected an Asian language, right? Chinese? Korean?"

"Are you Asian?" In my mind, no matter what ethnicity she claimed, she was beautiful. Stunning. I might have guessed Hawaiian.

"My grandfather's family is from Macau. You probably haven't heard of it. It's near Taiwan. My grandmother's family is from Brazil, but she was raised in Macau. They moved to the US before my father was born. My dad married an American. My mother and her side of the family are from all over. They've never really done the genealogy thing. Or, as my grandfather would have said, they are mutts."

I chuckled. "That's one way of looking at it."

"Anyway, in a roundabout way, that's why I took Arabic. My grandfather's family encouraged Cantonese. And I studied it. We went to a foreign language magnet school. But when I reached high school and needed to select my focus, I chose Arabic. It might have been the most rebellious thing I ever did. No, scratch that. Moving out of the house as an unmarried adult. My grandfather was mortified."

"Didn't go over well?"

"It's amazing I wasn't disowned. I mean, my mother's family couldn't have cared less. Actually, they expected I'd move out on my own because that's normal for them, you know? On your own after college. My grandfather didn't see things that way. He'd prefer we remained with our parents until marriage. But Dad took the brunt of it. He always had to work to balance his family and my mom's side. Are you close to your family?"

"My chosen family, yes. I went to West Point out of high school, then Special Forces. Some men I met from those years, they're my family. My mom passed away years ago. Heart attack."

"I'm sorry. And your father?"

"Don't really know him." I stood and cleared our plates. "Can I interest you in dessert?"

"What do you have?" She smiled in a way that could be interpreted as suggestive. I paused, then decided I most definitely read that wrong.

"Apple pie. From the market."

She rested her palm on her flat stomach. "Would it be rude if I passed? I'm actually quite full. You're an excellent cook."

"Well, meat and potatoes. If there's a grill involved, I can pull it off."

"Don't let me stop you from dessert."

As much as I might wish otherwise, she didn't mean herself. "I'm full, too. So, you mentioned a brother."

"I did?"

I dropped open the dishwasher. I thought she'd mentioned him, but maybe it was Poppy. She said something about her brother gave her the dog.

"Where does he live?"

"He lives abroad."

"Oh, do you get to see him much?"

"No. Do you go back to Chicago often?"

"There's no need. My buddies live all over, but none in Chicago." Besides, that was part of my divorce agreement…that I stay away. Not that I needed to share that on a first date. She picked up her pocketbook and took out her phone.

"Work stuff?" I asked.

"Thought I heard something. Here, let me help."

I tried to tell her to sit, but she insisted. Her lithe frame glided around the kitchen with a dancer's poise. The wine loosened me up, relaxed me, and I let my gaze follow the curve of her ass. She stood at the sink, rinsing dishes, as I wiped down the counter, stealing glances at her profile. The long lines of her neck, the way the silk blouse hugged the slight curves. The smooth quartz falling above the V, to those tempting, well-formed breasts.

She brushed against me, and my body reacted, instantly hardening. I wanted to hold her against the counter and trace kisses down her neck, hold her breast in my hand, brush my thumb across her nipple. I imagined what she'd look like naked, standing before me—

"I think that's it."

I blinked, and my back hit the refrigerator.

"I should probably get going home. I need to take Nym out for a walk."

"I meant to tell you to bring him."

"To your house?" She found the idea preposterous, as indicated by her wide, teasing smile.

"Why not?"

"You don't have a pet. You wouldn't want someone else's dog in your home, would you? Your home is so clean. It's pristine. Nym sheds everywhere."

"My place is clean because no one's here. I love dogs."

I followed her out the front door. "I'll walk you home. You walked, right?"

"Yeah, I did."

Our steps fell in line easily. Our arms bumped. I considered reaching for her hand, sliding my fingers through hers, but she slipped her hands into pockets.

"Is this your first date since your divorce?" She stared straight ahead, and I studied her, unsure she'd really asked. Her dark brown eyes held the question.

"Yes. Well, last night, if you count last night. What about for you?"

Several steps followed before she answered, "Yes."

"I enjoyed tonight."

"Me too. For what it's worth, I think your ex-wife made a huge mistake letting you go. A man who can cook—"

"Meat and potatoes." She grinned. "I don't want to oversell myself."

"A man who can cook and walks a girl home…"

"What about your ex? He must have been insane."

She flinched. Lots of people didn't like to talk about their exes. But something felt off. She stared off to her right, toward the ocean. Between the oceanfront homes, the dark waters glinted in the moonlight.

"That's a gorgeous waning moon," she said.

"It is." A woman who knew the verbiage for the phases of the moon. I liked that about her and, well, quite a bit more. So what if we were technically both each other's rebound? "Have you got plans for Labor Day?"

"No. You?"

"I'll be working. But I'll be here. Any plans to go visit your family soon?"

"I'm working on it. I miss my parents."

She stopped at the juncture of the road and her driveway. Her chin lifted. I moved closer, inches away. Her chest rose and fell. Those dark eyes met mine. The air between us intensified. My lips fell to hers. The entire date had been foreplay leading up to this. My lips against hers. Her silky strands between my fingers. Her body tantalizingly close. Our tongues dancing a slow, provocative dance.

Perfect. A perfect date, but without a long-term future. Nothing long term happened with your first date after a divorce, or so they said. Still, I wanted to treat her right. And for that reason, I ended the kiss when we were both slightly short of breath and with a promise for a second date.

ali

I smiled all the way home. Thank you.

I don't want to come on too strong. But at my age, games hold no appeal. I like how you make me feel. And I hope to see you again soon.

I LAY IN BED, HOLDING MY PERSONAL PHONE, READING THE BACK-to-back text messages over and over again. Smiling. A comfortable warmth settled within me, an infusion of… hard to believe it…happiness.

My BlackBerry vibrated on the bedside table, and an unknown number flashed. I reached over, picked it up, and declined the call. The phone vibrated again, and I lifted a pillow and placed it over my cell to smother the sound. Within seconds, the landline rang. No one ever called the landline. I lifted my middle finger and held my arm out, high and proud. The ringing stopped.

Wait. I'm in my bedroom. Did he see that?

In the kitchen, I fixed myself coffee. I had no proof he saw me. *Would he really put a camera in my bedroom? No. He wouldn't.* The seas rolled in calmly, with only an occasional whitecap all the way out to the horizon. The sun glimmered over the ocean, a big orange ball rising against a clear blue backdrop. The forecast called for clear skies, but they expected the temps to soar to the high nineties.

Nym lay sprawled at my feet, patiently waiting for his morning walk. I scratched below his ear and contemplated my translation workload. The landline rang, and the grating sound echoed throughout the living room. I slipped on shoes and exited the sliding door.

"*Hola!*" Poppy, from three decks down, shouted, waving her arm.

"Morning!" I shouted back. Nym's leash tightened. "You want to get out there, huh, boy?" Nym's tail wagged. Poppy matched my pace along her parallel boardwalk. When we reached the sand, I kicked off my flip-flops and greeted my blonde, bubbly neighbor.

"Gorgeous day, right?" she asked. "It's gonna be a scorcher."

I dug my toes into the still-cool sand. The lunch run would be a challenge. "I love the lights you've hung up beneath the branches of the trees on your patio. It gives it a magical feel." Poppy's restaurant was near my little office's location. Not that she knew that. I kept an eye on her restaurant's development. She had to be nearing her grand opening.

"Thanks. I like it, too. But my guess is the rooftop with the ocean view will be everyone's favorite."

"Maybe in summer, but not once it gets cold."

"Yeah, no doubt. Our outdoor heaters will be far more effective down in the cover of the trees. But I didn't hustle out here to talk about my patio."

"No?"

"No, ma'am! I heard ya'll had a date. And look at that smile. You have a glow. Yep. A glow." She reached out and pushed my shoulder. "Logan told Gabe he finally got up the nerve to ask you out."

"I doubt he said—"

"Who knows exactly what he said? Gabe is a piss-poor translator. But we've known since Howl at the Moon he wanted to ask you out. And he finally did. How was it? Does he open up and talk when it's the two of you? He's nice enough around me, but he pretty much just talks to the guys. He's hot… like, smoking." She exaggerated fanning herself. I grinned, silently agreeing with her assessment.

"It was good. We had a good time. But it was one date. Just one." Amusing as she may be, the girl needed to chill.

"Does that mean you don't see it going anywhere? Are you not that into him? That's okay if that's the case. There's another guy I know. A bartender at Jules."

"Isn't he in the middle of his divorce?"

She waved her hand, either dismissing me or waving at a fly. "Yeah, but it's behind him, pretty much. Another option. Did you really not like Logan?"

"Oh my god!" I screeched, and she laughed. "I liked him. We had a good time. And yes, we'll probably go out again. But it's, you know…"

"Hey, I get it. Take it easy. Take it slow. There's no rush." I side-eyed her. "It's okay. I get it, girl. I can see how dating again could be tough. I mean, after, you know…I bet you've got all these emotions. You can unload any time. I'm like a vault. I am not one of those girls who tells her fiancé everything."

"It's not about the divorce." It might be my cover, but I refused to play that card over and over. Somewhere out there were women battling real issues post-divorce. Hell, I suspected Logan was a person battling genuine issues. I wouldn't pretend to be torn up about a divorce that didn't exist. "I just…I'm not sure what my future holds. Or where I'll be. And I'm not in a rush."

"I love that about you. Aren't you, what? Over thirty, right? And not in a rush. I love that."

I side-eyed her once again. *Jesus. As if thirty is old.* She reminded me of my mother. "I'm thirty-two. How old are you?"

"Twenty-six. And I'm not in a rush either." I couldn't help but notice the sunlight reflecting on the enormous rock on her finger. "We've already agreed. No kids for years. I'm thinking around thirty-five. What about you?"

"Kids?" *Is she crazy?*

"Yeah."

"Poppy…"

"Yeah?"

"One. Date." The talking windstorm beside me blew my mind.

"Oh, I didn't mean that. Well, I guess maybe I did. At any rate, I like you aren't rushing things. But you had a good time?"

I laughed. "Yes. We had a good first date."

After the morning walk on the beach, I sat down to my translation assignment. Unlike so many of my corporate business assignments, this was a one-off project to translate an English romance novel to Arabic. Hours flew by as I pored over the text. Deep in thought, my personal iPhone rang, and on instinct, I answered.

"What the hell are you thinking?" Erik's angry tone riled up my defenses.

"Last I checked, I'm a grown woman. And you said I could go out with him."

"Then NSA visited the island. And now he's talking about going out with you again." *Wait...what?* "Cali, there's so many reasons it's not a good idea...in case you forgot, you are over there for your safety. People in the US government might not kidnap you, but if you show up in a database, others will find you. If someone found you, they could kidnap you to force our hand."

"Our hand, Erik? Our? Come off it. You're the one who's made the most wanted list. You're the one who's afraid they'll interrogate me and risk your being thrown in jail. This isn't about *my safety,* is it?" The surge of anger forced me into a standing position, and I paced the floor.

"Wrong. We've been over this. You're my twin. You could be collateral. And we're not just talking about the US. Remember? The Chinese would love to get hold of you, and trust me when I say you don't want them to. They'd either kill you or use you as a backdoor bargaining chip. Same for the Russians. As for the Americans...I don't like you spending time with him."

"You told me it was okay."

"That was before NSA came for an in-person meeting. When he's with you, what kind of questions does he ask?"

I huffed out air, letting the frustrated blow serve as my

answer. None of this made sense. *One date and he's ranting?* "Are you reading my texts?"

"I'm reading his." I was shocked, but I wasn't shocked. Erik had no boundaries. "Look, I've asked a tremendous amount of you. I get it. Can you hang tight for two more months? Just two more months. That's all I ask."

"Have you scheduled the flight for me to visit Mom and Dad?"

"Jesus, Cali, did you not hear anything I said? We have to be careful. I'm trying to arrange a private plane so you don't come up on anyone's radar. And believe it or not, I'm busy as fuck. We're doing a monster load of work with a wicked small group. But we're getting closer. Be patient. I gotta run. Love you, sis."

The line went dead, and I hurled the handheld phone across the room into a wall where it clattered on the floor. *Asshole.*

I closed my eyes in frustration. But behind my lids, I saw the photographs. The ones Erik showed me. Blood everywhere. The images grotesque, like something out of a dark television show. His terror that day had been palpable. He'd only shown me the photos when I brushed him off. Considered him delusional. Then he offered up his proof. She'd been murdered with a knife. One slice along the throat. A chill fell over me, and I rubbed my arms for warmth. He told me I could be next. Used for revenge.

I'd been out here for almost a year. He'd had no signs that his ex-partner still sought revenge. And all these other groups he dangled around to emphasize the threat? Even if the Chinese got to me—or the Americans, for that matter—it wasn't like I could lead them to Erik.

I had no idea where Erik was. He could be as nearby as Wilmington, or as far away as Bora Bora. I easily lied about his whereabouts because I didn't know the answer. And even if anyone out there tried to tap our communications, he always used a burner phone to call me. Half the time he used our stupid childhood code. And knowing Erik, he used a VPN with some complex server network that routed through a dozen countries. They'd never find him. Ever. But he might be right that if they found me, it wouldn't be pleasant.

Nym trotted across the room, and I rubbed his soft fur. My brother was a brilliant genius beyond compare. They'd never catch him. He'd never be stupid enough to use the same public library day in and day out until they triangulated his location and caught him. That was how I came to land here. He moved too often. I wanted peace. I wanted roots. The Taurus in me ran strong.

I closed my MacBook Air and sought tranquility through a long, sweaty run on the sand. I stretched my legs, ankle to toe, until my calves and thighs burned. In and out through my nose, deep, consistent breaths that pumped blood and oxygen as thoughts, once frenetic, mellowed to a dim void. My focus centered on maintaining my stride.

Beep. Beep. Beep. My pace slowed. My hands gripped my sides as I gasped for air then checked my time.

"You look like you had a good run." Still gasping, I held my hand up to my brow, sheltering my eyes from the bright overhead sun. Logan straddled an ATV. His shorts slid up above his knees, exposing tanned, muscular thighs and calves. He wore a baseball cap and sunglasses, giving him an athletic vibe. Everything inside me vibrated in response.

"Hey. I didn't see you."

"Well, I'm glad I ran into you. I bought too much fish to grill, and it's not gonna keep. Was wondering if you'd like to join me?"

Erik's angry *what are you thinking* floated through my mind. But I liked Logan. Clearly. My heartrate monitor provided the evidence. And Erik couldn't just change his mind. He didn't own my life. No matter what bullshit he'd wrapped himself up in. "Sure. I'd love to."

"Great. Seven okay?"

"Yeah."

"And bring Nym."

"Why?"

"Well, we might have leftover food. And I'm sure he doesn't enjoy being home alone, right?"

I couldn't think of a reason not to bring Nym, so I agreed and told him I'd be over later. As I stretched beneath the blistering sun, my thoughts circled my brother and all of his requests. I wondered how much longer I could go along with him. Two more months? What, exactly, would be different in two months? It was always the same thing with him. "Just a little more time, Cali." No, I didn't want to see my brother in jail. And our parents would be devastated if he were imprisoned. But I didn't intend to be a sacrificial lamb for him either. Yes, he got himself in way too deep. Yes, there'd been one mafia-esque attack on his partner's girlfriend. But that had been a year ago. I'd been sequestered, locked away long enough. Two more months? No, I didn't buy it. I'd been hearing it too long. At some point, the quality of my life had to factor in.

And in all my years in college and grad school, I'd never found a guy quite like Logan. In the past, I'd have a date and wait for a couple of days to hear from the guy, to see if I passed muster for a second date. And more often than not, I didn't even care if I did. Logan's text this morning was refreshingly different. I liked him. And while I'd grown to love Nym, the dog didn't qualify as the greatest conversationalist.

I would share nothing with Logan that would lead him to my brother, not that in his role in Public Safety he'd be interested in my brother, anyway. Without a doubt, there was a logical, simple explanation that explained his NSA visit. NSA wasn't even supposed to be monitoring activity in the United States.

At times, Erik's paranoia bordered on irrational. And this, his fears about a cop on a remote barrier island with a population below one thousand, qualified as irrational. Often, I found it hard to differentiate between Erik's irrational and rational fears. Were governments actually hunting him? Did this global crime syndicate truly want revenge? I had no proof of anything. Photographs of a murder. One long, heart-wrenching conversation over a year ago, and little bursts of insights and promises since. I loved my brother. I knew him better than any other person in the world. And I would never out him. But as I stretched my legs under the burn of the sun, I decided I needed a new normal. Or at least, I needed more.

Nym kept pace at my side, ears forward and alert. I'd kept him on a somewhat rigid routine, giving him long walks or runs in the morning, at noon, early evening, and late at night. It might have been my imagination, but the dog appeared nervous, maybe unsure about what we were doing off schedule and why. His tail wagged ever so slightly as we strolled down the black asphalt street. The black tip of his nose lifted, sniffing the air as the charcoal scent from a nearby grill wafted through the salty air.

I led Nym off East Beach Drive, into Logan's neighborhood. The white clapboard homes offered a casual and comfortable vibe, a more modern take on the traditional beach house. The front doors and windows reminded me of the modern farmhouse style of HGTV queen Joanna Gaines. Nym recognized the area, as I sometimes walked him through the streets and paths that cut through the neighborhood. I particularly loved this area during dusk. The interior lights lent a warm golden glow, and the scent of fresh-cut grass drifted through the narrow asphalt paths.

Towels hung out on porch railings to dry, and in some homes, surfboards leaned against sides and bikes were left out in the front yard, often haphazardly as the kickstands didn't do well against the sandy soil. Parts of this neighborhood were evocative—to me, at least—of some older Seattle neighborhoods filled with craftsman architectural style homes. Of course, the two locations couldn't be more different. Seattle was a burgeoning city, parking was scarce, and, well, it was a city. Here the yards featured palm trees and beach grasses, and parking wasn't an issue because there were zero automobiles. Still, in the evening, this area reminded me of home more than any other spot on the island.

As we approached Logan's house, I glimpsed him by his grill in his back yard. He looked up, and a fissure of energy burst inside as his gaze fell on me. My fingers scratched between Nym's ears to calm his nerves.

Logan wore gray linen shorts and a black V-neck t-shirt that pulled tight across his biceps and across his chest. The tips of his dark hair appeared damp, as if he'd recently emerged from a shower. I'd considered bringing food, but he'd said he had too much, so I showed up emptyhanded.

"What are we having?"

"Salmon grilled on cedar planks. I'm warming the wood now. Can I get you something to drink?"

"Sure." The table in his back yard was already set with placemats and white china. A large citronella candle rested in the middle, and all around the perimeter of his small back yard were lit torches. "It looks great back here." Two oversized doors opened onto the porch, and I followed him through the closest one into his kitchen, leaving Nym on the locked porch.

"As you can see, I'm at war with the mosquitoes and gnats. If they get too bad, we can come inside onto the screened porch, but I like sitting beneath the stars."

"Do you have bad mosquitoes here?" I had no issues at all on the beach, but I'd definitely smashed a few large ones deeper on the island beneath the tree canopy. Actually, some of those large mosquitoes reminded me of back home, or at least hiking near Mount Olympus.

"You know, it's more of what I think they call no see-ums. Little tiny flies. What can I interest you in? Red? White?"

"You're the chef. You pick."

"Okay. Chardonnay it is." He opened the stainless steel refrigerator door and lifted an unopened bottle. He held it out for me to inspect. "Have you had this?"

"Yes. It's good."

He poured us each a glass and lifted a prepared charcuterie board from the counter.

"Outside?"

"Sure."

Nym paced the porch, smelling the floor and the corners.

"Have you had any other dogs back here?"

"No. Nym's the first." His lips curved into a subtle smile. "You're the first woman I've had over, too."

"Ah, well, Nym isn't usually so nosy." He continued to pace the porch, sniffing every floorboard.

"Have you taken Nym to many homes?"

"No." I smiled and lifted my glass to my lips. "You're the first." The chilled wine had hints of oak, with very little sweetness, exactly like I liked it. "This is delicious."

"I'm not a big white wine guy, but I do like this. With the heat today, and the salmon, it seemed like a good pick." He tapped his phone, and music floated through the air. "Do you like Jack Johnson?"

"I do. I listen to him a lot."

"It's been ages since I bought music. But I have Sonos set up throughout the downstairs. I can choose playlists." He held up the screen of his iPhone for me to see.

"Jack Johnson's a fitting vibe for here, don't you think?"

"Yeah." I could hear Erik's reprimand, that those devices could be hacked and used to listen to conversations, but I brushed his irritating rumble out of my mind.

I settled back into a comfortable wicker club chair with thick cushions. My sundress slid up my thigh, and his gaze warmed my exposed skin.

"So, Logan, tell me something more about Chicago. I've never been there."

"Really? Well, you haven't experienced winter until you've spent a winter in Chicago."

"I went to college with a few folks from Minneapolis, and they said something along the same lines about Minnesota."

"Well, I suppose you could say we're cousins. It's one of

those places that has great people, restaurants, culture, you know, plays and museums if you like that, and to me, it's one of the more beautiful cities right there on Lake Michigan. But once you leave and you experience winter where people bundle up because the high is going to be fifty-one, well…"

"So, you don't plan on going back?"

"No. But I can't say I really came here with plans to stay here for the long haul either. What about you?"

"No long-term plans." I crossed my legs and thought back to the day Erik had recommended the East Coast, and I'd seen Wilmington on a list of top coastal cities. This island hadn't been the plan, but the job posting had tempted me, then I fell in love with this place. So close to the mainland, yet worlds away.

Logan whistled, short and quick. Nym approached him, and he scratched the dog's head. "I think that's the case for many who end up here. It's more of a place to take a time out. Rest. Unless, of course, you're a retiree like Chad and all his golfing buddies. Then I suppose that's another sort of long-term plan."

"The 'reap the benefits of all your hard work' plan?" I swirled my wine, comfortable and relaxed.

"Exactly."

His phone beeped repeatedly, and he tapped it. "Salmon's ready."

"Do you tie everything into your phone?"

"Pretty much. Doorbell, AC, I can lock and unlock my doors through my phone. If I'd wanted to, I could have connected the door on my golf cart shed to the phone, but I didn't think it was worth paying for a sophisticated garage door contraption on a golf cart shed."

I itched to explain how bad of an idea it was to have everything on one device. He was opening himself up to all kinds of security risks from hackers. Not to mention his data was probably being used by a hundred different companies to market him different products. No, that was the least of his worries. His biggest worry, as I considered the risks from such dependence on a hackable phone, came from a thief being able to unlock his house. And most likely the way they would do it was to figure out his password. Nothing high tech at all. Or simply steal his phone. Would a normal person have these thoughts? I thought of Poppy. If I used her as a benchmark, then no, she'd never, ever think like that. I refrained from saying anything that might expose my knowledge about risks, but I made a mental note to check out his phone to see if I could increase his security.

For dinner, he grilled salmon and covered it with a teriyaki glaze, and coupled it with a tossed salad and couscous with fresh sliced cherry tomatoes.

"You know, looking at these meals you're preparing, I'm feeling like I've been stuck in college-student mode."

"What's your typical meal?"

"Well, for dinner, I'm a big fan of frozen food."

He grimaced.

"It's just me," I said in defense. "I mean, I'd say I even eat a bowl of cereal at least once or twice a week."

"How old did you say you are?"

I laughed. "Thirty-two. There's no excuse."

"I can't say I've never done that myself. And I'm forty-two. If you were curious." His knee brushed mine at the same time a sexy smirk played across his lips. "But I eat out quite a bit. I'll meet up with someone from work or walk over to The Wisp. If I sit out there with a beer, most days someone I know will stop by."

"That must be nice."

Logan set his fork down and scratched at the end of his beard. "You know, it'd be easy enough for you to do the same. People here are friendly."

"I know," I said, purposefully upbeat.

His long index finger glided up and down the knife handle on the table. Slowly and deliberately, he raised his gaze to meet mine head-on.

"I don't want to pry. But I noticed your alarm system. The multiple locks. And you moved out here on your own and... I want you to know. If there's someone out there who treated you badly or anything..."

"It's nothing like that." Surprise at his conclusion hit me first, but then I considered how I must look to him with my locks and security cameras and German shepherd. "My brother works for a security company, and he's diligent." I half-laughed. "And that's an understatement. He's... he sees bad things, and he gets a little crazy, and then I think maybe I get a little uneasy with all of it?" There, that sounded like a good explanation, right? And nothing too accurate about Erik.

His hand found mine beneath the table. He squeezed, and in a contradiction of reactions, I felt oddly secure and comforted, while a fission of energy circulated up my arm.

"I'm a cop. I mean, it's not exactly like I see much here. But back in Chicago... I saw some of the worst. I get it. I can definitely understand how your brother might get carried away with your security. I mean, depending on what he might be seeing."

"Was it tough? It doesn't seem like it's tough here on Haven Island, but there are TV shows about being a policeman in Chicago." He scratched his beard, weighing his response. I presumed maybe deciding how deep he wanted to go with his answer.

"You see some of the worst aspects of human nature. And even some people you want to help, they don't trust you. It's a sort of thankless job." He licked his lips and closed his eyes, thinking. "But it's fulfilling. At least to me. Making the city safer. Fighting crime. It's fulfilling."

"Is there a lot of crime out here? On the island?" He got my question. This place was a small town, but it was also a step away from resort life. How fulfilling could his job here be?

"It's different here. But I still keep our little community safe. And this isn't forever. I'd say this was a needed breather." He fiddled with the napkin on his lap. There was something else there, and I thought he was about to open up. But he changed the subject. And I let him. "Well, tell me about your brother. I always wanted one, so I have to say, I'm jealous." He dug his fork into the food on his plate then waited for my answer. Erik's question from earlier, asking me about what kinds of questions Logan asked me, floated by. My stomach flipped. But no, I wouldn't go being paranoid. And some things are public record.

"Well, he's not just my brother. He's my twin. So I think of him as more. You know, more than just a sibling. We shared a womb."

"Wonder twins?"

"Not quite like that. But the connection you hear about with twins? We have it. Or we did, when we were growing up. Now, sometimes I'm not so sure it's… no, it's still there. But it's not as strong. We shared a bedroom until I was maybe eleven or twelve and someone told my parents girls and boys shouldn't share a room once, you know…"

"I can think of a few reasons a prepubescent boy would want his own room."

"Why do you say it like that? Do you think Erik requested his own room?" Some part of me had always wondered. Sure, there had been days when I wanted my room. Our parents painted our room blue and gray. But I loved hanging out with him so much, I never cared. I would've never asked for my own room, at least not at twelve.

"You'd probably know if he did." He scratched at his beard and smiled. "So, do you look alike?"

"I mean, we're fraternal… obviously. But we have the same hair and eyes. We're about the same height. He has a couple of inches on me."

"Is he a runner, too? Like you?"

"Oh, please. No. He's not into any sort of athletics. He's a computer nerd." I stopped myself from going on and on about how he lived in front of his computers, how he surrounded himself with computers and monitors when he was in one place long enough. "Are you finished?" He nodded, and I lifted our plates and carried them into the kitchen.

Nym followed me inside, hopeful for leftovers. The trainer had instructed me to not share human food with Nym, but it was just the two of us, and sometimes he gave me a look that brokered little discussion. And I was a sucker for those pointed fuzzy ears. "We don't have any leftovers, boy," I explained as the door swung open and Logan entered.

"Actually, if you let him have salmon, we do. There's another filet on the grill."

"Really?"

"I told you I had a lot of food. If it's cooled down enough, I can put it on a plate for him."

"No, that's okay. You can save it and eat it tomorrow."

"I'm not one for eating leftovers. Unless you want to take it home with you."

"No, it was delicious. But thank you."

"You have frozen food lunches?"

I reluctantly confirmed his suspicions.

He stepped up close to me, pressing me up against the counter and the sink. The pad of his thumb traced along my chin, and he lifted my head. His dark eyes looked down on me, and his fresh soapy scent lingered.

"I'd like to break you of your frozen meal addiction. It sounds lonely to me."

"It does?" I couldn't disagree.

He dropped his lips to mine. All my senses heightened, and my breathing intensified. I lifted my arms to his shoulders as the energy between us surged.

"Well, dinner was delicious. I'd say you are persuasive."

He kissed me again, soft and tempting.

"I like to think I can be. I'd like to think I have other powers of persuasion too."

"Huh?" I asked, breathless as his lips brushed the sensitive skin beneath my ear.

"You smell so good. What is that scent?"

"Shampoo. Rosemary." He trailed kisses down my throat as I repaid his compliment. "You smell good, too." He did. He had a fresh clean scent with a hint of a delicious woodsy aroma.

He lifted the hem of my dress and rubbed along my thigh. My core cinched.

"Do you have any idea how crazy this dress has been driving me? The hem bounces when you walk and shows off these long, lean thighs."

I shifted my leg, opening to give him greater access. The rough pads of his fingers were warm against my bare skin, and goosebumps spread like wildfire across my arms.

"Are you cold?"

"No," I breathed. I toyed with his soft hair on the back of his neck then tugged, guiding him back to my lips.

"Would you... Can we... Take this to the bedroom?"

"But what about—" A hungry, deep kiss silenced me. "The kitchen?" I asked, breathless, when he pulled back.

"Screw the kitchen."

"Are you sure?" My brain fogged. His thigh pressed hard between my legs, lighting a desire. But out of the corner of my eye, the dirty stack of plates nagged.

"Cali?"

"Yeah?" I brushed my fingers through the coarse strands of his trimmed beard, and he leaned into my touch.

"You're looking at those dishes, aren't you?"

My hips flexed against his legs, and I closed my eyes, reveling in the sensations firing off in my core.

"Now I'm not."

His rough beard scratched the delicate skin along my throat as he flicked over my sensitized nipple. Through the cloth, his touch teascd, and my body yearned for more.

His forehead pressed to mine. "Two minutes."

"Huh?" I groaned out as his nose toggled against mine.

He lifted me and placed me against the wall. Cold air encapsulated around my front in place of his warmth, and I stood, watching him, stunned as he moved at lightning speed. The chilly wall pressed against my back, and I alternated between crossing my arms and dropping my hands to my side.

Moments ago, I'd been ready to jump him, to beg him, to

drop all inhibitions. But the desperate desire to ease a long-buried need cooled, and my brain kicked in. *Shouldn't we take this slower? If we do this, will I be using him? I'm not about to get into a serious relationship. And he's so straightforward. He's a good guy.* He seemed to want more. If he wanted more, he deserved more.

Dishes clanged together. One singular swipe on the counters with a kitchen towel left the white gleaming. He closed the dishwasher with a dull snap.

"Clean," he announced as he stalked toward me. I halfway expected, or maybe hoped, he'd finish what we started and take me up against the wall. Hard, fast, and possessive. But he'd calmed down, too. He lifted my hand and pressed my knuckles to his lips. "Care to sit down? We can talk."

"Talk?" An uncontrollable smile spread.

"It's… we're both each other's rebounds, right?"

"Yes." I rationalized if you considered the shift from my life as it was, to the current state, as a divorcee, then I wasn't lying…he would be a twisted sort of rebound.

"This whole dating thing. To tell you the truth, I had no desire. Until you. I think I've been numb. Desensitized."

"You had a tough divorce?" The bow of his shoulders relayed an underlying pain as answer to my question.

"Is there any other kind?" Gentle, sensitive brown eyes searched mine.

"No, I suppose not." Apprehension he would see through me, see my lies, took hold. I dropped my gaze.

"I know they say a rebound relationship shouldn't…evolve. But to me, you don't feel like a rebound fling."

My fingers slid through his. A crushing weight rested on my chest. I followed him over to his sofa. He sat down first, and he tugged my hand, pulling me down beside him.

"You're not a fling to me either. But…"

"Sshhh. That's okay." Laughter from outside filtered through the walls, along with the high-pitched jingle of a bike bell. His arm wrapped around my shoulders, and he tilted my chin up. "I don't want to rush this. We can take it as slow as you want. But I like kissing you. A lot. Do you mind if I kiss you?"

My fingers skimmed his dark, thick hair at the nape of his neck, and he closed his eyes reverently. I pulled him down in answer. I tasted the faint hint of the cedar plank salmon, the chardonnay, and mint. His hands roamed over my dress, and I tugged on his shirt, pulling it out to grant access to the bare skin beneath. He groaned, and we shifted. Side by side on the sofa, his thigh pressed between my legs, and I ground against it. The tension and desire from earlier flamed back, but with a more controlled heat. He lifted my dress higher and higher, exposing me to just below my breasts. The soft touch of the rough pads of his fingers elicited an uncontrolled moan.

"Is this okay?" he asked in a low, barely audible, husky tone.

In answer, I brushed my fingers across his crotch and stroked the curve of his erection through his slacks. He groaned.

"How slow do you want to take this?"

Warmth from his roaming hand glided up my thigh and nestled between my legs. I leaned back and spread my legs wider. He slipped my silk panties to the side. One finger dipped inside, and I whimpered. My strokes over his erection became more frantic.

"Cali… I'm following your lead. Talk to me."

"Can we go to your bedroom?"

His body replaced his finger as he found his place between my legs, fully clothed, and pressed against me, a promise of what was to come. I wrapped my legs around his waist, and he ground his hips. *Holy shit.* He broke away, panting for air, his gaze hungry and raw. He stood and offered his hand.

I took all of three steps before he scooped me up and carried me past the kitchen, down a short hall, and into his bedroom. He set me down on his bed, against a stack of pillows, and my dress pooled around my waist. He tossed his shirt, and his focus fell to me. I lifted my dress over my head. I hadn't worn a bra, as the sundress didn't easily allow for one. I inched back on the comforter, leaning against my arms, in only my damp silk panties. He threw his shirt on the ground and unbuckled his belt, his eyes never leaving mine.

His pants dropped to the ground. He stepped out of them and stood before me in his boxers. Years of physical training and exertion shone in the lines of his chest, his firm pecs, and his taut, firm stomach. He climbed onto the bed, one knee at a time. My fingers explored his muscular chest and the smattering of dark, curly hair across those firm, hard pecs, those delectable abs and trailed down.

He stopped my hand when I reached the waistband of his boxers. "Not yet. Lean back."

He adjusted my body so I rested against the stacked pillows at his headboard. He trailed kisses from my lips, along my chin, and down my neck. His scruffy beard augmented the tantalizing sensations as he journeyed down to my breasts. He took turns working each nipple to a stiff peak with his tongue, and I pushed off the bed, crying out as his teeth grazed the tip.

"Sshhh," he coaxed. His lips caressed their way down my body, across my belly. He tugged at my panties, then distanced himself long enough to slide them off and toss them on the floor with the rest of our discarded clothes. He cast a mischievous expression then lowered between my legs. I spread my thighs, welcoming him.

His tongue, his fingers, and his beard brushed the sides of my thighs. The sensations cadenced, verging on overload, and I squirmed and mewled and gripped his hair, pushing him harder until my release pulsed through, leaving my limbs trembling and me gasping.

He kissed along my inner thigh as I recovered, then up my body.

"Oh my god. You are good at that."

"And you are responsive."

He laid his head down beside mine, a cocky smile on those talented lips. Once my breath evened out, I reached beneath the band of his boxers and wrapped my fingers around his stiff, hard cock and stroked.

He uttered unintelligible sounds and thrust his hips up into my hands. The boxers cut into my wrist, so I climbed up on my knees and removed them, sliding them down to his ankles and over his feet. He lay on his back, his arms crossed behind his head, his erection stiff.

"Your turn."

On my hands and knees, I crawled back up to him, then straddled him, placed my dripping wet core over him, teasing him, rocking my hips backward and forward. He reached up and caressed my breast.

With a pained grimace, he cursed and pushed me back. "I don't have a condom."

And neither did I. "Maybe it's the universe forcing us to slow it down. But I can still do this, right?"

I hovered over his cock, and his gaze heated as I lowered my mouth and licked the salty bead of cum on his tip. His Adam's apple shifted in and out as he nodded his consent.

I licked him up and down then took him in my mouth. He lifted my hair away from my face, groaning, his attention glued to my every move. He guided me as I licked and sucked, working him, giving him back a little of what he'd given to me. He expanded in my mouth and tugged roughly at my hair, pulling me back. His milky white release pulsed out across his stomach, his eyelids half closed.

I found my way up to him and kissed him. He fell against me into the kiss, and we ended up making quite a mess, which led to us cleaning off in the shower, each of us taking turns beneath the warm water, washing each other with his lavender poof.

He wrapped a towel around me and pulled me against his bare, damp chest.

"Stay tonight."

"But Nym…"

"Does he sleep with you?"

As my guard dog, the German instructor informed me, he shouldn't be allowed on my bed. But that heartless drill sergeant lived in Germany, and Nym slept on the end of my bed. So many rules came with Nym, I was destined to break some of them. Logan read the answer in my expression. He kissed the tip of my nose.

"He can sleep on the end of the bed. I'm not sure if you noticed or not, but it's a California king. He'll fit."

"As tempting as that is, I have to take him for a walk. I always take him on one late at night."

"By yourself?" He made a face that reflected disapproval. Nym entered the doorway, as if sensing he were the topic of conversation.

"I'm pretty sure no one's going to try to mug me with Nym by my side." I found my dress and pulled it over my head, then searched for my panties.

"I guess that's true." He slipped on shorts and an old West Point t-shirt. "If you want, you can crawl into bed, and I'll take him."

"Do you have any idea how tempting that would be on a cold winter night? How much I hate our late-night walks when it's freezing outside?"

"Well, by winter, I'll have the back yard fenced, and we can open the door for him to wander outside."

His natural assumption we'd be together in the winter infused a preposterous warmth through me. I liked the idea. Maybe too much. Because it really couldn't happen. Winter was months away, and if I let this go on, how could I possibly keep him at a safe distance? If Erik pulled through and remained true to his word and removed himself from his situation…would it all be okay then? Would Logan understand? Would I even choose to stay here?

ogan

"ARE YOU WHISTLING?"

Robert, part of the weekday shift, filled my office doorway with an amused smirk.

"It's a good day."

"Muggy as hell, and it's not even nine yet."

"Any day at the beach is a good day."

"Right." He clicked his tongue, and I opened my laptop, disregarding him, ready to get the day started. "Well, you may not want to whistle after I update you."

I leaned back in my office chair and waited for whatever crisis brought him to my doorway.

"We're receiving weird error messages. I've been on the

phone with the IT department for our servers, and someone's trying to hack in."

"Notices?"

I followed him over to the officer's office, a room which held three desks. We were a lean and mean staff, so folks shared desk space with alternating shifts. Robert was on an ancient desktop PC with a bulky monitor. Since I'd joined the department, I'd prioritized our budget for better servers to increase security, but upgrading these relics remained high on my wish list.

I scanned the error messages. Then I returned to my desk and accessed the code.

"Doesn't look like they got in."

"No. What do you think it is? Some bored teenagers? Or an attack?"

Every town in America had been upgrading servers for security over the last decade. I scratched my beard, considering what someone could want access to. Or what they could ransom. We had wealthy owners, sure, lots of CEOs of big business. But if someone wanted property records, we wouldn't be the first stop. However, our budget information could only be accessed here, and we were under fire right now from that budget responsibility group.

"What are you thinking?" Robert leaned over the desk.

"It could be a bored hacker up for a challenge." And it would be a challenge. Not only did I have a military intelligence background, but one of my best buds was NSA. When I upgraded our systems, I went with topline options. Every employee here utilized double authorization for accessing the Intranet.

"I read about how hackers could do real damage by

attacking our water or electrical." Robert made a statement, but the question hung in the air.

"Our water and electrical aren't on our grid. That's the power company. Ferry is private. I can't think of anything they could really do to us. Sewer, but that's private too."

"The activity halted about four a.m. There's nothing more for IT to do other than monitor. Weird, right?"

"Not much to do on it. I'll put a call in to my buddy and get his POV."

"A military guy?"

"Yeah, but he's NSA now."

"Nice. You know, my son's considering applying to West Point. You've followed an interesting career path, and so have several of your friends. I thought, if you wouldn't mind, it might be good for him to talk to you."

"Any time. I'd be happy to."

"If you had to do it over, you'd still go West Point, right?"

"It's an honor and a privilege." Robert nodded, and I focused on my laptop, effectively dismissing the conversation. *Would I do it over?* There was plenty I wouldn't do over, but I supposed West Point wasn't to blame.

I picked up the phone and dialed Matt.

"Morning."

"Hey, hey. If it isn't my favorite beach bum."

"Yeah, yeah." If he could see me, I'd flip him the bird. "Are you slacking these days?"

"Huh?"

"I got the live Matt. No voicemail."

"Oh, you caught me between meetings. I had a breakfast meeting near the Pentagon. Headed back to the office now. What's up?"

"Not much. We got some error messages that indicate someone's trying to hack in. Any suggestions on what they could be after? I know you see reports about this kind of activity."

"Not domestic. But…want me to look into it?"

"So far they haven't gotten in. My guess was it could be a kid? Some practicing hacker? I can't think of anything we store that's really worth accessing."

"They may not know that. Could be looking to see what you do have. Ransomware seekers or something like that. Your utilities, electricity, sewage…none of that is on the system they're trying to hack, is it?"

"No. That's all privately run."

"Well, as you know, when you have the net worth that you have in that area, you get some curiosity seekers."

"Yep." That was why I pushed to upgrade our security.

"Interesting. I wonder if someone is on a hunt for those servers I told you about."

"What servers?"

"Back in your office. If someone believes the boards…and they're trying to… I don't know. That doesn't make sense. It's probably coincidence." I didn't remember much of the specifics of the conversation we'd had. I'd been reeling from the Bethany pregnancy news. Nothing had jumped out as particularly relevant to our secluded little town.

"And this pod. Why would someone be hunting for it?"

"Well, the servers are used by a crime syndicate we've been tracking. They have servers in Iceland, Nigeria, Cuba, Argentina."

"You still haven't located the US location?"

"Nope. Realistically, they probably have more than one

location." He sounded like he was talking to himself rather than to me.

"Well, didn't I tell you before? This would be the worst place for a server farm. Our Internet connectivity is way too spotty. Wouldn't make sense."

"Yeah. And you'd notice if someone hauled in lots of equipment, right?"

"I mean, we don't inspect everything that comes off contractor boats. But most of what gets unloaded here is for construction. Still, I'm telling you, our connection sometimes comes and goes in waves. There are pockets on the island with zero reception."

"It's not ideal. But whoever is attempting to hack your servers may not know that."

"Common sense says the Midwest would be a better location."

"Why do you say that?"

"No storms to worry about. No earthquakes. You know this."

"They have tornadoes."

"A server farm could go underground. That's where I'd look."

"Yep. Any thoughts on joining our team?"

"NSA? Sounds like a desk job with either paper or meeting overload."

"And politics. You forgot politics."

"That's a sales pitch, right there."

"Right?" He chuckled. "Seriously. We're working on building blacklisted ops groups that could be right up your alley."

"Blacklist? As in off the record? Sounds borderline unethical to me."

"The fifth domain is the wild, wild west. We've got to adapt or sink."

"You and your fifth domain." Robert knocked on the doorframe, and I held up a finger to get him to give me a minute. "Look, I gotta go."

"Think about it. You can't hide away forever."

"Talk to you later." I hung up. Hide away. The way he said it, you'd think he forgot this assignment had been his idea. Admittedly, he did it to save my ass when I was facing potential censure.

"Everything okay?" Robert asked, his brow furrowed.

"Yep."

"What's the fifth domain?"

"Oh. Cyberspace." His blank expression begged for additional explanation. "You've got land, air, sea, outer space, and then, well, now cyberspace. As our attacks last night show, you have to defend all of them."

"Outer space?"

"Well, defend might not be the right word. But our country has a vested interest in outer space. And you know we have the Guardians now."

"The Guardians of the Galaxy."

We both chuckled at the terminology assigned by the US government. "So, did you need something?"

"No. Just wanted to tell you still no more error messages. I'm about to go on rounds."

My phone rang, and I checked the name. "Shit. It's Tamara. I bet she's calling about the proofs she left for me to review. Have you seen them?"

"No. Did you give them to Samuel?" Samuel worked night shift.

"No. Go on rounds." I waved him away and answered the phone.

"Tamara, I owe you comments. I know. I'll get them to you today."

"Comments? Oh, on the proof I dropped off?"

"Yep."

"I don't need those until next week. We're ahead of schedule. I'm calling because we have a PR issue."

I leaned back in my chair, not liking the sound of that at all. "What happened?"

"Do you read the *News & Observer*? Or the *Charlotte Observer*?"

"No." Both papers serviced cities that were hours away. Charlotte was at least a five-hour drive.

"Well, I'll email you the articles. We had a guest who stayed with us last week. It seems she received a DUI while on a golf cart?" Her raised tone at the end of her question conveyed disbelief.

"It's possible. You know what our guests can be like. Especially wedding parties."

"And you give them DUIs?"

"It's a moving vehicle under North Carolina law."

"Well, your department gave a ticket to the wrong woman. She works for a PR agency out of Charlotte, and her case has been picked up by the two biggest papers in the state. All that work I've been doing to be featured in *Condé Nast* and *Southern Living* is going to go down the drain if we get a reputation for giving out DUIs after two drinks on a golf cart."

"My team wouldn't do that. If she got a ticket, she was wasted." Nonsensical crap like this rubbed me the wrong way. My men were doing their jobs.

"She claims they wouldn't let her drive away. Her friend had to drive home."

"If she was drunk, they wouldn't let her drive. What do you want me to do?" I wondered if back in Chicago the folks on the traffic desk spent their days dealing with nonsense like this.

"I need every bit of information about the case that you have. I have to prepare a statement."

"Well, as a general statement, you need to reinforce that while people may be driving golf carts, they still have to follow North Carolina law."

"Logan, I'm not looking to get into a fight here. I'll let you read our statement before it goes out. But right now, I need information. She's making it look like we're not a good place to vacation. I emailed you her information and the articles. Do you think you have her alcohol level?"

"Maybe. Let me look into it."

My investigation led to one irate Samuel, who had a lot to say about the woman he pulled over last week. She also refused a breathalyzer, but he said she could barely stand. However, according to the newspaper articles, she had a witness who said she hadn't even had two glasses. It was precisely the kind of privileged issue that made me miss Chicago.

The blue skies and gently swaying palms by the marina contrasted with the turmoil and annoyance brewing inside me. I met Tamara in her marina-side office armed to argue. My officer did the right thing.

"Any chance you can drop the charge?" Tamara clapped her hands together in a praying gesture.

"Absolutely not." *Was she really gonna pray?* "It'll blow over by the end of the week. And as it is, these weren't front-page stories. They buried them. No one cares."

"It's being passed around on the internet. It's a wildfire, Logan."

As I went about my afternoon, arguing this bullshit situation with Chad and Tamara, my text exchange with Cali lightened my annoyance.

I enjoyed last night, too. I have too much work to do. That project I told you about? It's due Friday.

Of course, I hadn't convinced her to stay over. I knew the moment we left my house I was essentially walking her home. And when she stopped me at the top of her driveway, I could have taken it as an insult. But the hot kiss she gave me, and the little moans she made as she rubbed against me, well, actions spoke volumes.

So, can I take you out Friday night? We'll celebrate the completion of the project.

Looking forward to it.

So was I. And I planned to be fully prepared. I debated my best text response. There wasn't much to say, unless we got a stunning sunset over the marina. Then I could text her a photo.

"Hey, man, over here."

I slipped my phone in my pocket and nodded to Gabe. "You need a beer?"

"I'm all set."

I stopped by the pick-up window and ordered my Heineken.

As I sat on my stool, Gabe and I clinked beers. The Wisp overlooked the marina. Restaurant didn't accurately describe it. You could order food in from the nearby Delphina's, and they'd carry it over. But they offered beer and wine, and the covered patio and deck usually offered a nice breeze. A long wooden bar lined a portion of the deck, and Gabe, Tate, and I liked to sit out here, overlooking the marina after work.

"You must've had a good day at work today."

"Actually, no." On the annoyance scale, my day rated close to a ten out of ten.

"Well, then, that means things are going well with my neighbor."

"Did she talk to Poppy?"

"Said you guys were seeing each other. And that was one big damn grin on your face. Were you texting her?"

"Yeah."

"I recognize the look."

"I'm sure you do." Gabe and Poppy had only recently become a serious item. I started hanging out with Gabe after he'd moved here, so, after their relationship had started. Still, I picked up on enough comments from folks to know they'd moved noticeably fast. But they seemed really happy.

"So, what's she like?"

"You know her," I said.

"Nah, not really. She turns Poppy down more often than not. She's quiet." He took a swallow of his beer.

"Yeah, she is quiet. But she's wicked intelligent. She speaks five languages."

"I knew that. Tate discovered her first, you know. He told me about her when he hired her as a tutor."

"She's independent. Works as a contractor. I get the sense

she misses her family. Maybe Seattle. There's something more going on there. I can't put my finger on it."

"But you plan to." Gabe grinned.

"Yeah." I chugged my beer to hide my matching grin. "She's something else." I thought about her on the beach that night when I'd found out about Bethany. Her quiet way of helping me put that behind me.

"Is there a lot of crime in Seattle?" Gabe's question came out of nowhere.

"No. I don't think so. No more than most cities. Why?"

"Because. I figured maybe she came from a poor neighborhood. You know, her alarm system is more state-of-the art than what I have back in New York. I recognized the brand of cameras and the locks on her door. She hired someone who knew what they were doing when she had that installed."

"I noticed her alarm. Cameras too?"

"There's a glass bulb in front of the front door. On the back deck, too."

"Huh. Think they could be from a prior owner?"

"No idea. I've never been inside the house. Only at her front door. With Poppy." I swallowed the cold beer, considering this new information.

"She doesn't ever talk about her ex." I cut my eye at Gabe, curious to see if he knew anything.

"You should be grateful. There's nothing worse than a woman who won't shut up about her ex."

"Yeah, but I wonder if her hesitation means she's not over him? You know, some people need time after going through separation. It's like a war. A version of PTSD can accompany it."

"Well, what about you? She's the first person I've seen you even bat an eye at. We've been hanging with you all summer, and you've never once showed you had an interest in dating. We all assumed you were in recovery mode. Are you ready to jump into a relationship?" I didn't answer, instead choosing to focus my gaze straight ahead. A ferry entered the marina channel. Seagulls flew overhead. After a minute passed, he clapped my back and headed to the restroom.

The setting sun over the ridge of homes lining the far side of the marina lent a gorgeous hue of yellow and rose colors. *Am I ready to date? Absolutely.* But what would I bring to the table for someone like Cali? We didn't meet each other on an app. We hadn't answered questions about what we wanted out of life before meeting. Before investing any time. We'd actually gone into this as casually as you could.

At thirty-two, you could assume she'd have family on the mind. But maybe not. We'd spent a fair amount of time together, and the subject hadn't come up. If she aimed for a family, she'd move to a vibrant city, right? No one looking for a new relationship moved to a small town. Especially a reclusive island. So, it was conceivable kids weren't even on her radar. Not all women wanted them. On one hand, it felt too early in the dating process to have that discussion. What had I always heard? That after thirty the clock started ticking. I wouldn't want to waste her time. When would be the right time to lay my cards on the table? I supposed we should have some sort of talk. Was I ready to jump into a relationship? Hell, yeah. But what about Cali?

CHAPTER 13

ali

"WHERE ARE YOU?" BAREFOOT, THE COOL FLOOR NIPPED THE bottom of my feet as I paced my living area. Outside, the camera presented as a glass dome. The stark white twelve-foot ceilings inside housed only inset lights. White plastic covered each circular inset. *Maybe?*

Erik admitted to cameras inside. I didn't harbor any delusions he'd send someone over to remove them. But, if I found them, I could remove the intrusive devices. Erik crossed lines when he put cameras in my living space. Not that that should be a surprise. He was always crossing ethical and legal lines.

I lugged the borrowed ladder below the first light in the living area. The entire white circular center and metal rim were held in place by two stainless steel jut-outs. I removed the lightweight contraption and set it down on the top of the ladder. Dust sprinkled down in a cloud. I reached into the dark hole in the ceiling and twisted the dusty bulb. The backs of my fingers butted up against a hard object.

I climbed one step higher, straining to see. A small glass lens reflected the outdoor light. I fingered the cool metal around the lens. *Bingo.*

Erik's security team hid the cameras in the can lighting. I looked across the ceiling. Six…eight…twelve. *Holy shit. My kitchen, bedroom…bathroom? He wouldn't, would he?*

I gripped the camera lens and tugged. It didn't budge. *Strangers have been watching me inside my home?* A mix of nausea, disgust, and indignation stirred.

In a little red toolbox my twin so kindly put together for me, I located a small flashlight and a screwdriver. I took both, and with the butt of the flashlight in my mouth, I climbed back up the ladder, determined to disengage the device.

My knuckles butted against rough edges as I twisted and twisted. One by one, I removed the screws from the board in the ceiling. Only it didn't free the device. Wires connected from the back to something. I didn't know what and didn't care. With a solid yank, the wires snapped free from the camera, and a light cloud of dust filled the air.

"One down." Nym sat at the base of the ladder. "Aren't you enough protection, buddy?" His tail wagged back and forth.

I lugged the ladder to the next light. I didn't find anything. Then I repeated the process. After having checked six can lights, I studied the configuration of the room. Logically, a camera in every light wouldn't make sense.

With each ascension of the ladder, my irritation grew. I shared my frustration with Nym.

"This is my home."

"He has no right."

"I told him no."

"He didn't listen."

"He never listens."

Nym sat beside the ladder, ears perched forward.

"All right. Den's done. What do you think, buddy? Kitchen? Bathroom? Bedroom?" His pink tongue lolled outside the corner of his mouth. "He wouldn't dare put a camera in the bathroom."

Decision made, I hauled the cumbersome ladder into my adjacent bedroom. As I turned right, the back of the ladder swung wide, and a loud crash resonated. I set the ladder down and peered back into the den. Ceramic and glass littered the floor.

"Never liked that lamp much, anyway." Nym watched. "Oh, boy, your paws." I placed him on the dog bed in my room, far away from the broken glass.

As I cleaned up the shattered glass, I considered which bedroom location would be the most logical. I rolled the dice and selected the can light in the corner of the room, near the door that opened onto the deck.

Repeating my whole process, climbing up the ladder, removing the contraption, and flashlighting the dark cavity, an inferno of rage erupted with the bright white reflection. *A camera. Angled to view the entire room. My fucking bed.*

I gripped the lens and tugged hard, half-way ripping two screws from their hold in drywall. Out of my back pocket, I lifted my screwdriver and removed the two stubborn screws that remained in place. I yanked hard, ripping the wires from the back of the camera.

My BlackBerry vibrated. From my perch on the ladder, I could see the unknown number calling. And, oh… I wanted to speak to him.

I scrambled down and picked the phone up off my bed and screamed into it.

"What the fuck, Erik?"

"Calm—"

"Don't you dare tell me to fucking calm down."

"We don't monitor those cameras. They're just there in case we need them."

"Well, if you don't monitor them, how did you know I discovered them?"

"Cali. Stop. Think. You just disconnected two cameras. We get alerts if one is disengaged. They contacted me. That's all."

"They should have never been engaged."

He exhaled loudly, as if I was a nuisance to him. "It doesn't work like that."

"This is over the line, Erik."

Ruff, ruff, ruff, ruff. Loud barking, intermixed with a periodic low growl, announced a visitor at the front door.

"I've got to go."

"Logan's at your door. What's he doing there?"

"What the fuck, Erik? You're looking—"

"Jesus, Cali. You too can see your front door on your phone."

"Bye."

"Wait. I need to talk to you."

A sense of satisfaction filled me when I ended the call.

As I approached the front door, I quieted Nym. He stopped barking, sat on his haunches, and I breathed. Blue, cloudless sky shone through the windows on each side of the door. Calmer, I swung the door open to greet Logan.

"What are you working on?" he asked. His lips curved into a blatant mocking smirk.

"Huh?"

"Dust." He pointed. "It's here. There. And here." The tip of his finger brushed over my nose.

"Oh. I had to replace some light bulbs in the can lights."

"Gabe said you borrowed his ladder. I stopped by to see if you needed any help with anything. Am I too late?"

"It's all done."

"Well, I won't bother you. I have a reservation at Aqua at seven. Does that still work for you?"

A quick glance at my watch showed I'd blown an hour on the blockheaded camera hunt. Logan bent down to pet Nym, and the dog's tail wagged. I glared at the glass bulb over Logan's head.

"Sure."

"So, you need help with that can light?" He peered over my shoulder. I followed his gaze to the opening from the hall into the living room. One of the contraptions hung precariously from one slim galvanized steel hook.

"I can get it."

"You sure? I'm happy to help."

"Thanks, but I'm good." I still had all the bathroom lights to check, because, no, I couldn't trust he wouldn't do that. And downstairs in the hall. And those bedrooms. I planned to check every single recessed light. For whatever twisted reason, my obsessive brother liked having his security team watching me all day. I did not. Erik's intentions, while rooted in a place of concern for me, stemmed from a place of paranoia. It was the only logical conclusion. My parents should've gotten him therapy years ago.

"Hey, you okay?" Logan's dark brown eyes focused on me, and he tenderly brushed a finger against my cheek.

"Yeah. I'm good."

His lips molded to mine, ever so briefly, and my tight ribcage loosened.

"I'd better go get showered."

"Don't change on my account. I like this outfit."

I glanced down at my dusty jean cut-offs and white tank top. "I don't think this would really fit in at Aqua."

He stepped closer. His fingers grazed my cheek, then his lips found mine. My body awakened from his proximity, craving the pleasure he offered. His large hand curved against my ass and drew me against his pelvis. The lines of his erection pressed against my center. He broke our kiss with a groan. He clutched my hips, keeping me close.

"Were you and Gabe drinking?"

"We shared a beer on his deck. Why?"

"You taste lemony. Maybe lemony hops? I like it."

He bent down and gave me another taste. Our tongues danced slowly at first. As our kiss grew in intensity, our bodies melded together, seeking friction. He broke the kiss, his breath heavy.

"If you really want to get ready for tonight, I'd better go. Now."

I nodded, but my body begged to drag him into the bedroom. As if it had a mind of its own, my pelvis ground against him, ever so lightly, silently communicating what I really wanted. He gripped my hair and tilted my head back, kissing me deeply, owning me, stealing my breath, and inching me into the house, down the hall, into…

The bedroom—which still might have cameras. And a

security team lurking. Reality fell over me like a bucket of ice-cold water, and I pushed him away. He tilted his head, puzzled. His exhale hinted at frustration.

"We only have one hour. Should I pick you up?"

"One hour." He kissed the pad of his index finger and placed the finger on my lips. "Soon." After he drove away, I glared up at the security camera hanging nearby, then with a huff, slammed the door.

Moments later, my BlackBerry vibrated. I ignored it.

After I showered, dressed, and took Nym for a quick walk, I headed out onto the street. Waiting for him on the curb, on the edge of my driveway, qualified as anything but normal. But my landline kept ringing. This was what Erik and his damned security team had reduced me to. Standing on the curb, pretending to be normal. But the reduction started long before.

The day I came home to a ransacked apartment. My confidence, my strength—they both took the hit. Instead of calling the police, I called Erik. He'd been living abroad, but had recently returned home, temporarily living with our parents.

"I'll be right over. Don't call the cops."

"Why?"

"Trust me."

Moments later, he arrived with two friends.

"Where's your laptop?"

"In my backpack."

"So, it wasn't here?"

"No."

"What about your phone?"

I held it up with a shaking hand.

"They're after me." He said it like it was an answer.

"What are you into?" It had to be bad. Drugs?

He held both my hands. "I'm doing good things." He looked me in the eye. "Sit? Let me explain?" With an energy and zest I hadn't seen in ages, at least not since he lit up for achieving a higher level on Zeitgeist Battle, he said, "I'm a hacktivist. When a government threatens freedoms, or a company gets too greedy, we go in and attack."

I snatched my hands out of his clutches.

"Not with guns. No violence. It's the best kind of freedom fighting there is. Myanmar. Ukraine. Kazakhstan. That was us. We're making a difference, Cali. We're leading dissension in Hong Kong. And the reason someone broke in here...well, that's harder to explain."

"You're saying those people are here, in our country?"

"Some are. The physical location doesn't really matter."

"Why break into my apartment?"

"The group we started. The business we started. It is a business." He implored me to understand, eyes desperate. "My partner...one of my partners...he's off the range. He's pissed. He has this idea that now we're at war. And that if he doesn't teach me a lesson, others will be likely to not follow orders. He knows you're close to me. I'd hoped he would drop it after—"

"She's not safe." His friend, a guy I'd never seen before, approached.

I didn't agree to move that day, but I did agree to precautions. And Erik set about bringing me up to speed. Explaining the intricate world of the Dark Web, that part of the World Wide Web only accessible with special software, allowing users to remain anonymous and untraceable. And the unofficial role all of the world's governments chose to play and how they influenced public opinion. All the enemies he'd amassed while breaking laws via a keyboard.

                              .   .   .

I understood Erik's fears, but he'd taken it to an extreme.
I lived on a ridiculously safe island with fewer than three
hundred year-round residents. Even if someone kidnapped me
to draw him out, exactly how did those cameras help? His
security team was off in god knew where. I'd be long gone
before they could ever spring to action. It was just another sign
of the irrational overtaking Erik's brain.

"I promise you. We're doing good things." That was what
he'd said. As if the ultimate objective warranted the means. He
never denied he'd broken laws. Committed crimes. He'd aligned
himself with criminals, and they didn't take kindly to his
conscience acting without approval from the highest level.

Were his fears well-founded? Had I been in danger back
then? Or now? I still didn't really know. I'd succumbed to his
precautions for many reasons. Agreed to help him out where I
could. I still didn't understand it all. But these intrusive cameras
showed me one thing. The time had come to push back.

Logan escorted me past the throng of vacationers on the
outer deck of Aqua and directly up to the hostess stand. I
glanced over my shoulder, surveying the crowd outside. Many
held cocktails or beers. Some women wore shorts or skirts,
others wore colorful, flowing sundresses.

"Right this way." We followed the hostess to our seat,
directly in front of a window overlooking the pool below, but
high enough we also had a broad view of the expansive ocean,
punctuated by the occasional whitecap.

150

"Do you know someone here?" I asked as Logan held out my chair for me.

"I do. I know all the restaurant owners and their staff."

"Makes sense. I suppose they want to know you, in case they ever need to call in for help."

"We have community meetings. That's really where I'll meet the owners and managers. Now and then we've been called down when a patron has had too much to drink, but that's remarkably rare. This isn't really the sort of place where bar fights happen." He folded the napkin in his lap and leaned back in his chair, making room for the waitstaff to fill his water glass.

"Do you ever get bored?" He half-smiled and gave me a questioning expression. "I mean, compared to Chicago…"

"It's different. But no, I don't miss homicide. It's been a nice break. But I miss detective work."

"Do you think you'll ever go back to it?"

"Detective work? Yes. To Chicago? No. You could say I gave the city to my wife in the divorce."

"And your dog too."

"Yeah. I should've hired a lawyer, huh?"

"Wait. You didn't hire a lawyer?"

"No. She made more than me. We didn't have kids. I didn't want her money. No need for lawyers."

"What does she do?"

"She's a lawyer."

I choked on my drink then dabbed my mouth with my napkin. "Are you crazy?"

"Some think so." He grinned. "She wasn't a divorce lawyer. I'm not that crazy. She was a prosecutor. Then, during our marriage, she switched to defense."

"Ah, she switched to the dark side."

"You could say that. So, what about your ex? What did he do?"

Right as he asked, our server arrived. She uncorked the wine Logan ordered. I swirled it in my glass and sipped. A light taste with hints of vanilla and possibly oak. After nodding my approval, she filled both our glasses then took our order.

After she departed, I lifted my glass in the air.

"What are we toasting to?" he asked.

"To transitions. And finding our way."

Our glasses clinked.

I settled back into my chair and swirled the liquid in my glass, contemplating how to direct our conversation.

"When your ex became a defense attorney, did she change?" I could imagine if they ended up on opposite sides of the courtroom, it could be tense and difficult to leave the work scene out of the home.

"It would be easy to blame it all on that. But no." He scratched his beard, and after a brief minute, his gaze took on a faraway quality. Just as quickly, he shook it off and returned to our dinner. "The guy she was cheating on me with? That buddy of mine? He was a client of hers. They worked together closely."

"Oh. That's… I'm sorry."

"For a long time, I hated both of them. But there was a lot going on. Our marriage had some… challenges. And, at the end of the day, I couldn't give her what she wanted."

"What do you mean?" If she'd left him for someone with a high-paying job, I wouldn't have even asked the question.

"She wanted kids. And now, like I told you, she's going to have them. And I'm happy for her. I wouldn't go so far as to say I'm happy for him, but I'm happy for her."

I didn't understand at all.

"I can see the questions." He pointed at me and smiled. "Ask anything you want. We're dating. You should know." He shrugged as if to say, "It is what it is."

"You don't want children?" I struggled for the words, more trying to be sensitive in my question. But even as I asked about wanting, I sensed there was more going on than desire.

"No. I do. But… we were trying. Bethany and me. They say you should try for a year before going to get tested. The closer we got to that date on the calendar, it became more tense. We passed the date. Both of our jobs hit a rough patch. She switched sides, to the dark side, as you say. New job, new role. We let the baby thing fall to the back burner. We fought more. I assumed it was job stress."

"And then she ended up with your friend?"

"I should've known something was up. I think that's the worst part. I'm a detective. I should've known, seen the signs." He lifted his wineglass and drained it. I reached out for his hand and linked my fingers through his.

"It's not your fault. Relationships are tough. Multi-layered. And…" I hesitated, unsure what else I could say. I'd never been married, never had a truly serious relationship. I was out of my depth.

"That day out on the beach. When you found me?" He squeezed my hand, prompting my gaze to lift to his. It clicked.

"You'd just learned she was pregnant?"

"And I thought back over our fights. One after the other. We fought." He raised his eyebrows. "A lot." He swallowed his water and set it down. "But that day, I realized it was me. I spent so long playing victim. Telling people she cheated. And, I mean, yeah, that's all true. But she'd been right. I should've gone to get tested. She's close to my age. She didn't have time to play around with me not wanting to go jizz in a cup. Sorry, that's a bit too graphic."

"It's okay." His pain was evident, in his eyes, the way he bowed his head, as if in confession.

"For so long, I wanted to blame her for our marriage. But it was just as much my fault. I think it worked out the way it should."

"How do you mean?"

"Let's say I'd gone and gotten tested. We learned it was me. I'm infertile. Can you imagine that choice for her?"

"Huh? No, that's not. Logan, plenty of couples can't conceive. There are other options. Look at Jasmine and Tate. There are other Jasmines out there. It wouldn't've been a choice between children and you." True, disagreements over wanting kids broke people up, but not once they'd committed. I refused to follow his logic.

"She wanted her own. Now she's going to have her own." He exhaled and finished the water in his glass. He set it down on the table and rested against the back of his chair, forearms resting on the armrests. "So, it's early on for us. I didn't know when to share this. But you should know, I can't..." His gaze fell to the tablecloth.

"Logan?" I waited until he met my gaze, and I schooled the smile breaking out over the absurdity of the situation. "First, I'm not even sure where to begin. The most important part of being a father has absolutely nothing to do with sperm. If you want to be a father, well, there will always be children who need a home. It might not be an easy path, and you might not get the perfect male newborn infant, but if there's a will, there's a way."

"So, it doesn't bother you? That I can't, or—"

"No. Not at all." I wanted nothing more than to prop him up and eliminate any insecurities over this perceived weakness. "Has this…idea…prevented you from pursuing relationships?"

"Honestly, when I first got here, a relationship was the furthest thing from my mind. It's you…really. You got me thinking, that maybe…" He looked me directly in the eye, and a warmth infused me. With my free hand, I lifted my wine glass, not because I was thirsty, but because I didn't know what to say.

"Do you want kids?" In answer, I set my glass down and scratched my face, mimicking his nervous habit. Then my ear itched. Once I'd taken care of all the itches, I placed both hands in my lap and gave him my truth.

"Maybe? I'm not sure. When I see a baby in a stroller, or out and about, I've never wanted to pick it up. That's never been my… Even as a kid, I wasn't the girl who played with dolls. I've enjoyed tutoring. I like getting to know the older kids. In grad school, I also tutored area high school students. Jasmine and I have a friendship. And I've enjoyed watching her grow into her own. I think that's the most maternal I've ever been." He listened, expressionless. I swallowed. "It's not exactly a glowing endorsement for motherhood. And while my mother is constantly prodding me, I don't feel the same urgency she does about it. But I'm not against having children. I suppose I've always assumed I would one day." In all fairness, recent events had uprooted my life.

Our dinner arrived, and he excused himself for the restroom. His reaction to my answer had been indecipherable. But I had meant what I said. If he could or couldn't father children, it shouldn't impact who he has a relationship with. Agreeing on wanting children, that, to me, felt like a bigger hurdle. And did we agree? It wasn't even worth weighing possible answers. That was a bridge I could never cross with Logan. How would that even work? *Oh, yes, Logan, let me introduce you to our children's uncle. He's wanted for cybercrimes in countless countries. And yes, that includes the United States.*

When he returned to the table, a silence fell between us. We both ordered the grouper, which arrived with a mango and crab relish and ginger bok choy. His focus remained on his food. His broad shoulders held back, proud and righteous, like always. I suspected that for a strong military man, not being able to give his wife children must have felt like the ultimate failure. Even though it absolutely shouldn't have. Maybe I should've let the subject drop, but I couldn't. My heart weighed too heavily, and my mind wouldn't stop circling the heart of the matter.

"Logan, you know, you shouldn't let whether you can have children hold you back. From relationships, I mean. If you stop and think about it, no couple goes out and tests themselves for virility before getting married. They both love each other and want to spend their lives together, and that's what propels them forward. They may hope for kids, but if one of them can't, or together they can't, that's immaterial. It's like, I'm sorry, but that really bothers me that your ex made you feel you are less. Children aren't everything. For many happy couples, they simply aren't. You don't take a vow to be with someone forever as long as they can have children. You take a vow in sickness and in health. There's no mention of children." I set my fork down. My insides churned. The man before me was a good person, and he deserved more.

He reached his arm across the table and opened his palm to me. Tentatively, I placed mine over his.

"Thank you. I think I needed to hear you say that."

"Any time."

He stood and came around to my side of the table and pulled out the empty chair beside me. Before I could ask what he was doing, he sat down and lifted my chin. He pressed his lips to mine, soft and warm. His beard brushed my cheek, and I leaned closer. His breath tickled my ear.

"I also needed that." I pulled back enough to meet his gaze.

"Any time," I whispered.

"Well, look who it is." Poppy's boisterous voice rose high above the restaurant noise. "Look at you two!"

Gabe caught up with her and wrapped an arm around her back, pulling her into his side.

"Hey, guys." Logan didn't make a move to change seats. He merely nodded to Gabe and draped an arm over the back of my chair. "I checked the conditions for tomorrow. Perfect. Should be zero turbulence. You still up for going?" I turned to Logan, knowing the question had to be meant for him.

"Absolutely. What time?"

"You want to say seven? Is that too early?"

Logan looked to me, his warm hand sizzling under mine, and the temperature in the room heated.

"Can we push it a little later? Would that mess you up?"

"Nah, with the weather tomorrow, there's no need to hit it early. Ten? Is that late enough? You know, we could fly over to Savannah. Grab a late lunch, then fly back. That might be a long day of it, though. Let me think about where. Maybe Hilton Head. I don't know. I'd like some time in the air. I'll figure it out. Want to meet at the marina?"

"That works. We're finishing up now, but would you guys like to join us for a drink?"

Just as Gabe pulled out the empty chair beside Logan's empty seat, Poppy intervened. "Maybe another night." Gabe quickly pushed the chair back under the table. "We'll let you finish up your date. How about you both come over tomorrow night? I mean, you know, if you're going to be back from flying in time?" She squinted at the man to her right, questioning him.

"We should be."

Logan looked to me and raised a singular dark, thick eyebrow.

"Sounds good. Let me know what to bring," I answered for us.

After our friends departed for their own table, our server asked, "Can I interest you in dessert?"

"I'm full." I placed my palm over my stomach for emphasis.

"Just the check, please." His gaze remained locked on me, setting off a chain reaction of flurries.

My BlackBerry vibrated in my handbag. I checked it as Logan signed the bill. Three missed calls. No doubt Erik wanted to continue our fight. Explain to me his logic. How important it was that he have eyes on me. How much danger I could be in. I turned the phone off. Tomorrow, I'd deal with my brother. For the rest of the night, I planned to enjoy my date, uninterrupted.

We silently left the restaurant and climbed into the golf cart. Logan twisted the key. "Should I take you home? Or would you like to come back to my place for a nightcap?"

"A nightcap? Do people still say that?"

"I honestly don't know. It's been that long since I've dated." I laughed. I wasn't divorced, and I could almost say the same thing.

"Maybe we could stop by my house to pick up Nym? We could share a drink and go for a walk?"

If the request seemed odd, Logan never let on. He found my hand on the seat and slipped his fingers through mine, letting our joined hands rest on the seat between us. The warm night air breezed past us as he accelerated down the short road to my house.

Once we arrived, I told him to sit tight, and I ran up the five steps to my front door. I opened the door, and Nym's alert head poked through instantly. I re-tapped the alarm, picked up his leash, and locked the door once again. As I locked the deadbolt, light reflected on the lens hanging in the eaves above the front door. For the briefest of moments, I considered flipping the bird to my brother. But under Logan's watchful eye, I refrained.

I liked Logan. If I'd met him back when I was in college, his directness would've stood out as unique. Of course, back then, his younger self probably wasn't nearly as direct. Still, at this point in our lives, we had a commonality. Someone we loved had hurt us. Both of us found ourselves far away from our homes because of that hurt. But Logan had continued, looking out for others, doing the right thing. He hadn't talked to me about his time in the military or the police force, but I believed that, no matter what my brother might suspect or claim, the man beside me fought for good.

Yes, turning my phone off equaled defiance on my part. A setting of boundaries that were long overdue. Surely, I could date Logan without him getting suspicious about a brother who lived in another country? A thread of guilt weaved within me, thinking of bringing potential risk to my brother. He, too, believed in his cause and believed he was working for the good of humanity. But more and more, it felt like I had somehow become a casualty of an irrational war.

Tomorrow I planned to have a calm, rational discussion with that brother of mine. But tonight, Logan and I would cross a line that, had he had condoms, we would've already crossed.

An energy coursed between us, heavy with anticipation. The warm breeze sent my hair flapping behind me. Logan's beard brushed my ear as he leaned down, close to me, and with a hint of a smirk asked, "How long of a walk does Nym require?"

"Not too long. But we can walk him later." He flattened the accelerator.

ogan

MY BODY THRUMMED IN ANTICIPATION AS SHE ENTERED THROUGH
the back door of my home. The sheath dress she wore cupped
the svelte curves of her ass. The top of the dress dipped low,
revealing the smooth bronze skin of her back except for where
her glistening black hair fell. I ached to run my fingers through
the soft strands and to grip it just hard enough for intensity.

"What would you like to drink?" I kicked off my shoes by
the door as she floated down the hall.

"Did you buy a dog bed?"

"Yeah. I figured you might be over more, and Nym could use
a bed when he's here."

"That's really..." Her voice trailed off, and I wondered if she
thought I was overeager or pushing too hard. But, like I told

her, I didn't play games. She'd either like me or she wouldn't. "So sweet."

I stepped up behind her and brushed her hair off her shoulder, laying a light kiss on the exposed skin. Goosebumps sprung up along her arms. As I kissed her, I explored. The curve of her hip, her flat, smooth stomach. I inched up the fabric of her dress, little by little, high above the lean, taut legs I ogled on the beach during her noon run. The thin strip of her silk panties easily stretched, and she gasped as I slipped a finger beneath the fabric. Her head rested on my shoulder, and the curves of her buttocks perfectly melded over my arousal.

I toyed with her, pressing against her mound, circling the area I suspected would drive her crazy. She sighed and mimicked the movements of my hand with her hips, applying pressure to my very hard erection.

"Cali, you are dripping." I took her lobe between my teeth and gently bit down, and she quivered against my hand.

"I hope you went shopping." Her breathing quickened, and I sped my fingers to keep time with her husky exhales. "For condoms."

That made me grin.

I bent and scooped her up and carried her like a bride into my bedroom. Her feet hit against the doorframe, and for a split second, a memory of the same thing happening with Bethany and her white, silky heels flitted across. I shut the memory down. I'd always been a one-woman kind of guy. And I planned to focus on the one currently in my bedroom.

She leaned back on her hands, and her thin silk dress pooled at her waist. I reached over to the drawer in my bedside table and placed a condom on the edge. Then I moved over the bed, running my hands along her thighs, loving the smooth feel of her skin. I slowed at her white silk panties and put a thumb under each side then pulled. She rose ever so slightly, allowing me to ease them off.

Her dark eyes met mine, her lips in the softest of smiles, and my heart pumped double-time. After dropping the silk to the floor, I arched over her, with every intention of removing that dress. I wanted her naked, and I craved the taste of her breasts and the feel of them in my hands.

She had other ideas. She pushed up onto her knees. Her fingers found my belt and tugged. My knees butted up against the bed as she roughly worked my pants open and down.

Feeling more than a little ridiculous standing there with a shirt on and my dick sticking out at full mast, I helped her along. With determined speed, I undid my shirt buttons and shoved it off as she captured my gaze, her mouth inches from my aching cock.

As my shirt hit the floor, her tongue caressed her lower lip. Everything slowed as I transfixed on the sexy as fuck vision on hands and knees before me. My lower back muscles tensed so completely, I worried I might release right then and there, before she even touched me.

I roughly wrapped my fingers around my erection and stroked, aiming to gain some control. This was our first time, and we'd only get one first time. I kicked off my pants and reached for the hem of that dress, right as her tongue licked across the tip of my cock.

"Fuuuck." The wet warmth of her mouth surrounded the head, and the dress slipped out of my hand. I blinked to gain control and gently cupped the back of her head, careful to not apply pressure. My knees threatened to buckle. I focused on the ceiling. Her silky hair surrounded my fingers, and I scooped it back, away from her face. The hollows of her cheeks sucked in as she worked up and down my cock. Her fingers cupped my balls, and tightening sensations shot through me, from the pit of my stomach and down my spine. I pulled her off, and the suction broke with a pop.

She looked up, eyes dark and doe-like, questioningly.

"Baby, when I come tonight, I'm coming inside you." I found that hem and tugged it up and over her head. She wore a white lace bra that wrapped around her like a band, or like a sinful bathing suit top. Her dark nipples peeked through lace, and I gently pushed her back onto the bed, eager to taste.

I crawled along her legs, up the bed, making my way to her sacred apex. She spread her legs open for me, and just before dipping down, I told her, "And you're coming, too."

My tongue slipped inside her center, and she gasped. Her reaction urged me on. Her hands knitted into my hair and tugged, directing me as I tasted her, my tongue working her nub as my fingers slid in and out of her delectable channel.

"Right there, right there." She tightened around my fingers as her chest lifted off the bed, curling forward. A sense of elation filled me.

I grabbed the condom and quickly sheathed myself, eager to feel her around me. I positioned my body over hers, and her legs lifted, wrapping around my thighs, welcoming me. I paused, poised above her, and kissed her. Our tongues lashed against each other, and my hips pressed forward. She stretched around me, tight, warm, and better than I imagined. I pulled back and tenderly traced her cheek, slowing things down, even as our breaths raced ahead. Her hips lifted, and I sank deeper. She was plenty ready for me, but damn, the sensation robbed me of oxygen.

"God, you feel good." Her teeth grazed my shoulder, and her muscles tensed. "Am I hurting you?"

"God, no." Her nails raked down my back. She grabbed my ass and tugged.

I inched forward, studying her facial expressions.

"It feels so good. It's just been a long time."

Fuck. It had been a long time for me, but I'd been preparing myself for this all week, jacking off in the shower, envisioning this very moment, aiming to ensure I lasted long enough to blow her mind.

I pulled out, then pushed in, and fuck. Her muscles clenched around me. I stared at the headboard. She rocked her hips. I dipped my head and sucked on a nipple, still under the lace bra, then I yanked it down, revealing those perfect breasts.

With each plunge forward, I dipped to take a nipple in my mouth, sucking and twirling. All sorts of little noises came out of her and those nails on my back stroked up and down until we found our rhythm together. I pounded against her, my skin slapping against hers. Over and over until she tightened around me, on the verge. She whimpered as I pulled out and turned her onto her side and entered her from behind. From this position, I could tease her clit while I gave her the pressure she craved. It didn't take long with the combination of thrusting and working that sensitive bundle of nerves before she clenched around me and shuddered.

I sucked in air and stared at the corner, refusing to go over the edge. I bent and kissed along her shoulder and cupped her breast. She rolled onto her back and pulled me forward, kissing me, as her legs wrapped around my torso. I fell forward against her and thrust deep. She felt fucking amazing.

"I don't know if I can again," she gasped.

"Oh. You can." We transitioned to a slower rhythm, and our tongues followed along in a similar dance. As her breathing evened out, I lifted a leg, and lifted her ass, and watched. Captivated as her eyelids half closed, her mouth open, gasping in brief, ragged breaths. Her moans grew louder. Sweat dripped down my chest as I drove into her, watching her every sign, breathing deeply for control. My chest brushed against her chest, her pebble-hard nipples and the softness of her breasts in contrast to mine. Her nails sliced into me. She screamed. Her channel seized up, and I let her take me with her, releasing in a jarring, pulsing climax. I collapsed onto her, gasping for air.

"Holy fuck," she panted. It took me some time to catch my breath and to find the strength to lift myself off her.

I finally rolled onto my back and climbed off the bed to take care of the condom. When I returned, I stacked pillows against the headboard and leaned back against them, then pulled her up against me, taking care to ensure she was nowhere near the wet spot. The layer of sweat lent itself to creating a chill in the air conditioning, and I tugged at the ends of the comforter, pulling it over us both. It occurred to me we might have stained my comforter, but I was more than okay with the sacrifice.

With a hazy sense of satisfaction and elation, I settled into the vibration of her heartbeat pulsing next to mine.

"Wow." She said it low, as if she didn't mean for me to hear, or wasn't even conscious she said it, and a feeling of invincibility washed over me.

"Well, it was our first time. I wanted to be sure you didn't forget it."

"Trust me, I won't."

I loved the feeling of her silky strands against my chest,

covering me like a blanket. The tips of her fingers caressed my beard, then she tugged on it softly.

"I like this."

"You do?"

"I like the way it feels against my thighs."

"I'll keep it, then." I wondered if her ex, or other men she'd been with, had always been cleanshaven, but tonight I would not be asking about her ex. Besides, I'd been married before, too. I knew Bethany and I had had great moments, but they didn't undercut what Cali and I experienced. And Bethany and I had been great together, until we weren't. I had to believe the same would be true for Cali and her ex.

"When I first met you, you didn't have a beard."

"No. I also had shorter hair. Military style."

"You've loosened up since you've been here."

"I suppose." I wrapped a long strand of her hair around my finger, mesmerized by the contrast of her black hair against my skin.

"Me too," she said quietly.

"If this is you relaxed, I'm curious about what a tense Cali is like."

She raised her head off my chest, and a wide smile graced her lips. "What do you mean by that?"

"Cali, you have two deadbolts on your front door and an alarm. You run every single day at the exact same time. You live your life on a regimented schedule, and we live at the beach." A regimented schedule and the beach life clashed.

"Well, Nym does better on a schedule. And everyone should be secure. That's smart."

She dipped forward and gave me a playful nip.

I pinched her hip, and she squirmed. We both laughed in a lazy kind of way, and she settled back down on my chest.

"Did you install that alarm, or was it there when you bought the house?"

"I had it installed."

"Why? I mean, I'm not against it… Have you always been so security conscious?" I closed my eyelids, loving a naked Cali next to me.

"No. I just think it's smart," she said with an unmistakable edge. I kissed her forehead.

"Works for me. But if there's a reason for it…" What? What did I think? She was scared of something? Someone? Everyone in Chicago had an alarm. Seattle was probably the same way.

"I can get paranoid. I think it comes from living alone. But I feel like I haven't been so worried lately. That maybe I am relaxing. Maybe it's all in my head." The smooth pads of her finger circled over my nipple. "You're observant. Have you noticed a difference?"

"Hmmm…since we've gotten to know each other, the biggest difference I see is that when you see me, you smile."

"I do smile. I feel happy when I'm with you. I think I've been alone too long." I nudged her head, wanting her to look up at me. Slowly, she did.

"You make me happy, too. You know, I know they say that you shouldn't end up with the first person you date after a divorce. And I'm aware we're each other's rebounds, but right now, I'm really hoping we can prove all the naysayers wrong."

"What naysayers?"

"You know, whoever says you shouldn't end up with your first after your divorce."

Her bare chest glided forward across mine, and she kissed

me, soft and slow. Absolute perfection. The bed shook, breaking our kiss. Nym's pink, lolling tongue and dog breath infiltrated our cocoon.

"Oh, you want your walk." Cali scratched behind the dog's ears, and he wagged his tail. Choking down my annoyance, I offered to take him. But Cali insisted she come too.

Hands linked, we strolled down my street, allowing a long leash for Nym to wander. The stars shone as bright pinpricks cast far and wide. The far-off sound of the surf and the salty air surrounded us. Darkness shrouded all but one or two homes on our brief lap around the block. As I locked my door for the night, she studied her watch.

"Do you need to do something?"

"I should probably check email and voicemail. It's what I normally do before going to bed." She strode up to me and looped her hands behind my neck. Her fingers toyed with the hair at the back of my neck, sending a prickling sensation along my spine. I closed my eyes to better enjoy it while pressing her against my chest. Her lips pressed against my throat, warm and soft. "I think tonight I'll skip it."

"Now that's the kind of relaxing I want to see more of." I bent slightly and walked her backward into my bedroom.

This time, I pulled back the comforter and the sheets. We watched each other as we each undressed, this time folding our clothes. She slid the lace bra right down her body and wriggled it over her hips. *So that's how you take it off.*

I crawled into bed next to her warm, soft, naked body. I wasn't sure if she would want to do more, but her leg brushed over mine, and her fingers fondled me. At forty-two, I needed more rest before re-engaging, but the post-intimacy appealed as much as our foreplay. We kissed slowly this time and explored each other. Her touch and her tongue proved too tempting, and my cock twitched back to life. When we came together, it felt like we'd been lovers for years, not hours. And I knew, with every fiber of my being, that I wanted to be with her for years to come.

CHAPTER 15

ali

THE RICH AROMA OF BREWING COFFEE FILLED THE AIR. I BLINKED repeatedly, squinting in the bright white light. Sunshine poured through the open blades of the plantation shutters. I stretched and automatically checked my wrist for the time.

Nym cocked his head.

"It's time for a walk, right, boy?" His tail flopped left, then right. "You're wondering why we're here. I know. We're off routine. Doesn't seem right, does it?"

Logan's deep timbre responded, "I beg to disagree. Nothing has ever felt more right to me." He bypassed Nym in the doorway and handed me a white ceramic mug with steam rising from it. "I wasn't sure exactly how you take your coffee. I noticed an almond milk in the recycling bin that day Nym got wrapped up in burrs, so that's what I used. Is that okay?"

"Do you use almond milk, too?"

"No. I like mine black. But I bought some almond milk, so I'd have some on hand. I also have regular skim and cream."

"You're prepared, huh? Ready for whatever your lady friend wants in the morning?" My tease came out of nowhere. Out loud…it sounded icky.

"Lady friend?" He smirked. It sounded like something Mom would say. "Prepared for you. No other woman. I think I've been pretty straightforward and direct." His pointed, unwavering gaze sent my insides fluttering. He sat on the edge of the bed and pressed his lips to mine, the pressure just right. I think I may have moaned.

"What can I make you for breakfast?"

"What were you thinking?" My dress hung on the low post on the end of his bed. I reached for it. He handed it to me, then passed me my panties and bra.

"Scrambled eggs. Anything you don't eat?"

"No, not really. I try to limit the amount of meat I eat, but I eat anything."

"So is bacon not your favorite?"

"I'll eat it, but rarely. It's not very good for you, you know."

"I think with your workout routine you can swing it."

"I'll eat whatever you make."

"I'll fix it while you get ready."

Proving he couldn't be more perfect, in his bathroom lay a brand-new toothbrush and toothpaste, his facial soap, moisturizer and a pristine white washcloth. His brand struck me as too harsh, so I scrubbed my face with water. I read the bottle of his men's facial moisturizer and finally decided I wasn't quite brave enough to put it on my face, but his thoughtfulness brought on an incessant smile.

I emerged from the bathroom refreshed. Two plates of steaming scrambled eggs, buttered toast, and no bacon awaited me.

"You're really kind of amazing."

He shrugged, like it was no big deal. "I'm trying to make a good impression."

He scrolled through his email as we ate, and I contemplated turning my phone back on. But I knew damn well an influx of angry texts awaited, and I wasn't quite ready to face the impending fight. So my phone remained off, tucked inside my bag, to be dealt with later.

"Can I give you a ride home? It's on the way."

"Thanks, but Nym needs to walk."

Outside, the palm tree in his back yard swayed beneath clear blue skies. Birds chirped. The high *tink* of a biker's bell cut over the distant sound of crashing waves. He'd have a perfect day for his flight with Gabe.

On his porch, he kissed me goodbye. His hand cupped the curve of my ass, an intimacy he now claimed, and my insides melted.

"Can I see you tonight?"

"We're supposed to have dinner with Gabe and Poppy, remember?"

He grinned, looking so happy it twirled my insides. On the walk back to my place, my cheek muscles stretched from my wide, uncontrolled smile. Two kids pedaled by, barefoot with towels precariously perched over rusted handlebars, and I edged Nym over off the pavement. A golf cart loaded down with surfboards on top and filled with a family passed by. Saturday at the beach was in full swing.

I turned right into my drive and halted. A golf cart, not mine, parked in front of my front door steps. A familiar man stood beside it. He wore cargo shorts, a dark gray t-shirt, and sunglasses. I'd seen him before. Where? The memory clicked. Next door. He rented his house out, so people were in and out of it all the time, but I'd seen him enough to expect he had to be the owner.

"Hi." I approached, ready to extend my hand. I slowed my step several feet away, as it occurred to me my neighbor wouldn't need a golf cart.

"Cecilia? Cali?" An uneasiness settled in my gut.

"Yes?"

"Your brother sent me." *Oh, no, he did not.* My jaw clenched. What, exactly, did Erik expect this guy to do?

"Your mother has been admitted to the hospital." The world stopped. "She's in critical condition. You have forty-five minutes to get ready. We have a plane ready to take you. I'll wait outside." I didn't move. "I'll wait right here. You need to get moving."

"Who are you?"

"Douglas. I work with Erik. He tried calling, but you turned off your phone. I'm assuming you'll want to shower and pack. Cali, you need to get moving. We have to fly out of the Wilmington airport. It's busy this morning."

"What happened?"

"Excuse me?"

"To my mom."

"They suspect a heart attack. That's what I was told yesterday evening. They probably know more now. Erik knew you'd want to go home to her."

I held the lifeless phone in my hand, the one I'd refused to turn on because I'd been pissed.

"I had instructions to pick you up from Logan's house if you weren't home by nine. You look like you're in shock, but I need you to move. We really need to get going."

"Right." I flicked the phone on as I climbed the steps into my house. The man stood in my drive, arms crossed, scanning the yard from left to right.

Nym followed me into my bedroom.

"You never growled at that man. You must think he's okay." I scratched behind his ears then turned on the shower. The water ran from cold to hot.

I picked up the phone and dialed Dad. Voicemail clicked on. I flicked over to my missed calls list. None from Dad. Five missed calls from Erik and a slew of texts.

Steam swarmed the bathroom. On a normal day, Nym would remain in my bedroom. But, proving that today was anything but a normal day, he sat beside the shower, ears forward, alert.

The tepid water poured over me. The thick cloud in my head cleared. Verification. I needed to verify Erik knew this guy. Erik's text—all of them—said to call him. None mentioned Mom. And surely if something happened to Mom, my father would call me. I'd be on the short list of people he would call right after 911.

I got dressed quickly, pulling on leggings. My outfit could work for a long flight, but it could also work if I needed to run. I pulled the laces on my running shoes tight. I glanced up at the ceiling, scanning the glass insets of the lights above. Was someone watching?

I dialed the number that sent Erik's most recent texts. My back rested on the closed bedroom door. I chewed on my thumbnail. Waves crested in the distance. The beach. I could escape out the back.

"Cecilia," Erik answered, stern. Sirens rang in the background. "Do what Wolf says."

"So, it's true? How's Mom?"

"If you would've picked up your damn phone, you would've learned about it last night. You could be with her right now."

"Is that what you were trying to tell me yesterday?" A weakness penetrated, and I locked my knees in response to the shaking.

"No. It didn't happen until later in the afternoon Pacific coast time. She hadn't been feeling well all day. She thought she ate something wrong. Dad wanted her to make an appointment with her doctor, but she wanted to see how she felt in the morning. You know Mom. When she vomited, Dad called 911. Then he called me and asked me to get in touch with you, which is really hard to do when you turn off your phone."

"I thought—"

"I know. It's fine." A hint of exhaustion colored his statement. "But you need to pack. Get moving."

"How do you know I'm not moving? Are you watching me?" I peered up at the ceiling.

"No. I'm listening to you, and you don't sound like you're moving. Plan to stay a while." *Right.*

I pulled down a suitcase from the top shelf in my closet, with my phone tucked between my ear and shoulder. A horn beeped, and distant, muffled voices filled the background, only the voices, I could swear, spoke something other than English.

"Where are you?"

"Stuck on a project. Dad knows."

"You're not coming home?" *Our mother is in the hospital!* Ire rose along with a desire to scream.

"I don't think I'll be able to. But if she gets worse, I'll be there. You'll need to tell me, but know if I come, it will be with grave risk."

Grave risk, my ass. I opened the suitcase and headed to the closet, going straight to the hangers to throw in my standard clothes for visits home. I tripped forward over Nym. *Nym!*

"What should I do about Nym? Should he come with me?"

"No. He's a security dog. He needs to stay with the house."

"But…"

"Shit. I'd say Wolf could feed him, but he's got an assignment." He muttered, as if running through names. "Can any of your friends take care of him? Those neighbors down the way?"

"I'll ask Logan."

"Fine." I suspected he'd like to say more, but all the background noises ceased. "I've got to go. Listen to Wolf. If you text me, use our code."

"Who is Wolf?"

"The guy outside."

"He said his name was Douglas."

"Douglas Wolfgang. We call him Wolf. Do what he says."

Then the line went dead.

I dialed Logan.

"Morning. I was just thinking about you."

I clutched the toothbrush, absorbing his words, then with a shake, threw the brush into my toiletry bag and snapped open drawers.

"Unfortunately, I've had some bad news. My mom's in the

hospital. I was calling to see if you could take care of Nym while I'm gone."

"Absolutely. Is she okay?"

"Yes—I don't know. I'm short on details. But I've got to rush to make my flight. I'll text you instructions for care. His food gets delivered each week. Amazon delivers to the post office, so you'll have to pick it up there."

"That's fine. He can stay with me."

"No." Erik wanted Nym here. "The house will be empty. It's better that he's here. And he'll feel more comfortable in his home. I'll text you the alarm code and leave keys… not under the mat. Underneath the steps that go up to the front door."

"All right. How're you doing?"

"I think… It's not… my mom is healthy. She's thin. You wouldn't think she'd have heart problems."

"I'll be there in a few minutes. I'll drive you to the marina."

"No. It's okay. I'm on my way."

"Which ferry are you getting?"

I glanced at my watch. *Shit, we just missed the outgoing ferry.*

"The first one I can get. Thank you for watching Nym." I zipped up my suitcase, lifted it, and it fell to the ground with a thud. "I'll text you when I land." I should've said more…given a softer goodbye.

Knock. Knock. Knock.

The distant sound echoed in the open living room. I rushed to the door and flung it open. Within seconds, Douglas Wolfgang had my suitcase on the cart.

We flew toward the marina at a speed that would most certainly get him pulled over by Public Safety if we crossed the path of an officer. The man didn't say a word. Stared straight ahead. A man on a mission. I checked out his waist, expecting a gun holster, but didn't see one.

In the marina, a cloud of smoke rose behind the engine of a small ski boat. The water churned behind it. Another man, in cargo pants and a Navy SEALs t-shirt, waved from behind the wheel. A smooth white rope looped around from his hand to his elbow. He lifted a seat and dropped the coiled rope underneath the cushion.

Wolf passed my suitcase over, and he stowed it in the berth. He returned and held out his hand to assist as I stepped over the water gap from the dock to the boat.

"Nice day for a boat ride." The man smiled broadly, relaxed and friendly. Wolf boarded and untied the boat.

"Let's go," Wolf directed.

We putted slowly out of the marina. Wolf gestured for me to take the front captain seat, next to the amiable driver. He took a place in the row of seats along one side of the back of the boat.

"So, you are flying her out?" the man steering the boat asked Wolf.

"No. Jones is." He slashed his index finger across his throat. Stone-faced.

"What's that about?" I asked. Wolf shrugged. "You told him to be quiet. Why?"

The man driving the boat chuckled and extended a hand. "I'm Trevor. Good to meet Erik's infamous sister."

"Infamous? What do you mean by that?"

"Oh, nothing. I've spent a fair amount of time with your brother over the years." We passed the "no wake" signs, and he pushed the lever forward. The nose of the boat dipped down, then soared as we bounced from wave crest to crest. I clung to the edges of the seat and braced my feet against the front wall.

Trevor expertly maneuvered the boat through the inlet at a speed that would normally have me screaming, but under his command, my fear remained dormant.

"Are you a SEAL?"

He glanced down at his chest. "No. Found the shirt at a thrift store."

The shirt didn't look that old. But I dropped it. No reason to ask questions, because I couldn't trust the answers. Besides, the more I learned, the greater the risk I would endanger Erik.

I searched for the familiar harbor across the inlet. But the shoreline flanked our right.

"Where are we going?"

"Further down toward Wilmington. We'll get closer to the airport."

I settled back into the seat. The wind whipped my hair, and the boat picked up speed, lessening the bounce as we tore down the waterway.

After docking, and with curt goodbyes, I found myself in a black truck headed to the airport. Douglas, or Wolf, showed credentials at a gate, and we drove through. He parked and pulled my suitcase and another one out of the bed of the pickup truck.

"Are you coming, too?"

"To Seattle, yes. Not to the hospital. A car service will take you from the airport. Sound good?"

I nodded, mystified as I followed two steps behind him. We walked through a side building onto the tarmac. A small, navy blue jet awaited us.

"We're taking a private plane?"

"Erik called in some favors. Direct flights from Wilmington to Seattle aren't available on commercial."

He shook hands with the uniformed pilot. The pilot smiled. As if this was normal.

I sank into the soft, plush leather of the first seat in the first row, beside a window.

"I'm going to set an extra blanket for you. There's no flight attendant on board, but I'll be up front. That galley area? It has a microwave, and the freezer has several meal options for you. Beverages are across the aisle. There's ice and glasses on that side."

"It's okay. I got her." The pilot gave a quick nod to Wolf and closed the door behind him.

"You need anything, you knock on the door. You should get some sleep." With that, he joined the pilot.

Mom. I called my father. His voicemail picked up. Then I settled in for the ride.

I fastened my seatbelt. The plane jerked and rolled forward, inching away from the hangar. I scanned my texts, pausing on the most recent one.

I'm at the ferry station. Are you here?

Logan's text tightened around my throat. I tapped out my response.

At the airport. A friend took me over in a boat. About to take off. I'll text when I land.

After hitting send, I wondered if a flight departed at this time to Seattle. The half-truths agitated. Little white lies. When dispersed, they cast a haunting shadow.

CHAPTER 16

ogan

*At the airport now. A friend took me over in a boat. About to
take off. I'll text when I land.*

A friend. *Poppy? Gabe?* They owned a boat they used to get
back and forth. So did Tate and Luna.

Robert tapped on the door. "I'm going out. Plan to sit off
Timber Bridge. Look for some newbies in their rentals."

We were constantly pulling people over who seemed to
forget a golf cart was actually a motorized vehicle and subject
to the state's driving regulations.

"Sounds good. I won't be in long. Stopped in to check on
some things, but something's come up. My girlfriend's out of
town, and I need to take her dog for a walk. Then I'll be out of

touch this afternoon." I'd be gone all day on that flight with Gabe, so Nym would miss his lunchtime run.

"You've got a girlfriend?" Robert smiled and settled against the frame, clearly waiting for more. That was the first time I'd uttered the word—at least the first time in many, many years. It felt a little juvenile, but mostly good feelings surfaced, maybe even pride.

"Yeah. Her mom's in the hospital."

"You know, if you need to go out of town to be with her, we can cover."

Yes. We were a streamlined crew, but we had to have enough coverage to carry on if someone got sick or needed to take a vacation. Our team could get by, and I hadn't taken a vacation day since I arrived two years ago. "I'll let you know. If things are bad, I probably will head out."

"What hospital?"

"Seattle. That's all I know." I needed to get more information from her. When she landed, I'd ask.

"If it's serious, you may want to make plans to get out there. That's a haul. Not easy to get to from here."

"Yeah. You're right." With the time difference, it was a full travel day. If things took a turn for the worst, it would be impossible for me to get there quickly. I scratched my jaw and pulled out my chair, keen to do some research on flights. *That must've been why she hauled ass to get to the airport. She probably didn't have many flight options.*

"Well, let me know if you need me to do anything."

He paused at the door, and I slowed my fingers, sensing he had something to say. "Yes?"

"You're always scratching that beard."

"Yeah?" I wasn't sure why he cared.

"Well, I have this great stuff you can put on your beard. It's like a moisturizing salve. Helps with that. I'll leave you a sample."

"You don't even have a beard." He'd sported the cleanshaven baby face for as long as I could remember. To me, he looked super young, but after hitting forty, I'd noticed all the twenty-somethings looked young.

"Didn't work so well for me. I was like you. Scratching all the time."

I turned my attention to the keyboard, and he took the hint, disappearing down the hall. I scratched my beard as the time capsule on the screen indicated the search for flights was in process. As I scratched, her words from last night came to mind—she liked it on her thighs. Nope, this beard was here to stay.

Scrolling through flights, I discovered that almost every itinerary option included two stops. I located a single flight with one stop that departed at 8:48 a.m. and got in at 2:51 p.m. I booked it. That would give me the rest of the day to get things settled here. Find someone to take care of Nym. The possibility this was overkill given our new relationship definitely lurked in the back of my mind. But she might need me. I needed to be closer to her, just in case.

I also knew hospital time was hard time. I'd seen that firsthand in both the military and the police force. And with my knee, I'd lived it.

I could book a hotel room near the hospital so she and her father would have a place nearby to get showers. Ideally, across the street. Of course, I needed to know which hospital. And based on the flights I saw, she probably wouldn't land until maybe one in the morning her time, which was more like four here. I'd be up and preparing to get to the airport by then.

I knew she'd tell me not to come, so I pointedly didn't mention my plans. But I asked her for the hospital name in a text. If she texted me that her mom was fine, and all was good, I could cancel a flight. Transfer it for the future. But now, if she called and said that things were bad, I had a plan lined up.

As I left our office building, Chad flagged me down, waving his arm to catch my attention.

"Logan. Just the man I wanted to see."

"Oh?" I paused on the plank board sidewalk, waiting for him to park his cart.

"You got a minute?" Chad's minute equaled about thirty minutes on a clock.

"I've actually got to head. My girlfriend had a family emergency, and I'm heading out to be with her in the morning. I've got several loose ends to wrap up. Can it wait?"

"Well, won't take long. Can I walk with you? Where are you headed?"

"Timber Bridge. What's up?"

"I heard about the folks trying to hack into our servers."

"Yep." I rocked back on my heels, waiting.

"Well, that's a little scary, right?"

People got scared about the damnedest things. Always blew my mind. They'd worry about someone hacking into their accounts, but then turn around and freely hand over their credit card to a waitstaff person who could walk off behind closed doors with it and easily write all the information down. That most basic level of credit card theft happened all the time. Or the gas station attendee who took the card and swiped it in a device that captured all the info—that had been one of the most successful crimes going for a while.

"They haven't gotten in. We haven't seen any attempts in the last few days either. Probably just a bored kid."

"Bored kid, huh? Yeah, I've read about some of those hackers. That makes sense. So, you're not worried about ransomware or anything like that?"

"No. Remember when I came here, I upgraded everything."

"We have some high-profile residents."

"Yes. But, to answer your question, I'm not worried."

"If you're not, I won't be. But I still find it disconcerting."

"Chad, the only way to be absolutely secure is to not have an internet connection. Your phone, your laptop, that Apple Watch on your wrist, your Alexa? By having all those items connected to the Internet, your data is exposed to some level of risk. Don't know about you, but to me, the good things from those outweigh the risks."

"Yeah, yeah." He rambled down the walkway with me all the way to my cart. He slapped the top of my cart after I slid down onto the seat. "You have a good trip. Where you going?"

"Seattle."

"Oh?"

"It's my girlfriend's hometown." *And I need to get going.*

"When'd you get a girlfriend?"

Even in my hurry, I couldn't stop the grin. "Recently."

"Do I know her?"

"Cali. She lives a few houses down from Gabe."

"Yeah, the green house, right? Nice plants on the steps."

"That's her."

"She has Cujo for a pet."

I chuckled. "Yeah, that's her."

"Well, good for you. Let me know when you're back. The missus and I would love to have you both over for dinner."

"I'll let you know, Chad. I'll have access to email when I'm gone, so if anything comes up, reach out."

"Will do."

After going over the revised schedule with Robert for the next week, I stopped off at Gabe's. No one answered the door, so I called him.

"Hey, where are you?" We were supposed to meet at the marina, but it was still early for him to be over there.

"Sitting out on the beach. Getting some reading in. A few new quarterly reports I wanted to get through."

"You in front of your house?"

"Yep. You here?"

"Yeah. I'm gonna come around and find you. I have a favor to ask."

CHAPTER 17

ali

The front entrance of Sacred Heart Memorial Hospital matched any other hospital. Lots of glass, high ceilings, circular drive in the front. The location was at least thirty minutes from my parents' home—without traffic. With traffic, I'd bet it could easily push an hour.

Why this hospital? A framed poster near the reception desk flaunted, "Voted #1 for Transplants." That wouldn't be it. But maybe the cardiology department here is also top-notch?

I rushed my suitcase up to the information desk, patting the handle with twitchy hands. A nice woman with spectacles assisted me at the long desk in the lobby.

"Let's see, Dahlia Lai is in CCU."

"What's CCU stand for?"

"Cardiac Care Unit. And you're family?"

"I'm her daughter."

"Well, we allow family to visit." She peered over her silver-rimmed glasses. "Don't worry, dear. She's getting excellent care." She informed me they were limiting visitors to a maximum of two and gave instructions for locating cardiology. She also offered me a mask and explained that it was a holdover from the pandemic. I didn't mind wearing one at all. I wanted to do everything I could to keep my mom and all the other patients safe.

Once I arrived on the floor and checked in at the main desk at the front, they checked my temperature and directed me down one of the long halls with white square linoleum tiles. Low level beeps invaded the hush. Harsh, frigid air conditioning infiltrated my clothes. The abrasive scent of ammonia, or some similar cleaning agent, filled my nostrils. A man in scrubs and a white lab coat nodded absently as he passed. I wandered farther down the hall, following the arrows. A door on my right remained open. Inside, a wrinkled, frail person lay on a hospital bed with a thin blanket tucked around his legs.

Several doors down, I arrived at room number 389. I peeked through the tall, narrow glass pane in the closed door. Nerves sparked, generating fear. Senseless fear.

I pressed the stainless steel handle and pushed forward. A curtain hung fully covering the bed. *Dad.* A fiercely private man, he wouldn't have it any other way. The pale green curtain waffled, and my father appeared as the heavy door slowly closed on automatic hinges behind me.

Dad's jet-black hair held an oily sheen. Dark circles sank

below his eyes. My father had never been a large man, but he appeared smaller and frail, as if he had shrunk in height and breadth. He held out his arms, and I rested my head on his shoulder. He patted my hair, up and down, while he repeated my name, "Cecilia, Cecilia." My heart split in two when he added, almost in disbelief, "You came."

"Of course I did. I've been trying to call you ever since Erik told me." I pulled back and held his wrinkled hand in both of mine. "How is she?"

"Sleeping. Do you want tea?"

"Can I see her?"

With a slow, stilted nod, he slid back the curtain. A faint mechanical noise reverberated as the chain on the ceiling circled through the track. My mother lay on the bed, a pale blue blanket over her. A needle poked into the back of her hand, visible beneath the clear tape holding it in place. Her chart hung on the end of the bed. On the opposite end of the bed, a monitor with numbers and graphs across the screen attracted my attention. Her oxygen showed at 96, and her heartbeat graph, at least to me, looked good. I didn't know what I was looking at, but it wasn't a flat line.

"She needs surgery." My dad's whispered words belied his worry.

"For what?"

"She has two clogged arteries."

"But she eats so healthy. That doesn't make sense." Clogged arteries belonged to people who ate fried foods.

"Her doctor will come by again in the morning. You can talk to him with me. Erik is stuck at work. He works so hard." My father squeezed my hand, and while he sounded proud of his son, a sadness laced his words. "He is an important man. Very successful."

"Yes, he is." Deep wrinkles dented my father's slacks. His shirt sleeves were rolled about midway up his forearms. The straps to a mask hung out of a pocket on his shirt. He wasn't wearing one in her room, and given they lived together and he probably hadn't left her side, him wearing one didn't feel necessary.

"He paid for this room. When she is in a regular room, she will have a suite. He has been generous with your mother. He bought her a Cadillac last Christmas." He sighed and patted my hand. "How are you?" He brushed his hand across my cheek and tenderly draped my hair behind my ear. He always tucked my hair behind my ear, as if he couldn't see my face otherwise.

"I'm good. Scared for Mom."

"Me too." He shuffled over to one side of the bed and pointed for me to go to the other side. "Touch her hand. She'll want to know you're here."

I brushed my fingers over hers. They were cold, almost freezing.

"Dad, she needs another blanket."

"The nurse says she's fine." A folded blanket rested on top of a storage unit against the wall. Ignoring Dad's stare, I pulled it down and draped it over her legs, and over her arms, close to her chin.

My father's lips contorted. The lines around his lips flexed. He didn't like what I had done. But he said nothing.

My BlackBerry vibrated, and I slipped it out of my pocket. An unknown number shone on the screen.

"Answer your brother out in the hall. I'll stay here."

I nodded. As I closed the door, the curtain enclosed the bed.

"Hey. I'm here."

"How is she?"

"She's asleep. I haven't learned anything yet."

"I've been researching surgeons."

"Did you find one?"

"Not yet. It's in progress."

"Is this surgery a big deal?"

"It's heart surgery. She suffered a heart attack. There's damage."

"Is she a transplant candidate?"

"Her doctor hasn't mentioned it. They wouldn't do that unless it's absolutely necessary. And the heart transplant list—I mean, I could hack the system, but they have so many protocols in place I don't think she'd get the heart before someone caught on."

"Erik." I closed my eyelids and my eyes burned. "You can't… It's unethical." I paced, my head down.

"I know. And right now it's not necessary. I just want you to know I've thought of everything. I'm doing all I can."

The annoyance that had risen dissipated, and tears blurred my fatigued eyes.

"I know. I wish you could be here."

"I'm closer by. If something happens, I'll be there."

"Thank you."

"You know, your cop is on the way."

"What?" I'd texted him when I landed. I pulled out my iPhone and clicked to my messages, to see if I missed a return text. When I put my BlackBerry back to my ear, I picked up Erik's ongoing conversation mid-sentence.

"Probably not a bad guy. I got into his PD file. His presence on the island is because of a censure. But I don't have an issue with what he did. And he's definitely not there on behalf of NSA. I've figured out the connection between him and that guy. They're old friends. He's just your basic cop."

"Are you saying you're once again okay with me dating him?"

"I'd rather you didn't. But it's not my call. Obviously, there are things you can't ever tell him. But he's a glorified traffic cop. He's not going to pick up on much. And I think he'll be good for you right now. He cares about you. Enough to fly across the country." I actually grinned in the hall. Probably the only grin on the CCU hall at that moment. "His flight gets in tomorrow afternoon. He's planning to surprise you."

"Well, why did you tell me?"

"Because we don't like surprises."

"No, we don't. But yet you put cameras in my home without telling me." A woman about twenty feet away glanced my way, and I paced away from her. It wasn't the time or place to have it out with my brother, but I couldn't stop the words.

"Cali. You knew I had a security team outfit your home."

"Yes. But not inside. My bedroom." I gritted out the word.

"You knew."

"No. I didn't. There's a glass bulb in the office. Above the front door and on the back deck. You hid the others." How did he not see this as a wild invasion of my privacy?

"For aesthetics. It's the best placement."

I rested my head against a wall. Exhaustion overwhelmed me. Mom mattered. Not this.

"When I get back, I want you to tell me where every single indoor camera is."

"Cali." His harsh tone warned me.

"Don't Cali me. You had no right."

"It's for your own good. And you should've realized."

"What? No." *Asshole.* A nurse smiled at me as she passed me in the hall, and I forced a smile in return. "Where are you on putting this behind us?"

"Close. I promise."

CHAPTER 18

ogan

WHEN I ARRIVED AT THE FRONT DESK AT THE CCU, THE FIRST thing I noticed was a sign with limitations on visitors. They allowed only one family member to stay overnight. And only two visitors at a time. I should've thought of that. But I could still make myself useful. Surely they could use a break.

"If there are two visitors right now, what's the process? Should I wait for one to leave the room?"

The nurse peered over her computer screen. Multi-colored hearts dotted her pastel scrubs.

"In the afternoon, we're lenient. After dinner we try to keep things quiet and limit the number of visitors. Ms. Lai needs her rest. But a short visit won't be a problem."

"Good. I'm hoping I can relieve Mr. Lai and his daughter, so they can go home."

Her eyebrows raised high. "Good luck with that. But if you can get Mr. Lai to take a break, you'll be earning your keep. They're right down that hallway. Room 389."

My knuckle wrapped against a heavy, shut door, the dull thud of each knock hardly registering. Through the glass pane, a curtain hung from the ceiling. The fabric wavered, then she appeared. Dark hair behind her ears, curled into the neck of an oversized sweatshirt with a hoodie. The door opened, and she threw her arms around my neck, standing on tiptoes, and pressed her mask against my throat.

"Thank you for coming." Her words came out as a breathy whisper.

The door, attempting to close, pressed against my arm, which was looped around her back. She smelled like fragrant flowers, an unusually potent scent for her, but it was still Cali, and I could swear her heartbeat against mine soothed us both.

When she broke our hug, I studied her, looking for signs of exhaustion. She wore leggings, and thick socks rode halfway up her calves. Tiny gold crosses dotted her ears. Without thinking, I reached up and ran my thumb over a lobe. She bowed her head and clasped her neck.

"My mom's family gave them to me. Years ago."

"How's your mom?"

Four fingers clasped the doorframe and opened the door wider. An older gentleman with short black hair, flattened to his scalp, and dark eyes, stared me down.

"Dad, this is my friend, Logan."

"Cali told me about you. Thank you for coming." Her father's eyes glassed over, and he bobbed his head and opened his mouth as if he had more to say. "Come in. Dahlia has been looking forward to meeting you."

Dutifully, I followed them both into the room. Her father swung the curtain out of the way, unveiling the room. A slight woman with long white hair lay in the hospital bed, blankets pulled up to her shoulders. Whisper-light blue eyes blinked, lost in pale, colorless skin.

Her father stood at his wife's head. The darker olive skin tones contrasted against his wife's almost lucid skin as he lovingly brushed loose strands of hair out of her eyes.

"Can I get you something to drink? Would you like tea?" Exhaustion coated the man. His rote question went unnoticed by all. Just looking at his bloodshot eyes burned mine.

"Mom, this is Logan."

"Logan. It's so nice to meet you."

"Thank you, ma'am. I wish it was under better circumstances. Are they treating you right around here?"

"Yes. Such nice nurses. But that doesn't mean I'm not ready to leave. Can you do something about getting me out of here?"

"No, ma'am. I'm afraid not. But I was hoping I could do something about getting Mr. Lai and your daughter to take a break. I'm available for night duty so they can get some sleep." Figured I might as well put it out there. The man hovering at her side looked like he might fall down standing. I'd swear color flowed through her pale skin at my suggestion.

"That would be wonderful."

"It's not happening," Mr. Lai responded, stern, lips in a flat line, hand on her shoulder.

Cali absently massaged her mother's foot through the blankets. The two women gazed at each other, and a soft smile graced her mother's lips. Cali wore a mask, but I sensed her return smile.

"Last night I stayed at my parents'. Dad refused to leave."

"Oh, do you live nearby?" I asked the room.

"About thirty minutes away. It's too far," her father answered.

"Well, I got a hotel room that's down the street. Less than a five-minute walk." I whipped out the plastic key card. "I have a key for both you and Cali. Two queen beds. Whenever you want to use it, you can."

"Dad, you need a shower." He rubbed his jaw, which drew my attention to spotty growth along his face. Longer black strands clustered along his chin, but you could see he'd never grow in a full beard.

"Ronin, you do need a shower." Her mother's words were gentle and teasing, but sincere.

"I don't have my shaving kit."

"Dad, we can go back to the house and get you anything you need. Then you can go to the hotel and shower. You can stay overnight."

"I can't sleep without your mother. But she might appreciate it if I had a shower."

"Dad wasn't happy with the clothes I brought back for him this morning." Cali cast her dad a loving smile.

"She brought me sweatpants." He shook his head. "One step above pajamas." Her dad wore a white button-down oxford and formal black slacks with a slick black leather belt. I wondered if somewhere in the room a tie lay cast aside.

A nurse tapped on the doorframe and entered.

"Good evening, Ms. Dahlia. How're you doing?" She lifted her chart and checked numbers on the screen.

"Want to get out of here."

The nurse chuckled. "That's what they all say. You'd think we treat 'em badly." She hung the clipboard back on the end of the bed. "You're scheduled for some tests this evening. Probably in less than an hour I'm going to come and get you."

"You're letting me out of bed?"

"Where'd you get an idea like that? We're wheeling the entire bed down the hall. We've got you down for an MRI and a CT scan. It'll take a little while. So, if anyone wants to head out for a bit, that would be a good time to do it." The nurse looked pointedly at Mr. Lai.

"I don't have my—"

"Dad, tell me exactly what you need. We'll run back to the house. While you're getting a shower, Logan and I will wait here. If anything happens or you're needed, you can get back here in five minutes."

Mr. Lai frowned. He sucked in his lower lip. Then he shuffled to the sofa and fumbled around in a duffel bag. He pulled out a pen and paper and scribbled out a list.

"Logan, it looks like you're about to be whisked away, but I'm sure I'll get some good visiting time in before you leave. Doesn't sound like they're letting me out too soon. You'll stay a bit, right? I want to get to know you."

"Yes, ma'am. I'll stay as long as I'm needed."

Her fingers brushed her throat, and Cali sprang into action, gathering a small pink plastic cup with a straw and holding it close so she could sip water. Her mom's head sank into the pillow, and her eyes closed.

"She gets exhausted so easily," Cali commented to herself, and the weight of the words fell around her. She bent and placed a masked kiss on her mother's forehead, then looked to her father. "We'll be back as soon as we can."

Out in the hall, Cali pulled out her phone and tapped the screen.

"I have a rental car. I didn't know if we'd need it or not."

"Great. Where are you parked?"

"At the hotel."

"This'll be faster." She resumed tapping. "I'll have the driver stay at the house while I run in and get some things."

"Okay." I didn't agree, but I wouldn't argue. If this was faster, and what she wanted to do, I'd follow along.

The Uber met us at the entrance to the hospital, and we both climbed into the back seat. After discussing the directions with the driver, and he let us know traffic on the 5 freeway wasn't bad at the moment, Cali relaxed into the seat.

She held a hand out to the middle of the seat and flipped it over, welcoming my hand. I placed my hand over her palm. I wanted to tug her up against me, but she'd already fastened her seatbelt.

"It was really nice of you to come."

"I wanted to be here for you. I worried about how you'd take it. But you didn't even seem surprised."

"I...it felt completely natural to see you there. Flying out here...I was blown away. It's sweet. Who's taking care of Nym?"

"Gabe and Poppy."

"Was he okay with them?"

"I think so. I introduced Gabe. Had him feed him."

"But not Poppy?"

"She wasn't around."

"Maybe we should tell Poppy not to come over."

"Really? Does he bite?"

"If he thinks she's breaking into the house, he'll attack her. Did you give them his commands?"

"Yes."

"Okay. I'll text Poppy. Emphasize a few things."

The sun lowered across the city landscape, and a dull pink haze mixed with cream filled the horizon. The light had grown dim enough most cars had turned their headlights on, and brake lights occasionally blinked red up ahead.

After she quit texting, I asked her, "How're you holding up?" Her lower lip quivered.

"It's tough. I don't know if it's tougher seeing my mom sick or my dad so worried. She has to be okay, Logan. I don't know what my father will do if she's not."

"She looked pretty good to me." It wasn't the complete truth, but she didn't look like someone at death's door.

"I know. I agree. And I think she's better than she was yesterday. Periodically, they've given her oxygen, you know, through the nose, just augmented oxygen, I guess, but she's doing good. I just worry because she tires out so easily. And she sleeps so much."

"Are they giving her anything to make her sleep?"

"I don't think so. But it's possible."

"Heart medication can have all kinds of side effects. Or at least, that's what I've heard."

"Yeah."

The driver exited the freeway and drove through an urban neighborhood, filled with newly constructed apartment buildings and townhomes. The newer area transitioned to an older neighborhood with a more traditional feel, with mature trees in the yards and dated architecture. The driver pulled up to a gated entry. Two brick pillars bookended the iron gates. She gave him a punch code, and the gates opened.

"Is this where you grew up?"

"No. I grew up nearby, though. In a much smaller house. Erik wanted our parents in a gated community. Actually, he tried to talk them into a high-rise, but Mom loves to garden. This house has a water view from the back yard. It's an older home, but it's completely remodeled. It's nice. Really nice."

The driver drove slowly as he read the mailbox numbers, and Cali leaned forward, directing him. "That one."

"Here, I'll be just a minute."

"I'll follow you. I need to use the restroom."

"Okay."

I followed her in, and she pointed to a half bath then jogged up the stairs. The house wasn't at all what I would have expected. The minimalist modern design didn't match her parents' persona. The enormous modern kitchen boasted stainless steel appliances offset by white cabinets and marble countertops. Over the island, the marble cascaded from the top to the floor on two sides. The floors were yellow pine, the only element that showed the home's age.

I entered the den, searching for some sign of Cali and her family. I discovered a portrait of a boy and girl, most likely in elementary school. On the other side of the window, two stacked portraits hung. Judging from the black drape over Cali's shoulders, I guessed they were high school senior portraits. Her brother wore a suit. He, too, had black hair. He bore a noticeable resemblance to her father.

"You ready?" From the base of the stairs, she called out, "You're lucky you're seeing the remodeled home. If you'd seen our old home, family photos lined every inch of the walls. My mom loves photos. Photography is one of her hobbies."

"Not too many now. It almost feels like your parents have it staged to sell." There were no knickknacks, nothing to reveal a history or a personality.

"If I took you upstairs, or even downstairs to the basement, you'd find all of that. I think they caved to Erik's designer on the main floor living areas."

"It is beautiful."

"Yeah, it is." I sensed hesitation. Maybe she wasn't such a fan? "Come on. I'll bring you back here later. The back yard is the best spot."

"Did you get clothes for yourself?" I asked because she only held one duffel. She shook her head. "Stay with me. We'll be close by. They won't let more than one person stay overnight, will they?"

"Good point. You're good at this hospital stuff."

Back at the hospital, when we entered her mother's room, her father sat in the hospital room chair, bent over, his forehead resting on his palms. Without the bed in the room, an uneasy vacancy remained. His shoulders curved downward, creating the profile of a broken man.

"Dad?" Her voice, low and soft, sounded childlike. She touched his shoulder, and he slowly lifted his head, groggy and out of it.

"They'll bring her back here in about an hour," he said with a glazed expression.

"We got your things. It's right in this bag. We'll stay here and wait for her. She won't be alone. Okay?"

He nodded, but his eyes held a vacant, faraway stare.

"Go get a shower. And lie down in the bed. See if you can get some rest. You won't be any good to Mom if you collapse. No one can go without sleep."

"I sleep at night. The sofa, it folds flat. I sleep."

I didn't broach the discussion between the two of them, but when I blew out my knee, I spent about a week in the hospital. No one slept well in a hospital.

"Come on, Dad. I'll walk you out."

He slowly stood. When he looked at me, he blinked, and the wrinkling around his eyes made me think he was trying to remember who I was and why I was there. But he smiled.

"Logan, you'll stay here? Just in case."

"Dad, they have our numbers." They exchanged a single glance. "But of course, Logan will stay here while I walk you out. Someone will be here waiting for her at all times. I promise."

Thirty minutes later, Cali returned. The plastic-like cushions crinkled as she joined me on the narrow sofa. She settled in against me, her head resting on my chest. The night shift transitioned in, and with the lights in the room dim, even with the bright fluorescent haze in the hall, it felt like we'd approached the twilight hours.

"Your father okay?" I asked to break the silence as much as anything.

"Yeah. I'm hoping he lies down and sleeps through the night. And it's your hotel room. I'm sorry about that."

"Don't apologize. I'd actually hoped you'd take the other bed and sleep too. Let me carry on with night duty."

"You are being so good to us. To me. I can't believe you actually came here." Her arm wrapped around my waist. A warm sensation washed over me. It felt right. There was no other place I was supposed to be. No other place I could be other than by her side as she went through this with her family. I brushed a kiss across the top of her head, and she sighed into me as I held her.

"Did you ever see the film *Lost in Translation?*" I asked.

"Years ago."

"Well, when I first asked you out, I think I thought we were a bit like those two characters. Two people lost in life at the moment, and that we might help each other."

"I don't remember the details…"

"The details aren't important. She suspected her husband was cheating, and she wasn't happy in her marriage but wasn't dealing with it, and he didn't have the most functional relationship either. And they're in a foreign land for a couple of days and a friendship forms. I wouldn't say the film ends with everything working out, but they're stronger because of the friendship, maybe better able to handle the future. And, since we're both divorcees, and find ourselves on this odd little island, almost a bubble unto itself, I guess…"

"You thought we would help each other get to a better place?"

"A rebound version of the film." I smirked. If she didn't get the comparison, I couldn't blame her. "You didn't want to date me, remember? But I pushed because I think I had that in the back of my mind. That we could be good for each other. That it was time for us, or for me, at least, to move forward."

She didn't raise her head. She didn't move. I had no idea what she was thinking. But we were in a hospital room, so I figured the chances were good her thoughts were with her family.

"Your heartbeat is strong and steady." Her head lay against my chest as I combed my fingers through her hair. "I'm so grateful to have you here. I don't think I could do this alone." Her voice quivered.

"You don't have to."

"I care about you, too. I don't know what the future holds, but please never doubt that." Emotion overflowed in her words, and I tightened my hold on her, soothing her beneath harsh fluorescent lights.

Minutes ticked by. The long hand on the white wall clock documented every single one.

"Tell me about Chicago."

"Why?" Her out-of-the-blue question threw me.

"We've got time to kill. And I'm hungry, and I'd rather not think about that."

"I can go get you food."

"If Dad returns, we can eat together. For now, I'm too content to move."

"Got it. So…Chicago." I didn't like to think about the place, because then I remembered. But she wanted to talk cities. "It's great. You ever been?"

"Once for a conference. I liked it."

"Yeah, I love the summers there. The winters I'm not missing so much."

"Is that why you left? The winters?"

"No. I told you. My ex wanted me to leave." A pummel pounded my chest at the admission. I pushed forward, laying it out there in the most non-melodramatic way possible. "What I didn't tell you is that I lost my temper. Anger management issue. That's what the psychologist called it. Leaving the state was part of my divorce agreement. Because Bethany feared for her lover's life. My buddy stepped in, pulled some favors. He said someone with my background would be useful down on

Haven, but I've always known it had nothing to do with being useful. He believed I needed something low-key so I could, you know, regroup."

She had raised her head, but I didn't notice her change in position until I finished my re-cap. Warm brown eyes sought mine.

I looked away, to the white wall. The crack of bone. I heard it like I was there, all over again. It was a sound that was impossible to replicate. They couldn't even do it in the movies. The splatter of blood. His deformed nose. Bethany crying. Tugging on my shirt. And my fists. Over and over and over. Striking him like a prostrate punching bag. Nausea edged within. I blinked, attempting to block the memory.

"That's my deep, dark baggage. He spent a few days in the hospital. I wasn't on duty at the time, but they worried about my stability. Bethany struck a deal with me. Said he wouldn't file assault charges if I moved." Saying it out loud hit harder. I fucked up. I'd been blind with rage. And as a result, I lost everything. But the truth of the matter was I'd lost everything before I ever raised a fist. My marriage had been decimated long before that day. I just didn't see it at the time. "I'll never return to Chicago."

Her lips brushed against my jaw. Her fingers linked with mine. She rested her head on my shoulder. I closed my eyes, reveling in her comfort. The physical, and the internal.

ali

MY FATHER KICKED US OUT OF THE HOSPITAL ROOM WITHIN minutes of returning. An uneasy calm encapsulated the brightly lit hall. The mechanical beeps suffused into the fabric of the building. The inner rooms darkened, and human voices fell to murmurs. Bone-deep exhaustion permeated my entire being. I could only imagine how exhausted my father, at his age, must feel after so many days in the cavernous hospital.

"Are you sure you can sleep here, Dad?" After a shower, the thick black hair I remembered replaced the oily mat, but other than that slight improvement, he remained unchanged. His shoulders caved in. His freshly pressed button-down and dress pants were now wrinkle-free, but he still appeared frail. Physically smaller than I ever remembered.

"Once you leave, I will sleep. The longer you stay, the less I sleep."

In the hotel room, Logan opened a binder which held a brief room service menu.

"Order whatever you want. I need to go to the restroom." My eyes burned, and the lids weighed heavily. My muscles ached, and my feet throbbed.

On the toilet, a dark red stain smeared my panties. I stared in disbelief. I'd been so in my head I'd forgotten my period. As if punishing me for forgetting, the tension in my shoulders evolved into throbbing stomach cramps. I wadded up tissue and put it into my ruined underwear, washed my hands, then exited the bathroom and picked up my pocketbook.

"I've got to go down to the store."

"What do you need? I'll go. You're exhausted. Take a bath or shower. Room service will be a minimum of thirty minutes."

"It's okay. I'll be quick."

His large hand fell to my shoulder, and concern etched his eyes. "What's wrong?"

Blast it. He'll find out, anyway. We're sharing a hotel room.

"I got my period. I just need to run downstairs—"

"I got it. You go get in a warm bath. Is there a particular brand you like?"

I stared at him in disbelief. "You're volunteering to go buy my sanitary products?"

"You look surprised? Did your husband never do that for you?" His lips turned up slightly on the ends, amused. He picked up his wallet from the desk and slipped it into his back pocket. "Tampons? Pads? Both?" He stood, waiting patiently for an answer.

"Ah, I doubt the hotel store is going to have a great selection. Whatever they have will work. Tampons. Thanks."

"Sure thing. Go get in the bath. You'll feel better."

In the tub, the steaming hot water warmed my chilled bones. The heat eased my stiff muscles, tight from the combination of uncomfortable hospital chairs and the weight of worry. A vision of Logan downstairs, picking up tampons from a shelf, flitted through my mind's eye, and I smiled.

I'd dated other men, but none so seriously they would have bought me tampons. I'd never dated anyone over forty, someone already trained by a wife. He'd long ago come to understand menstruation is a fact of life.

I sank down in the water, closed my eyes, and quieted my mind, pushing out all thoughts other than the repeated *drip, drip, drip* as water leaked from the faucet into the tub.

When the water chilled, I reluctantly drained the tub, dried off, and dressed in pajama pants and a long sleeve pajama top. When I opened the bathroom door, I discovered Logan had set up our dinner on the table and lit a small candle.

We ate dinner, and I brushed my teeth, then I got into bed. The crisp, white linen on the bed, beneath the thick comforter, combined with the shower running, lulled me into a groggy cocoon, broken by the click of the bathroom door. Steam shrouded Logan in the doorway, and he hesitated. I took a moment to appreciate his muscular chest and the smattering of black hair creating a trail to the white towel wrapped around his trim waist. I patted the empty side of my bed.

"Come to bed."

He dropped the towel near his suitcase, his back to me, exposing his muscular buttocks for the briefest of seconds before he pulled on loose boxers. He clicked the light, and pitch-black darkness enveloped the room. He slipped into bed behind me and pulled my back to his front.

"How are you feeling? I bought Midol and Advil. I wasn't sure which you might use." He brushed flyaway hairs off my cheek.

"I'm good right now. But thank you. Thank you for being so thoughtful."

"Well, I don't know if you've noticed or not, but I care about you. I want to take care of you." He kneaded my shoulder muscles and the tight muscles leading up my spine, into the base of my hairline. I reached behind me, feeling for him, wanting to return the favor, but he stopped my wandering hand.

"This is about you. And only you."

IN THE MORNING, LOGAN'S MUSCULAR FORM CLOAKED MY smaller frame. The red letters on the digital clock on the side table read six forty-five. The reality of the day cast a dark shadow.

An intermittent buzzing sound, faint, repeated in bursts across the room. My phone. With care, so as not to disturb Logan, I pulled out of his reach and slid out of bed. Along the floor, I found my iPhone, charging.

A text shown on the screen.

Found a surgeon. Surgery this afternoon.

The message arrived from an unknown number, but I knew it was from Erik. Given it was from an unknown account, in accordance with agreed-on protocol, I didn't respond. I did feel grateful he didn't use our annoying childhood code that required deciphering. And he'd clearly deducted I wouldn't be toting two phones around Logan.

"Is everything okay?" Logan stood behind me, in view of the phone, and I jerked. The phone dropped, face side down.

"Yeah, it's fine. I didn't mean to wake you."

"Did you get some news?" He gestured to my hand.

"Surgery is this afternoon." I offered a soft smile and studied him, holding my breath, wondering if he'd seen the unknown number. If he'd ask questions. But seeing an unknown number would be so much easier to explain than a coded message.

Logan entered the bathroom and closed the door. The unsettling certainty that Logan wouldn't be here for me, wouldn't want a relationship with me, if he knew the truth rooted itself into my conscience. And I'd known this…but now he was here, and we felt serious. Like we'd gone from casual to serious in a blink of an eye, and yet I had a family member he wouldn't accept. Could never accept. Erik had been worried about the implications of Logan turning him in, but what about the flip side of that coin? If Logan ever learned the truth, would I disgust him? Would he expect that I would turn my brother in? Because I couldn't. I would never.

"Hey, hun, it's going to be okay. Your mom's going to be okay. You hear me?" His fingers brushed my cheek. "Bathroom's yours. I'll go get us coffee."

I faintly nodded. Nerves fired off, and I wasn't sure if it was the impending surgery or Logan. An unknown number…easy enough to explain. It's Erik…he lost his phone. Easy explanation. But…when we got back? Would Erik stay true to his word? Would this be behind him soon? Would he ditch the burner phones and join the land of the legal?

Coffee awaited me when I exited the bathroom, freshly showered and hair dried. "You're too good to be true."

"Trust me. I have a list of shortcomings. If you stick around, you'll discover them all." I didn't have to ask who had provided him with this list, and once again, I bit back any commentary, not wanting to invite the ex-wife into our space. But something had to have been wrong with the woman. To me, he couldn't be more perfect. Unfortunately, part of that perfection was his integrity and his commitment to uphold the law.

His fingers laced with mine, and I pushed back the swirling concerns. Today, I needed to be strong for my father, and here for my mother. Those relationship concerns hovered, but I'd deal with them another day. Today…I needed to be present for my family.

JUST AS WHEN WE'D LEFT THE NIGHT BEFORE, THE CEILING curtain wrapped around the bed, blocking any view of the people within. The knob clicked as I opened the door. My father's head peered around the curtain.

"Morning. Where's Logan?"

"He went to get us breakfast. I'm going to text him your order. What do you want?"

"Coffee and an egg sandwich. Don't let me forget to give him money when he gets back."

"I think he'll be okay getting you, Dad." I looped my arm around his, holding him to me for a private question. "How's Mom?"

"I'm fine. Come, give me a hug," Mom answered, her voice raspy. I bypassed Dad and ducked behind the curtain.

Fear pierced me with the sharpness of a knife blade, and tears welled up. An oxygen mask covered her face, and her skin had become paler, almost translucent. She lifted her mask to speak, and her lips held a bluish tinge.

"Don't let the mask scare you. I'm quite all right."

I wrapped my hands around hers, the one without tape and wires. "Did you sleep okay?"

"All I do is sleep. Your father—you need to get him out of here so he can sleep."

"Oh, Mom." I kissed her hand, so cold within mine. She lifted her mask and pushed it lower, below her neck.

"Honey, don't be scared. It's not my time yet. I'll be all better after the surgery today. You wait and see." A sob escaped me. "Cilia, listen to me. I don't have grandchildren yet. I'm not leaving this Earth without meeting them." I kissed her knuckles as warm tears ran down my cheeks. "I. Like. Logan."

Her breathy words caught my attention, and I raised her mask back over her nose and mouth.

"I think you need the oxygen. Keep it on, okay?" She nodded. "You don't like it, do you?" She shook her head, half an inch back and forth. "Well, let's keep it on so you're in tip-top shape for the surgery. What time is it?"

"Right after lunch. One p.m. They'll take her back about an hour before. Your brother found the world's most respected surgeon. From Ohio. He's going to be doing the surgery with the chief surgeon from here. Your mother is going to be just fine. I'm researching options for recovery."

"I'll be here, Dad. I'll help you."

"Can you do that? What about work?" Wrinkles formed between his brow as he asked, and my face heated.

"Dad, I'll be here for you and Mom."

He wrapped an arm around me and kissed my forehead, like he used to do, years ago, only now we were almost the same height.

Logan entered the room as my mother drifted off to sleep. Reluctantly, I dropped her hand and accepted the coffee.

"Her body is in a battle. The conversation with you taxed her. She needs her rest. Why don't you two take your food outside? Maybe go for a walk? Enjoy the blue skies?"

A crushing fear ricocheted through me.

"We'll be quiet. We promise." Logan's words were gentle, but I searched my father's expression, wondering how he'd handle a contradictory response. Dad batted his eyelids, and his lips pushed together. Then he dragged a chair up to my mother's bedside, assuming his position, leaving Logan and me on our own.

We resumed our spot on the stiff sofa. We ate with the utmost care, as quiet as we could be. Mom drifted in and out of sleep, and we waited.

A little before noon, a cheery nurse entered the room and checked my mother's vitals then began adjusting cords as she prepared to wheel my mother off.

Mom's eyelids fluttered, and my father hovered over her, whispering. He backed up for a minute, allowing me my time.

"Mom, I love you. You come through this." Her light blue eyes met mine, and my lips brushed her ear as I reminded her, in my lowest whisper, "You've got to meet those grandchildren."

Sobs wracked through my frame as they pushed her bed out into the hall. My father walked by her side, holding her hand as the nurse maneuvered the bulky bed. No doubt he would be by her side as far as they would let him. Logan pulled me against his chest, and I bawled. All the things I should have said came to mind. She was the best Mom I could have ever had. I loved her more than life itself. She was my everything. And I was so sorry for not being around more.

"Hey, sshhhh." Logan coaxed me the way you would a small child. "She's going to be okay."

"I should've said more."

"You'll get to tell her everything you want after the surgery. She's going to be feeling so much better. You just wait."

ali

My father joined us in the surgical waiting room about half an hour later. My head lay against Logan's broad chest, my arms wrapped around him, and he soothed me with gentle strokes. Growing up, I would have never conceived of holding on to another man like this in front of Dad, but he didn't give us a second glance. He sat down in a chair next to us, silent.

"Dad? Did you see the surgeon?"

"Briefly. Erik says he's got the best ratings. He's done thousands of these surgeries. He almost seemed to think your mother's case was beneath him. Which is good. He doesn't expect any issues."

"From what I understand, unclogging arteries is pretty commonplace these days," Logan volunteered. I squeezed his knee, only now remembering his mother had died from a heart attack. She didn't have the opportunity for surgical repair.

"Dad, do you want to go with us to the cafeteria?"

"No. I'll stay here."

I settled back against Logan. My father remained stone still.

Logan tugged on a strand of my hair. "Do you want to go?"

My stomach felt heavy, as if filled with lead. Food struck me as borderline repulsive.

"Why don't you go? I'll stay here. I'm really not hungry."

"I'll bring you back something. Maybe hot tea? Some soup, if they have it? Crackers?"

"Tea. Hot tea would be good. Thank you."

"What about for your dad?" he asked me, even though my father sat three feet away. But, while he was physically present, his heart and soul were down the hall in surgery.

"Hot tea? Potato chips?" I guessed my answers.

Logan left us in the waiting room. A woman sitting on the opposite wall had a large kaftan wrapped around her, and I wished I'd brought blankets. An older couple a few rows over carried on a whispered conversation. A pre-teen sat with headphones on, tapping away on a device, clearly playing a game, a light, repetitive tapping on keys the only noise generated by his activity. I fell into a meditative trance, much like my father.

The heavy door swung open, and a surgeon in scrubs stepped through. I looked to my father, searching for signs of recognition. He returned his stare to the wall. Seconds later, the nearby couple rose and followed the surgeon into a private room.

Logan returned with food. I wrapped my icy fingers around

the warm paper cup and occasionally sipped at the tea. Whatever else he bought remained in the white paper bag.

The heavy door swung open, and a different surgeon, in teal scrubs, entered. My father stood. The surgeon's eyes—I would never forget them. His expression said everything.

The rest of the day proceeded in a blur. I followed my father and the surgeon into the private meeting room. The doctor explained complications from cardiac catheterization were rare but could happen. She suffered what they called an air embolism and died almost immediately. There was nothing that could have been done. My father asked to see her.

My father bent over her, visibly trembling from his audible sobs. I stood back, watching, both numb and aching. Logan asked me if I wanted time alone with my mother. I told him no, I'd have time at the funeral home. We gave my parents privacy.

Erik arrived. Tears ran down his cheeks, and we hugged, clinging to each other. I sobbed harder, to the point my breaths altered, gasping. Erik's dark eyes, behind his thick glasses, shone glassy and thick with emotion. He asked about Dad, and his question reminded me we weren't alone.

"He's still with her." I backed up and held a hand out toward Logan, where he sat in a nearby chair. "This is Logan."

He nodded knowingly. Of course he knew. Logan stood, and the men gazed at each other.

"I'm sorry…for your loss." Logan added the last part as my tears streamed.

I wasn't sure who offered a hand first, but they shook hands, and Erik said he'd go find Dad and help take care of some hospital matters. I didn't have any idea how long we remained in the waiting room before Erik returned with Dad.

Back at my parents' house, I wrapped myself in one of

Mom's old crochet throws and curled into a ball. Erik joined me, stoic and serious. All business. I expected tomorrow we would make arrangements, but he entered with a distinct focus. I sensed he had a checklist and he wanted to go through it.

"Where's Logan?" I pulled my feet closer to me so Erik wouldn't sit on them.

"Checking out of the hotel. He should be here soon." That made sense. I sniffled then reached for a tissue.

"Cal, I'm taking Dad with me." Did he mean taking him out for dinner? He couldn't… "He wants to go. He's decided against a funeral. He doesn't want to spend any time in this house without her. We'll put it on the market. I've found a real estate agent who will handle everything. Before you leave to go back east, go through the house and gather anything you want to keep."

"Wait." The walls and floor waffled and spun, and I braced myself against the sofa armrest. "What?"

"Dad wants to return to Macau. I'm taking him."

"Is that where you've been living?"

"Sometimes. He wants to be near his family."

"But no. No. When someone loses a spouse, they say you're supposed to stay in the home for a year. Not move to another country."

"His visa is current. We're leaving late tonight."

"What? No. We have to have a service for Mom."

"She's being cremated. You know Dad is fiercely private."

"But her family? Her friends?"

"This is what Dad wants." Erik's somber expression hinted he might not agree completely, but he wouldn't fight it.

I poked a finger through the crochet and wiggled the

knuckle. In an out-of-body experience, the protruding finger appeared as someone else's, not my own.

"Your visa isn't current." He said it matter-of-factly. "But I'd like for you to join us."

"Move?"

"Dad thinks you should stay here with Logan. I disagree. It's up to you."

"That's very kind of you both to come to that conclusion."

"Don't be like that. If you don't join us, if you choose to stay here, it's possible we won't see each other again." I gasped, and the tears returned. "In a worst-case scenario. We can see each other again in non-extradition countries. I just want you to be aware of the risk."

"Is Dad aware of it?"

"To some degree."

"You told him?" My insides, wracked with pain, couldn't take any more. My question wasn't rooted in concern, but simple curiosity.

"This is the course of action he's chosen. At least for now. We leave tonight."

"Why tonight?"

"It's best to stay moving. And I'm not lying, Cal. Dad wants this. He hasn't said so, but I don't think he can stand the thought of sleeping in their bedroom."

"Where is he now?"

"Packing. There's a closet downstairs. And Mom's basement room. Those are the two places you'll find the sentimental stuff. Any of the stuff you want to take. I mean, if you want this furniture, you can have it. But it's not like it's what we grew up with."

No. The designer Erik hired pushed my parents into the

modern era. Truth be told, a lot of the furniture we grew up on had served its purpose.

I looked down at my lap. "I want this. Mom made it."

Erik's dark eyes shone like mirrors. I saw a distorted version of myself in his pupil, just as a lone tear fell down his cheek.

When my father entered the den, Erik hurried to wipe his face. His rush to hide his tears reminded me of my eight-year-old brother. He'd fallen when we were both learning to ride our bikes without training wheels. Somehow, maybe because Dad held on to my bike longer than Mom held onto Erik's, I hadn't fallen. Tears soaked his cheeks, and bright red colored one knee and thigh. Dad scolded him. Gave him the "boys don't cry" spiel. He didn't tell me the same thing, but I tried to stop crying from that day forward, too. At some point, though, I'd shed that outdated mode of thought. Erik apparently hadn't.

"Cecilia, there are two boxes I've set out down in the hall. One has photographs. You remember how your mother loved them?" Yes, she'd loved the real thing. Dad bought her a Polaroid. She had another camera too, a real one with multiple lenses. She'd referred to herself as a hobbyist. To my knowledge, she still took in film to get developed. Or she had. I nodded to answer his question. "Well, those are two boxes for you. Stay here as long as you want. We won't list the house until you're ready."

"Dad, this isn't the house I grew up in. I don't have any attachment to it."

His lips tilted downward on the ends. I suspected his lips would angle downward for a long time in the future.

"I understand. I have tagged a few items I want shipped to me. Anything else you can take."

"Dad, I don't—are you sure about this? Can you stay a few

days so we can give Mom the service she deserves? Her family—"

"We will give her a service back home. I'm having her ashes sent to me."

"But—"

"Cecilia. We're in shock. But I need to move. Forward." He stood, arms at his sides, head tilted down. "I like Logan. I've always wanted you to be with someone good. Who deserves you. I think you are like your mother in that you will be happiest here in America. It's good to see my daughter in love." He stopped speaking and looked at the ceiling as his bottom lip trembled. His chest rose and fell. I stood to go to him, and he raised an arm, motioning for me to stay away. "I'm glad Dahlia got to see you with him. She told me he's the one. That's what she said. But it's up to you. You can have an expedited visa in three days. We'll make it happen if that's what you want. At any time. But I like Logan. He is protective." He grimaced then transformed before my eyes. His shoulders rose, his lips flatlined, and his chin jutted out. "Erik, are you ready? The car is on the way."

ogan

"Welcome back." Gabe held up his glass beer bottle in greeting, and I pulled out the stool in front of the beer waiting for me. I picked it up and clinked the neck of the bottle against his.

"Thanks. And thanks for this." Drops of condensation on the glass dripped onto the wooden deck. The cold liquid quenched my thirst, and my muscles relaxed at the end of the workday signal.

Post-Labor Day, the crowds had cleared, and the marina didn't hold as many boats. But the skies were blue and the days still long and humid. Everything around us reeked of summer, except for the noticeable absence of vacationers.

"How's Cali?"

She's good was on the tip of my tongue, but I held it back. I didn't know how she was, but good didn't qualify as remotely accurate. She'd taken the last two weeks off work. Had walked a ton. Hadn't been for a noon run since we'd been back. She'd dropped a few projects and extended the deadlines on a couple. I didn't really know what she did during the day. In the evening, she cuddled up against me while I flipped channels.

"That bad?" Gabe asked.

"It's tough." I shrugged. "Her mom died. And, I mean, unexpectedly. She didn't really get to say goodbye. I don't know. What's someone supposed to feel or do?" I might've sounded defensive, but I didn't mean it that way. I asked because I didn't know if I should be concerned or if I should get her help. Or if time was all she needed.

"How's her dad taking it?"

"Her father and brother both left the country. Sounds like for good. Moved to Macau. It's near Taiwan."

"I didn't know she was from over there."

"She's not. She's from Seattle. Her grandfather on her father's side is from Macau. Don't repeat this, but her family's an odd crew."

"Other people's families always seem odd. I think I can count on one hand the number of people I've ever met who didn't have issues with the in-laws."

"No. It's not that. I mean, I get they were emotional. And meeting me for the first time. Her dad, a typical older businessman. Consumed with grief, as you'd expect. Her brother...he didn't..." I thought back to Erik's demeanor around me...but he'd just lost his mother. "They didn't even have a funeral."

"Maybe COVID showed people you don't have to go

through all that. I know I've always felt badly for the family standing there shaking hands on a receiving line when they've just lost someone they love."

Memories of my mother's funeral surfaced. It had just been her and me, but one of her friends planned the funeral. I'd been inundated with her friends introducing themselves. Her church friends served plates of cookies and lemonade after the funeral. I shook a thousand hands. I knew they all said funeral-appropriate things, but damn if I could remember any of those words of wisdom.

"I think it would've been good for Cali, though. I'm not the biggest fan of funerals, but I do believe they provide closure. And the way her dad and brother left—who does that? On the day she died. It was bizarre." I shook my head, still grappling with it. If I didn't know better, I'd assume they were on the run. "Cali said her dad couldn't handle being in the house after her mom died. Which sucks. It's almost like she's mourning them too."

"Why doesn't she go out and visit them?"

"She might. She applied for a visa."

"We never see her at the house. Poppy's been by every day."

"She's basically living at my house."

"Why don't you guys stay at hers? Don't get me wrong, I like your place, but she's oceanfront. And you'd be two decks down."

I swallowed my beer and thought about that. I wasn't sure how we fell into our current rhythm. I'd offered when we got back to get her settled in at her place, and she'd said no, she wanted to stay at mine. We went over to her place together, and she packed up some more clothes and picked up Nym.

"There's something about that house. I can't put my finger on it, but she doesn't feel safe in it."

"I don't know why not. She's got more security than most houses in the Hamptons. It's like a five-minute process to get through the front door."

I scratched my beard, thinking about that. "It's not so odd that she has an alarm system or multiple locks. It's that she's always turning it on. She locks her door when she goes out on the beach." She still hadn't told me anything about her ex. Not even his name. I learned she had her maiden name when I met her family, but I didn't know if she'd changed it back or had never changed it to begin with. Not that now would be the time to ask questions. She had enough on her mind without digging up bad memories. Come to think of it, she must've gotten divorced quite a while ago. Nowhere in the house were there any photographs of her with another man, not even a photo of her as a bride. Only that high school graduation portrait. I wondered, if my mom were still alive, would she have removed all traces of Bethany?

"It's probably habit."

"What?" Gabe's question threw me, because it was nowhere near where my thoughts had gone.

"Locking up all the time. An ingrained habit."

"Yep." I took a long swallow of my beer. She didn't lock the doors at my house, but she also didn't seem to leave it much since we'd returned. "Poppy should stop by my house. Does she know where it is?"

"Yeah. She pointed it out to me one day when we cut through your area."

"Well, if she gets a chance, ask her to stop by. I know they say to expect dark days. I just don't want her to unpack her suitcase and live there."

"Maybe Poppy and Luna can get her out for a girls' night. Nails or something."

"That'd be good. I made reservations for dinner tomorrow night. I mean, I don't want to push her…"

"Nah, I think that's a good idea. Have you bought her flowers?"

"No."

"Poppy loves flowers. Get her something cheerful, though. Stay away from, you know, anything people send to funeral homes. That's…" He shook his upper body in mock revulsion.

"I'll keep that in mind. You want another beer? I'm gonna place an order for a to-go pizza, but I'll hang until it arrives."

Back home, I peeked through the window on the back deck while I kicked off my shoes. Cali lay on the sofa with a blanket over her and her head on a pillow. Nym stretched out on the floor beside her, ears pricked forward, listening. He knew I'd arrived home, but Cali showed no signs of awareness.

After two or maybe three bites of pizza, Cali went to bed. The sense of helplessness stifled me. The whole situation fell far outside of my wheelhouse. A box with a cardboard lid sat on the coffee table. I flipped off the top.

Photographs filled the box. Some Polaroid, with the white frame, some regular prints. Most of the shots were of Cali and Erik growing up. I'd thought all photos these days were online, stored in a cloud. As I dug into the box and found younger photos, Cali and Erik became virtually indistinguishable, with identical haircuts. In several pictures, they even wore matching outfits—the same t-shirt, shorts, and shoes. Cali had a touch of tomboy, and her brother probably wouldn't appreciate me saying so, but he had a feminine quality. I found one shot with them both holding dolls. And another photo of them both holding water guns. Right about the age uniforms infiltrated the photos, it seemed Cali's hair grew longer, and Erik got a haircut. A photo of Cali in braces, smile wide and open, standing behind her brother, caught my attention. He sat at a large desktop computer with a mammoth monitor, oblivious to the person taking a photograph. While he was oblivious, she was all joy. Light and happy.

Bethany had been all about the photos and had done some cool things with our wedding photographs. She had some apps that let you create books and gifts. *If I scan these photos, I could do something like that for her. Bring back a little of the lightness...and a smile.* I pulled aside a solid selection and set them in an old shoe box to take to work. So many photos filled her box, my selection didn't make a dent. She'd never notice.

"Hey, you ready?" Friday night, I held out a wrapped bouquet, all multiple colors. I picked it up from the market on my way home.

"What are these for?" Cali's lips turned upward, into a soft smile, and I'd swear my insides lightened, just from seeing more life in her.

"Just because." I pressed a kiss to her lips then broke away, aware we were about to be late. I'd gotten pulled into a discussion about someone's barking dog and didn't get home as early as planned. "Let me take Nym for a walk, and we can go."

"I already walked him. He's actually back at my place."

"Oh, yeah?"

"I went back there this afternoon to pick up a few things and check on some stuff. He trotted around from room to room. It could all be in my head, but I felt like he missed the place. I knew we were going out to dinner, so I figured I'd leave him. His breed is territorial. While I think he loves me, I think maybe he loves that house more. We can swing by and get him after dinner. Or let him sleep there."

"Works for me." Her long black dress fell down her lean frame in an elegant column, and she wore black leather sandals to match. Her dark hair formed a smooth curtain past her shoulders, completing her polished, refined look. I lifted her hand to my lips. "You know, Nym's not the only one who loves you. I do too." The moment didn't feel romantic, and I should've said it with more impact. I'd wanted to say it earlier, but I didn't want it to come across like I was saying it because her mother died. But every single day, the feeling surged.

Her fingers brushed through my beard, and those dark eyes bored into mine. Her gaze cut to my core.

"I don't think I could have—you've been wonderful."

"Because I love you." I gazed into her dark eyes, and I hoped my expression reflected my words. I didn't need her to say it back to me; I simply had to let her know.

She pushed up onto her toes, and her lips found mine. She laced her hands behind my neck, and I roamed her gentle curves. Our tongues danced a familiar dance, soft and slow. A part of me ached to carry her into the bedroom, but I had a mission. I broke our kiss and ran my nose along hers, then my fingers through her silky strands. "We have a reservation." I whispered against her ear as I guided her out of our home, "We'll finish this after dinner."

"Promise?" She flicked her tongue over her lower lip, and

the movement reverberated in my groin. I'd been holding her at bay, unsure. She'd had her period, and then she'd been so sad. But my body remembered hers, and it ached for her.

"Oh, I promise. We'd better get out of here, or we won't make it to dinner."

She linked her fingers through mine and tugged.

"Well, let's go. I'm hungry." As we descended the steps, she said, "I accepted a new project."

"Oh, yeah?"

"It's a children's textbook translation. Cantonese."

"Wasn't Arabic your great rebellion?"

Her white teeth appeared as she bit her lip through a smile. "You're a good listener. Yeah, I took the project as a way of brushing up on my Cantonese. It'll be intensive for me. It'll take a lot of work to pull it off. I have an old professor who is going to help. But my grandfather taught us Cantonese. I learned it when I was learning English. It's not like I unlearned it when I chose a concentration in Arabic."

"But you don't list it as one of your languages?"

"I don't. I understand some of it verbally, but I have years of studying the writing in front of me. It's a tough language. It's one of those that you can study for a lifetime. Anyway, it makes me feel closer to my family. When I was little, my grandmother would sing to me. It was more of a mix of Cantonese and Portuguese. As I grew older, both my grandparents were so different from other people's grandparents." She chewed on the corner of her lip, then with a loud exhale continued. "Looking back, I think I owe my love of languages to my grandmother. When I was little, before I cared what others thought, I felt like she was magical. Her language was like a secret code that no one else knew, and when she sang it…" As she trailed off, a faint smile graced her lips. I understood. She may not have seen eye to eye with her father's family, but that didn't mean she didn't love them and they weren't a part of her.

"It goes without saying, if you want me to apply for a visa, I'll go with you to visit them any time." She smiled and led the way to the door. I didn't press.

On the way to dinner, a sadness emanated around her. Less than before, but still undeniably present. Her lips lay in a flat line, and she looked off in the distance. But she also looked more alive and aware than she had since we'd returned.

We entered Starlight, Poppy's recently opened restaurant, with our fingers linked. Poppy personally seated us at our table. She'd just left us with menus when Cali's slim black pocketbook began humming. Her eyes widened, and her fingers trembled as she unzipped the leather bag. She appeared startled, and I slipped into high alert mode, one hand braced on the chair, my weight angled forward, prepared to respond. Not many people called her.

She read her phone, and a perplexed expression crossed her features.

"Someone set off my alarm. Do you think someone tried to break into my house?"

"Or could Nym have set it off? He hasn't been left there alone in a while."

"I don't know, but we need to go." She pushed her chair back. "We've got to get a check."

"We've only had water. We're good. Let's go."

She dashed out, heads turning in her wake, watching her speed out of the place. I waved a hand at Poppy to catch her attention.

"We'll be back," I called, pointedly ignoring a couple staring nearby. I caught up to Cali in time to slide into the passenger side of my golf cart. She flattened the accelerator. I held on to the roof of the cart for balance as she whipped around the parking lot and onto the road.

"I'm sure it's nothing." There weren't many alarms on the island, but back in Chicago, false alarms were common.

"Maybe. But if it's something, Nym's trained. I mean, what if someone noticed my house has been dark? And they just want to go TV shopping? And Nym attacks?"

"Cali. We don't have that kind of theft here."

"Well, why would someone break in?" She rushed her words, and if I didn't know better, I'd say I frustrated her. Her left knee bounced, and she leaned forward, almost on top of the wheel, as if urging the cart to go faster.

"First, you don't know if someone broke in."

"The alarm isn't wrong."

"A tree branch can set off some of those alarm systems. A bird against the glass."

"There's an intruder."

"Why would someone want to break into your home, Cali?" She scowled. A mix of annoyance, probably at me, and an on-edge apprehension. "Why do you have such a sophisticated alarm system?"

"Because it's smart!" She lashed out at me, and I quieted. I braced my foot against the front of the cart as she flew along, for certain breaking the eighteen-mile-per-hour speed limit. A block away from her house, a shrill, high-pitched alarm greeted us, and she paled. My heartrate jumped, the same way it did at the sound of a siren. I wished I carried my gun.

Before coming to a complete stop in front of her house, she

leaped off the cart, leaving the ignition on, and darted up the stairs. I ran after her, pissed at her lack of caution.

"Stay back." She ignored me and swung open the front door.

"Dammit, Cali!" I reached for her and shoved her against a wall. "Stay. Here," I gritted out. "Right. Here."

She gave me the briefest nod, along with a stunned expression. *That's right, you will listen. I'll be damned if I'll let you put yourself into a dangerous situation.*

I crouched low, scanning the living area and kitchen, arms raised, ready. The corner of the rug had been kicked back. The sliding door was open. The sound of waves crashing wafted through the opening along with a slight breeze.

I scanned outside.

And ran.

Gabe held both arms straight up in the air, as if held at gunpoint.

As I stepped onto the deck, I discovered the issue.

"Dude?"

Nym growled, white fangs gleaming, the growl unnerving and fierce.

"*Sitzen!*" Nym sat, dropped the growl, and wagged his tail.

"Holy shit, am I glad to see you guys." Gabe bent over, hands on his knees. "I thought I was dog meat."

"What're you doing here?"

"I couldn't find my watch. Then I remembered I took it off when I fed that dog. Wouldn't you think he'd remember I fed him?"

Cali wiped her hand across her brow, and her chest heaved. "Gabe, he's not trained that way. You're lucky you're alive."

"Why on Earth do you have a dog like that? He bit me!" He held out his foot, and his flip-flop dangled. Red marks spotted across his ankle. No blood, but you could see where it looked like teeth had clamped.

Cali bent over his leg, checking out his ankle while rubbing between Nym's ears.

"He didn't break skin. He wasn't trying to hurt you. He wanted you to stay."

"For what?" Gabe crowed.

"For me to come home." She stood. "Why didn't you turn off the alarm?"

"I didn't get a chance. I didn't know he was home. I knew you guys were out to dinner, and I didn't think you'd mind. He came out of nowhere, and his lips did that thing where he shows his fangs, and I backed away, and he started growling. Fuck! He chased me through your house."

"Well, you're lucky. Did you find your watch?"

Gabe's mouth dropped. "Lucky?" He turned to me, palms splayed out. "Are you hearing this?"

"Yeah. I am."

"The dog bit me!"

"He nipped you. He wanted you to heel. You're lucky." Cali bent over her dog, and Gabe's eyes bugged out.

"You're insane. You're both insane." He shook an index finger at both of us, and I suppressed a laugh. He looked like a frenzied madman.

"Let's get you inside. I'll check out your wound, and we'll find your watch. Why would you take your watch off here?" Cali sounded lighter than she had in ages. Amused.

Gabe looked like he could strangle her. "I got sunburnt. It itched."

"Well, I'm so sorry about Nym. Why didn't you use any commands? I texted you all of them before."

"Well, let's see… you try having a growling canine at your heels and try to remember the *German* commands!"

"Gabe, I really am sorry." She touched his arm, and his anger deflated.

"Don't worry about it. I'll be fine. He really just nipped at me. Scary as fuck, though."

We went back to Gabe's place, and Cali used his fully stocked medicine cabinet to apply ointment and bandage his ankle, then we ended up eating chicken salad sandwiches and drinking a couple of glasses of wine with Gabe and Poppy. Poppy returned home after Gabe texted her and told her we were over at their house. After dinner, we stopped back by Cali's house, picked up Nym, and headed home.

Nym trotted into my house, tail wagging. To me, the dog looked happy to be back.

"You know, maybe you should keep him here. Maybe he's unsettled, going back and forth between two homes." I couldn't help but think of all the folks who gathered on the beach in front of her house. I'd prefer to eliminate the risk of the dog actually turning into a Cujo and terrorizing the beach.

"It's not that he's unsettled. It's the way they trained him. You get that, right?"

I followed her into the bedroom. She lifted her hair, and I undid the top button on her dress and unzipped it. She let her hair fall down in a silky, seductive veil.

"How was he trained?"

"Didn't I tell you? In Germany. Both Nym and Astra. I'm lucky he didn't really hurt Gabe. My guess is he knew Gabe, because he'd been feeding him, so he resorted to keeping him there until we arrived. If Gabe hadn't run from him, maybe he could've gotten his watch without issue. But I suspect Nym wouldn't have liked him taking an object from the house."

"Where's Erik keep his dog?"

"Back where he lives."

"Isn't that a big deal moving an animal between countries?"

"It's not cheap. And yeah, it's a process. Astra has gone from Germany to the US to Taiwan. I think my mom has the photo of the two dogs together as babies."

"Were they cute puppies?"

"So cute. The trainer sent us pictures. I didn't get Nym until he was eighteen months old." She placed a kiss against my throat, and a shiver of need laced down my spine. I forgot all about the dog. Her dark eyes found mine, and her dress glided over her shoulders and down to the floor, in a pool at her feet. A sheer black bra and tiny black lace panties remained. *Sexy as fuck.*

Her fingers tangled in the hair on the back of my neck, and she pulled me down as she raised on tiptoes. She opened for me, her lips insistent and her tongue demanding. I'd been treating her with kid gloves, giving her space to mourn. It'd been too long…for both of us.

She stroked my chest, then set about working the buttons on my shirt, one by one. By the time she gripped my belt buckle, I lifted her fingers to my lips, slowing us down. For weeks, she'd been drowning in sorrow. I had ached for her. I desperately wanted her, but better than anyone, I knew she hurt.

"Are you sure? We don't have to." I'd be content to hold her, to fall asleep like we had done, with her in my arms.

In answer, she slipped off her bra and lay back on the bed, offering herself up to me. Her tantalizing nipples were erect, waiting for me. She spread her legs, and her fingers dove beneath the black strip of lace covering her pussy. Her head tilted back, and her eyelids fluttered closed as she showed me exactly what she wanted. *Fuck.*

I didn't think it was humanly possible to undress faster than I did. My mouth, my tongue, my fingers worshipped her. I caressed, comforted, and cherished her. I brought her to the edge, trembling, over and over, all with my fingers and my mouth.

"Logan. Please. I want you." And god, I wanted her, too.

"Condom." I reached for the bedside table, but she grasped my wrist.

"We don't need one. I'm on the pill. I'm clean."

"Me too. I haven't been with anyone since Bethany, and I was tested… after I found out."

"I won't cheat on you. Ever." Her words, yes, they were only words, but god, hearing them unleashed a surge of emotion. For her, for us.

I entered her, bare. I let out a guttural moan as she stretched around me. God, it had been too long since we'd loved each other in this way. We moved in unison, working each other into a frenzy, a light perspiration coating our skin. Her hands roamed my back, her nails grazed my skin, she gripped my ass, begging me to go deeper, to take her higher, and as we both found our release, and I pulsed inside her, I knew. She was all I needed and all I wanted. I didn't think I'd ever find this again, and somehow, I'd found it.

She cuddled against me on her side, one arm around my chest while I fingered her silky soft hair, our legs tangled. Our breathing slowly regulated. One phrase circulated, over and over, until I couldn't hold it in any longer.

"I love you."

In return, she tilted her head up to look at me and smiled. I pressed my lips to her forehead and held her. I'd said it. She hadn't. Earlier or now. But she still lay wrapped around me.

We were ensconced in an afterglow, but my head didn't quiet. The dog, the alarm, the locks she cared about on her house and only her house. My curiosity got the better of me, so I probed.

"I get the sense there's something about that house." Her fingers toyed with my chest hair. A minute or two ticked by. I wanted her to open up to me. To tell me about her ex. What happened in her first marriage? How did it unravel? I wanted to know everything about her. But at her own pace, when the timing was right. Her reluctance to mention anything about that time in her life led my imagination to wander, to suspect it must have been traumatic or painful. Or maybe she was ashamed. But I believed there was no way she could have something worse to admit than my admission that I possibly couldn't father children. I had bared myself to her, and I couldn't shake the hunch her walls remained intact. "I'm not pushing you for information. I trust you'll open up when you're ready."

She didn't say yes. She didn't say no. She pressed her lips to mine and whispered, "I love you, too."

ali

"WHAT ARE YOU FROWNING OVER?" HE WASN'T ONE TO TAKE work home with him, yet he had his archaic laptop open. I gently squeezed his shoulders. "Wow. You are so tense." I dug my thumbs into his trapezius muscles, eliciting a deep groan.

"Keep doing that." He dipped his head low, stretching the back of his neck. The movement exposed his computer screen.

"What's got you so tense? Facebook?"

"It's a political group. This woman, she's from Raleigh. She tweets. She posts. She's got a lot of people riled up. Because of this group she's leading, I'm having to jump through hoops with budget justification. Thought I'd look into her more, and this group she's in. But she's in a ton of groups. Random causes. I suppose that's normal for an activist."

"Is she anti-police?" These days it seemed people could be

pro or anti anything, but I guessed police, as her cause increased his tension.

"She's aiming for more fair distribution of police resources. I understand her argument, but I have to say I'm not sure where she's getting all her information. She's sharing articles from sites I've never heard of. I guess bloggers? The claims are sensational. One article claimed they make police department budgets each year after a big BDSM party. Another theorizes the United States is run by elite members of a cartel and the cartels dictate police policy. It's ludicrous. Where do people get this stuff? But her more sensible posts are the ones that seem to get the most likes. Logic appears to be winning out."

I burrowed my elbow into his shoulder, and he flinched.

"Too hard?" I laughed as I fell forward from his movement.

"A touch."

I froze, close enough to the screen the woman's profile picture came into focus. I knew her. And several of her friends. My breathing stalled. "So, what's her end goal?"

"I don't know what this woman's end goal is. She's all over the place. She's a regular contributor to a group called National Budget Watchdog Group. That's the group that's done an analysis of police budgets in affluent areas. Essentially, they're advocating to redistribute budgets, but they don't seem to understand how budgets work. That some of those funds are county, some city. Taxes pay for those services. I mean, on the outset, you think budget watchdog, that sounds good to me. But then, digging into it, it's like they don't understand how things work. It's just odd. A few of the beach towns, like Haven Island, have come under particular scrutiny. But the deeper I dig, I feel like we're up against someone who'll pick any fight.

And she has a lot of followers. This budget group, not so much, but this woman does."

I tapped him on the back. "I'm gonna go out on the deck and try to reach Erik. Check in on Dad."

He nodded and continued scrolling Facebook.

Outside on the deck, with my BlackBerry, I called Erik on the number he'd most recently called me from. I backed up on the screen porch, providing myself a direct view into the house.

"Cecilia?" Dad's voice came through the line.

"Dad? Where's Erik?" I blanched, wracked by a pang of guilt for not chatting with Dad, but I needed to speak to my brother.

"He's busy."

"Why do you have his phone?"

"He stepped out for a run. I'm in his apartment."

Erik ran? I exhaled as my stomach bottomed out. I pinched my nose and focused. Erik told me those fake profiles were being used to counter the propaganda efforts of his old syndicate. But this account was what I'd call anti-police. What would that make his old syndicate? Pro-police? Why would Erik be against that? Or was this about undermining a political candidate?

"Cecilia?" Dad's concerned tone pulled me back.

"How are you doing?" I asked.

"Good. It's good to be with family. How are you and Logan doing?"

Through the glass, Logan's dark hair bent over the laptop.

"We're fine. He's fine."

"Good. I need to run, sweetheart."

"Can you have Erik call me?"

"Is everything okay?"

"Of course. Love you, Dad."

Across the dunes, waves rolled and whitecaps peaked. The gentle breeze rustled the grasses along the dunes. Off in the distance, a pelican dove into the dark water with a white splash. The tranquil scene clashed with my rampant thoughts.

Erik said he was using my profiles in his efforts to counter the efforts of his old company. Had he been full of shit? Did he pick this up as a pet project aiming to remove Public Safety back ages ago, before I even met Logan? Did having a police presence on the island threaten him in some way? What, exactly, was he up to?

$\mathcal{L}$ogan

Several of the guys on my team gathered around the conference room table. Matt had returned, and his drop-in visit had me on edge. The last time he visited he announced Bethany was pregnant.

"Did you see that hurricane that's out in the Atlantic?" Matt asked offhandedly. I recognized it as office small talk. Samuel, one of the guys on my team, did not.

"Yep. Saw it this morning before I came to work. Red arrows everywhere. Could go to Florida, the southeast, the northeast, or hell, for good measure it might go into the Gulf. That's one job I wish I had. I'd have fun drawing those arrows."

Matt smirked, appearing amused at Samuel's statement, but I knew enough of his world to know he lived with a myriad of what-if scenarios on a day-to-day basis. He chugged from his water bottle, then addressed me.

"At what point do you prepare?"

Samuel piped in, "Not until they're down to one or two arrows. When they don't know continent yet, we just watch."

I nodded. He wasn't wrong.

"It's late in the season, isn't it?" Matt asked.

"No. Not really. Hurricane season officially lasts until the end of November," Samuel said. "It's been a quiet season here. Not for Florida, though. I'd bet those folks are tired of evacuating."

Matt smiled, but he shuffled his feet. I got the sense he wanted to talk about something other than the weather.

"Hey, Samuel, can you do beach patrol today?" I asked as nonchalantly as possible.

"Sure thing, boss."

I gestured to my office. "Want to sit?" I pointedly asked Matt, ensuring no one would follow us in.

In my office, I closed the door behind Matt and shifted the cardboard box to the side of the desk so we could see each other's faces across the desk. Ever curious, Matt peered into the box.

"What's this?"

"Cali's family photos. I brought them in so I could scan them. It's hard to believe anyone these days would have anything other than digital."

"Yeah. I can't imagine paying to develop photos. Although some of these are Polaroid. Still, expensive."

"Yep."

He held up a photo. "Her dogs?"

"That one on the left is Nym. He's living at my house now.

The one on the right is her brother's dog. Astra." I sat down in my chair and rolled it up to the desk. Matt remained frozen in place, the photo lodged between his thumb and index finger.

"Nym. And Astra?"

"Yep."

"Do you have a photo of her brother?"

I dug around and located the one I loved, the one where he was on a computer and she stood behind him. You could see the similarities between their facial features, even though in the photo they held markedly different expressions. He took it from me and ran his thumb over it.

"Logan. She named her dogs after hackers."

"What?"

"Anonymous. Astra."

A low-level quake flared beneath my rib cage. Her constant turning off her phone. Not feeling secure in her home.

"Her brother. He's on our watch list. Logan, she's a hacker." He spoke low. His words acted like a wind funnel, sucking the oxygen from my lungs.

"What kind of computer does she use?" His gaze remained on the photo beneath his thumb.

"It's nothing. Slim."

"Then you haven't seen her real computer."

"She has an iPhone." My head hit the back of my chair. She didn't spend inordinate amounts of time at the computer. This didn't make sense.

"She's a hacker," he confirmed. "I'd bet she has devices you haven't seen."

Her dad used a BlackBerry. And at the hospital her brother had a small Android, the cheap burner phone kind. *Fuck.*

"Logan, she could be the one we're looking for. If she is, and the chatter we picked up is correct, she could have those servers on this island."

"She has an oceanfront home." Being a hacker might explain her nervousness and an attack dog. But storing servers in an oceanfront home? No one would do that. A numbness fell over me. As my brain slowed, Matt dug into the box of photos, rapidly flipping through image after image.

He held up a photo of five guys on a sofa. Each held joysticks in their hands.

"Do you know any of these guys?"

I pointed to Erik, the second from the end. "That's Erik. Her brother. They're twins. See? Same guy as in the photo I showed you."

Matt's face hardened and his lips fell into a straight line. "We've been searching for this guy. He's in the CIA database under a different alias. Didn't have his real name but had his photo. He slipped up about six weeks ago, searching for organs on the Dark Web, but also on legitimate sites for surgeons. Made a mistake of crossing requests on two different accounts. Traced one account with a Lord Nikon alias back five years to this photo with friends. But we're still working on identifying everyone. So, his real name is Erik?"

"Erik Lai. What's he wanted for?"

"He's senior management in Spectre. He's known as Zero Cool. Whole group loves pop culture names from that nineties film *Hackers* and, of course, Bond films."

"What exactly is Spectre?"

"Think modern-day mafia. Digital underground."

"Chinese?"

"No. China wants them. They're pro-Hong Kong. Ties to some outfits connected to Russia. But they don't need government funding. They're the best thieves out there. This guy," he waved the photo in the air, "goes by Crash Override. Another alias he uses is Wilson Fisk. We believe he's CEO. We've been watching him for years. The entire business has imploded. They've stolen from Russia, China, Venezuela, UK, US. Name a government, they probably want them."

Black spots faded in and out in my periphery along the ceiling. I spread my palms out on my thighs.

"You think she's involved?" It physically hurt to ask the question.

He breathed in deeply, and his eyes slanted, bandying back and forth between the photo in his hand, the box of photos, and me. "Chatter is just chatter. You know that. But given who her brother is…"

"But she stayed here. Her brother and Dad are in a different country. She stayed here." But for how long? Hadn't she just mentioned she planned to visit them? Was she staying behind for clean-up? Did she plan to leave for good? She hadn't asked me to join her. I offered. *Holy shit. All the signs. Once again, I missed all the signs.*

"What country did they move to?"

"Macau." Nausea circulated. I'd heard of Macau. Never had a mission there, but the country had a reputation for being purveyors of crime. I just didn't even think. Matt flicked through the photos, but his mind had moved ten steps ahead. I dropped my head to my hand; I couldn't watch him. I couldn't absorb this. *How the fuck?*

"We don't know anything yet. She looks suspicious. She's a person of interest. Having a dog named after a hacker doesn't make her a criminal." I recognized his calming tone.

"Holy shit." The room spun as I remembered the day I teased

her about being one of the few who used a BlackBerry. After that day, I'd seen her with an iPhone. I just never gave it any thought. She never once said anything about her ex.

"Can you run a search for me? Can you find out if she's ever been married?" He remained frozen. "I need to know if she lied to me."

In my gut, in the churning pit of my stomach, I knew. Cali lied to me. Possibly in every single way. She may have been using me for some as yet unidentified purpose. The realization hit harder than when Bethany lied. And she'd been fucking my friend. Anger, vitriol, furor all swirled together. The worst kind of anger because it wasn't at her. No. These emotions, they were all aimed at me. For being a fucking dumb ass. *Again*.

"She doesn't even have an ex-husband." I spit out the truth. "God damnit."

"I'm going to bring her in for questioning. I think you should stay away from her until I've talked with her."

"Her photo hasn't come up on any wanted list?" He'd met her once before, but I shuffled through the box, searching for a recent photo to thrust into his face.

"No. We're still working on identifying all the players in Spectre. You know how it is. There aren't directories. But you need to calm down."

"I am calm." I gritted out the words and glared at him.

"I'm just saying—"

"You don't think she's got some guy out there, do you? Like a boyfriend or a husband? You don't think she was targeting me?" I rose out of my seat and leaned across my desk, desperate for him to reassure me.

"I don't know. I need to talk to her." What he didn't add to his statement was, "You need to calm down."

"Do whatever you want. You need the key to my house? That dog. It's from Germany. I'd bet she has a kill word."

"Are you saying you think she's dangerous?"

"I'm saying I don't fucking know anything. At all. About her. Who she is. What she wants."

"Okay." He tapped away on his phone. "I'm calling in back-up."

Fuck, how did I not see this? I'm fucking military intelligence. Or I was. Fuuuck. A sucker. A fucking moron.

ali

"HURRICANE MELBA TRAJECTORIES HAVE BEEN UPDATED. YOU can see here on the map the potential storm paths. Portions of the Florida coast are now under a tropical storm warning."

My phone vibrated, and I muted the television. An unknown number.

"Erik. We need to talk. Are you alone?" I asked before he spoke. It could have been a telemarketer, but I'd been waiting for his call. I wanted honest answers from him, and if he was anywhere near our father, I suspected I wouldn't get them.

"We'll talk later. You've got to get out of there. I'm sending Wolf over. Where are you? At Logan's?"

"What are you—"

"Cali, you don't have time. Get moving. Out the door. They know. They're coming to get you."

"Who knows?"

"NSA. Get outside. Now. Leave the dog."

"Erik, you're not making any sense."

"Dammit, Cali. Listen. Matt Rodriguez, Logan's friend from the NSA, is on the island. Logan had pictures of us. He somehow recognized me. Now he knows my real name. He knows you're involved. He's called for back-up, and they are coming to get you. Get out of that house. Now."

"Hold on. How do you know this?"

"We monitor all of Matt's calls."

"How?"

"We have a chip on his phone. Cali. Get. Moving."

"But wait, have I done anything illegal? You told me I wasn't breaking the law. You told me the profiles I was creating were to sway public opinion for pro-democracy causes. To counter the propaganda from your old company. That's it. I was helping you. That's all they were supposed to be used for. And I just saw three profiles being used for American politics. Anti-police. What are you doing?"

"It's all related. Cali. Get with Alex. He'll hide you. We'll figure out how to get you here. We can talk about it all then. I'll explain everything. Get out of there."

"Hide me? Erik, I didn't break any laws. And if I did, I did so in ignorance. I'm not going to run."

"Cali. They could scapegoat you. You could be interrogated endlessly. This isn't public safety coming to get you. It's FBI. It's NSA. I'm sure Homeland's not far behind. Get. Moving."

"I can't disappear. That would kill Logan."

"Cali, leave him. You can do so much better."

"Dad likes him."

"He likes the idea of someone taking care of you. Logan's

going to help them lock you up. If you think he's choosing you, you're wrong. He's helping Matt right now. Whatever you think you have with him…it's over." I leaned against the window frame, looking out into the empty yard. I kept circling the fact that yet again Erik asked for more time, and once again his solution was for me to pick up and run. *Over with Logan? No. He loves me. I can explain this. All of this. This is Erik's nightmare. I'm done hiding.*

"Let them interrogate me. Fake accounts are all over the Internet. That's my worst offense." I paced the floor, thinking through every random favor Erik had asked since that faithful night when he came clean, in a panic, worried I'd be the next victim. Research, article writing, and image creation. Little things, all because his team dwindled. His so-called splinter group.

"The servers. What's on them?" I monitored the machines. But I wasn't a hardware girl. But I could see how they could implicate me, depending on what data was routing through them.

"You need to F7 them."

A knock on the door sent Nym into a barking fury.

"*Sitzen.*" Nym obeyed. The phone line went dead.

Nerves vibrated through me. My fingers quivered. I glanced down at my socked feet, then over to the back door. One of the public safety officers that worked for Logan stood on the back porch, his frame filling the glass pane. The repeated knock on the front door continued.

"Cali? Are you inside? We just want to talk."

ogan

"Have you heard of TLG Enterprises?"

"No."

"Are you familiar with TJX?"

"No."

"Do you have any contact with the PLA?"

"No."

"The People's Liberation Army of China?"

"I know what it is. And I told you, no."

"What about the NEC?"

"You can keep throwing acronyms out at me. I don't know anything of value to you. I am not a hacker." Her index finger and middle fingers tapped the table, the only movement she'd made for the prior thirty-plus minutes.

The FBI agent interrogating her maintained an indecipherable expression.

"Not the kind of hacking you're worried about. I do sock puppetry. That's it. Fake accounts. You can keep me here for however many days you want. You can lock me away for months. You can waterboard me. Torture me. Cut off my fingers. Pull my teeth. Whatever you people do. My answers will remain the same." She stared straight ahead at a wall, no doubt doing exactly what they had trained her to do.

Matt and the agent exchanged a glance. Matt pulled out a chair to sit, while the other agent stood. A changing of the guard.

"What do you think we're going to do to you, Cali?" Matt asked with a gentleness to his tone. Too gentle to garner any trust, but it was easier to judge an interrogation than to conduct one. She sat there, simultaneously stoic and sad.

"Cali?"

"Lock me up?" There was a question mark in the lilt of her last word, but her chin tilted upward. Defiant. Her defiance stirred some of the anger that had been simmering within me, ever since I discovered the truth about the woman I'd essentially been living with.

"Is that what Erik told you we would do?"

"Yes."

"Do you believe this of the entire US government? Or only the NSA?"

"It's all the same, isn't it?"

Matt pinched the bridge of his nose, and I could tell that after two hours of questioning, he was unsure which direction to take. We had one holding cell.

A knock on my door pulled me away from the computer

monitor where I watched the video of her interrogation. We didn't have an interrogation room, so I'd rigged a camera in our small conference room. As the head of the Public Safety Department, Matt had invited me to watch the interrogation. An FBI agent named Jill Matera watched with me. She had been taking notes, but she stopped making notations about an hour ago.

I opened the door and stepped out into the hall. Samuel peered past me, no doubt curious. This kind of activity was far more interesting than the standard issues we encountered on a daily basis.

"Hey, just wanted to make you aware we've received updated information on Melba's track. It's looking like it's going to be a direct hit on either North or South Carolina. Both governors have started voluntary evacuations."

"Okay." I scratched my beard, thinking through our steps. "What's the timing looking like?"

"It's three days out. We'll know more tomorrow morning."

"Okay. Can you do me a favor and make sure we have everyone on staff tomorrow morning? Just in case? And call Chad for me? See if I can meet with him end of day? After he's done with his afternoon round of golf. We should review evacuation plans."

"Sure thing. How's it going in there?"

"Not making much headway."

"You gonna need assistance?"

"This is out of our department's jurisdiction." By a mile. "Once this is done, I'll call you." He took a few steps down the hall. "Hey, what are they saying are the chances it'll hit here?"

"Oh, it's coming to the Carolinas. They don't know where the direct hit will be."

"Start tying stuff down. Okay? Have everyone spend today tying anything loose down or getting it put away. PSD property first. Then we'll start combing the island to batten down vacant homes."

"Yes, sir."

I pushed open my office door. Jill remained in her same position, staring at the screen.

"Did I miss anything?"

"She's asking for you." Her gaze lifted from the screen. "Are you two close?"

"She's my girlfriend." I would've expected Matt had already briefed them. But maybe not. She picked up her pen and scribbled on her yellow notepad.

"Matt. I am telling you. I have no knowledge of malware, Trojan horses, wiretapping, or any kind of coding, okay? Yes, I know how the game is played. I know that hacking is often done with phishing, screen manipulation, and even more mundane techniques like stealing a username and password. I understand how the world works, but that doesn't mean I'm guilty. My brother is not a bad guy. He's not working to attack the United States." Cali's volume increased. Her arms remained folded in front of her.

Matt crossed his leg and laced his fingers over his knee. "Ms. Lai, you are wrong about your brother. His efforts have everything to do with sabotaging the United States. We have been monitoring his alter ego for years. He is a part of one of the most dangerous crime syndicates in the world. We believe he functions as the CIO, the chief information officer."

"So, you know about Spectre?" Her question made me want to vomit. My insides churned, but everything else stilled.

"Yes. What can you tell us?"

"Not much. My brother believes the less I know, the safer I am. He got in over his head. He's been working to dismantle Spectre. He has several partners who are all actively working to counter their efforts. That's what I was doing. Helping them." The FBI agent appeared to believe about as much of what she said as I did. He leaned forward, over the desk, in an intimidating position.

"Ms. Lai, that's an interesting spin. Are you aware his group recently pulled off a three-million-dollar ransomware operation in Spain?"

"No."

"But you still think your brother is good?"

"If he did it, he had reasons. It met his ultimate objectives in some way. I'll grant you his ethics are off-kilter, but he's looking at the larger picture."

"Is that how you justify it?"

She glared at him. She hadn't asked for a lawyer yet, but this would be a good juncture for her to request one. The two interrogators waited, possibly expecting her to ask for a lawyer. Minutes ticked by, then Matt resumed the questions he appeared to have listed in front of him.

"Who owns the house you currently live in?"

"I do."

"Ms. Lai, we have access to financial records."

"It's part of a trust he set up, but I still own it."

"When you flew out to Washington State recently, you didn't fly commercial. How did your brother get you out to the West Coast?"

"The company jet."

"Did you see a logo for the company? Anything inside the jet that would show what company owned the jet?"

"I wasn't really paying attention. My mother was in the hospital." Her words slowed, and her gaze dropped to the desk. "My brother…" Her eyes fluttered closed, and she bowed her head. I leaned forward, closer to the monitor, watching. It could be an act, but she looked emotional. Broken down. "What other things do you believe my brother has done?"

Matt glanced directly into the camera, and his lips scrunched. He once again transitioned to a different interrogation approach. "Spectre started out earning most of their income from drugs. You've heard of Dread Pirate Roberts? You mentioned him earlier, when you asked if we planned to scapegoat you. So, you're familiar with what he did? The network he set up that allowed the trade of anything on the Dark Web?"

"Yes. Are you saying my brother deals drugs?" Her brow wrinkled, and she examined him.

"It would be simpler if that was the only thing he did. No, dealing drugs, organs, slaves, stolen goods, information, credit card data, Spectre does it all. Your brother is a part of one of the more sophisticated crime corporations in the world. But we believe their ultimate game is to create an unstable United States. Really, an unstable world. The group has ties to arms dealers."

"I just told you that he's trying to dismantle Spectre."

"Okay. And how do the profiles you created fit into his plan for dismantling Spectre?"

She rubbed her forehead and winced. *Did she think she could somehow lie her way out of this?*

"I'm not sure. He didn't get to explain it to me before you picked me up. I created them. I don't know what he did with them." She was good. I'd interrogated plenty of people, and she had a believability quotient. Clearly, I was susceptible to her game.

"How did you think he was using the accounts you created?"

"Like I told you. He was using them to counter Spectre's propaganda machine. To promote pro-democracy rhetoric to undermine Spectre's ultimate objectives. At the worst, it generated political discussion."

"Political discussion? That's one way of phrasing it." Matt stood and paced, the first sign he was beginning to lose patience. "No, groups like your brother's, they foster false information on both sides. In the US, it's the Democrats and the Republicans. In Great Britain, it's the Conservative and Labour; in Canada, it's the Liberal and Conservative. In any country, there are different political factions. Groups seeking instability ultimately feed all sides of the spectrum, fostering division, feeding hate groups. It's a long-term plan in a country like the United States. But we've already seen it destroy smaller democracies like Myanmar."

"But why?"

"Our profile on your brother suggests he is doing it for personal freedoms, possibly a long-term plan for Hong Kong independence. Some groups believe an unstable world gives Hong Kong its best chance at prolonged independence. But I can tell you that the profiles of the other men in his company do not match your brother's. They have their own agendas."

"I told you. My brother is trying to take them down. He got in over his head. He wouldn't…" She raised her hand over her eyes and let her head fall back. Her lips trembled. When she lowered her head and revealed her eyes, she held a new resolution. "Are you pressing charges against me?"

"No. Not right now. I'm in the process of obtaining a warrant to go into your home."

"So, I'm free to go?"

"Yes."

Cali pushed her BlackBerry across the table to him. "You don't need the warrant. Nym is at Logan's house. You're welcome to search the property and take my computers."

"Is there a safe room in the house?"

"Yes. Upstairs in the attic. Accessible from the master bedroom. Can I see Logan?"

"Cali, do you maintain servers?"

"Yes. I'll show you where. Can I see Logan?" I couldn't breathe.

Matt looked to the other agent, but where the man stood in the room, I couldn't see his face. Matt stood and exited. Moments later, my office door opened.

"You want to see her?"

I didn't. But I'd been down this path before, and I welcomed my first meeting with her on camera. My anger would remain controlled.

"I'll go in. Anything you want me to ask her?"

"No." He stared me down. "You okay to do this?"

"Yes. You want to come?"

"No. I'll be here. Watching."

"Okay." My hand fell over the doorknob, and I paused. "It looks like that hurricane is going to hit. If you want to check out her house, do it now, before we go into evacuation mode."

I entered the conference room and made eye contact with the agent. His badge read Zayerdon. I couldn't remember his first name. He stood in the corner like a prison guard. I pulled out a chair across from Cali, outside of the view of the camera.

"You wanted to see me?" Her dark brown eyes held the telltale sheen of sadness. Inside, a hard wall blocked my emotions. She could cry all she wanted, but she lied to me. The person I loved didn't exist.

"I have done nothing wrong." Her words, by complete chance, happened to be the same words Huxley, my Chicago PD colleague, said to me when I first asked him about the Hildebrand case. He'd hired my wife as his defense attorney, and she got him off. But to this day, I believed they should have convicted him. He hid evidence on a case, all to build a stronger conviction against a man who may have been innocent. The thing about innocence in the United States—it could be bought.

"You can tell that to your lawyer."

"Logan, you know me. Please." Her voice broke, and she sniffled. Disgust prevented me from looking at her.

"I thought I knew you." I lifted my gaze and found those brown eyes staring back at me, pleading. The liar wanted forgiveness. "Tell me, were you ever married? Or was that part of the sock puppet profile you created to get close to me?"

"I never." She closed her eyes, and lines formed around her mouth as her lips puckered. I hoped for anger from her. I'd like to have it out right here and now. But when she opened her eyes, the tears trailing down her cheeks reflected the overhead light. "I told people I was a divorcee before I ever met you. It was a simple explanation for how I could afford the house on the beach. An easy explanation that gave me space. If you think about it, I never added to the story. I hated I couldn't tell you the truth."

"Your brother didn't ask you to get close to me?"

"No. No." Her tone rose an octave as she worked to convince me. "He didn't want me anywhere near you. He wanted me to stay far away from you. And I swear, I think they're wrong about him. He believed I was in danger. They killed his colleague's girlfriend. He sent me here so I'd be safe. He's not a bad guy. He's not. And he didn't have me doing anything illegal. He promised me he didn't."

"So, let me get this straight. He's a top-level executive at an organization that's essentially a modern-day mafia crime group, but he didn't know they were bad? He didn't know they were breaking the law? And then he pisses off someone out there, and he realizes his sister might be attacked in retribution. You know what that is, Cali? That's gang mentality, right there." I'd love to believe she was that stupid, but the problem with that was that she was all kinds of brilliant. Her bottom lip trembled. I'd had enough of the damn trembling lip, the tears, the whole devastated bullshit routine. I came in here to hear her out, but I couldn't deal with her playing the whole 'I'm innocent' card. I got up and paced the room, clutching my fists behind my back. Keeping it controlled. Breathing in and out. "And you… go along with it? You believe he never did anything bad? You believe he's only on the good side?"

"No, I did. But I just thought… he was hacking into websites illegally. I knew he was afraid of the Chinese government. And maybe he was bending some US laws."

"Bending? Bending?" My anger threatened to boil into rage.

"My brother is not a drug dealer." A hint of matching anger lit her words. "He made some bad choices. He got in too deep. He's trying to correct things."

Enough anger resonated in her defense that I believed her. Well, I believed she honestly thought her brother was innocent. Innocent in her frame of mind. Criminals rarely recognize that by definition when you bent a law, you broke it.

"Here's the thing, Cali. I've dedicated my life to my country. To stopping people like your brother, who want to tear this country apart. Whether it's from propaganda or drugs, it doesn't matter. It's all criminal intent." I exhaled loudly and ran my nails into my beard. "Did you have a question you wanted to ask? They said you wanted to see me."

Tears ran down her cheeks, freely flowing. I didn't so much as flinch. She lied to me. I didn't know this woman. I hoped Matt and his team were over in her house finding evidence to lock her away for years. I wanted them to lock her up and send her far away from me.

ali

I OPENED THE DOOR AND PRESSED THE KEYS TO THE ALARM keypad. Four strange men stood behind me, and oddly enough, I felt safe entering my home. Erik had built up NSA in my mind as some evil waterboarding organization, a group who would create a case against me to build their careers. But they had yet to slap handcuffs on me.

Logan's eyes—I'd never forget them. I couldn't unsee them. He'd been so cold, so angry. Worse than I could have ever imagined. The Logan who held me in Seattle, who told me he loved me, he was no more. His absence hurt more than that of my brother and father.

The men passed down the hall. One had a camera—a real camera, not his phone. And he snapped away. Another had a phone to his ear. Matt, the agent I knew, stood at my side.

"Do you…" I stopped myself from asking the naive question. Of course he believed what he said about Erik. "Can you show me more about Spectre?"

"I can." He led me to his kitchen table and opened his phone. He handed it to me. It was open to a page on a site. An internal NSA document.

"What's this?"

"It's an overview of what we know about the organization. There's nothing on there that requires clearance." Of course. So, this was what they had available for anyone to read. Which meant he had more evidence that couldn't be shared.

I scrolled through, reading in detail about the global organization. The document concluded with a list of cybercrimes the NSA had credited to Spectre. Notations were made if there were disagreements about the responsible parties.

I found it hard to swallow and hard to stomach. All that concern, for all those years. It turned out that worry had been warranted. This was all so much worse than I'd ever comprehended. This was what he'd meant by never seeing him again unless we were in a non-extradition country. But had he been full of shit? Did he not extricate himself? Was he not working to dismantle the organization?

I had two options. I could believe my brother was good and sharing information would ultimately help him. Or I could believe my brother had been lying to me. And if he was lying to me, would I really help him continue as a criminal? No, ultimately those two options funneled into one solution.

"There could be cameras in here." I handed Matt his phone.

"What do you mean?"

"My brother's company installed the security. I discovered several hidden cameras. I think I found most of them. I disengaged any I found inside. Except for the ones on the porch." I pointed out the door we'd just come in. "The company, or whoever is monitoring the house, they know you're here. The cameras outside definitely still work."

Matt's brows came together as his forehead wrinkled. I expected another round of questions, but he gave a quick, "Wait here," and hurried down into the living area. He spoke to his colleagues.

I leaned against the wall, staring out at the deep blue ocean. Erik had always been a genius. Fantastic with computer code. Obsessive to a fault. But how did it come to this?

"Cali, can you show me your safe room?"

"Sure." I led the way to the bookshelf in my bedroom, which moved to reveal a secret staircase, up to the panic room. I'd never used it, but my brother had insisted on adding it to the house.

"Oh, and your computers. Do you mind if we look at your computers?"

"No problem. I have nothing to hide." A small part of my brain said I should force him to get a warrant, that I should seek a lawyer. That they might find some technicality to lock me up for life. But the larger part of my brain, and all of my heart, didn't care. If my brother lied to me, if he didn't recognize his mistakes, as he said he did, then I had no choice but to assist.

Outside, the whitecaps and the angled waves signaled strong winds and a coming storm. The grasses over the dunes whipped in the wind, and the sky over the horizon loomed grayish blue. I stared out the windows as one man tapped away on my laptop. Jill, the FBI agent who had been back at Logan's office, entered the front door without knocking. All the agents wore gloves.

I left Matt and some others in the safe room. It turned out those monitors connected to cameras all through the house. If I'd ever stopped to explore that claustrophobic room, I would've been able to figure out exactly where cameras were. Erik hadn't tried very hard to hide the cameras from me. Jill approached, all business.

"Can I show you some photos? See who you recognize?"

"Sure. I haven't met many of my brother's business associates." *Business associates. Is that what you call criminals?*

"We're going to try to get through what we can before the hurricane hits."

"It's coming here?" I hadn't been in front of a television. And I handed all my electronics over to Matt.

"It's looking like it. It's making it hard for us to get a full team here. We might take a little longer going through everything. I hope that's okay."

"You don't need to pretend to care."

She didn't respond. She opened a laptop and clicked away, presumably preparing to play "do you know" with me.

Matt joined us, his phone to his ear. I snapped my fingers to get his attention.

"Your phone. It's bugged."

"How do you know my phone is bugged?"

"Erik called me before you came to Logan's. He told me you were on the way. I asked him how he knew. If you look on the motherboard in your phone, I'd bet you'll find a chip that doesn't belong."

"Any others?" I shrugged. He inched forward, wanting an answer.

"I'm sure." *What did he want me to say?*

I sat down on the leather sofa beside Jill. I rested my head on my hands, leaning forward, spinning from the day. Telling on my brother felt so wrong. He loved me; he was my twin. We shared a womb. And here I sat, no doubt under his watchful eye, selling him out. Sharing his secrets.

A tissue box appeared below my knees. "It's gonna be okay."

I looked up and sniffled. *No, it's not.*

"Give Logan some time. He'll come around."

Did you see him with me? I wanted to ask her. But I didn't. She wasn't my friend.

Hours passed as they opened drawers and looked behind photos. Jill gave up on me recognizing anyone. I wandered around my house while officers invaded.

A framed photograph of my brother and me sat on a desk, and I picked it up. I held the photograph, trying to remember where we were when it was taken. Based on the hairstyles, we'd been in grad school. My hair was still the same. But Erik's was now cut short. Back then, he'd been shaggy.

A hand on my shoulder shook me. Matt peered down with a concerned expression.

"I think we're going to head out. I think we've got everything, but we'll be back tomorrow." He thrust a piece of paper in my hand. "If you want to do some research of your own, check out some of these links. Do you know how to access the dark web?"

"No."

"Tomorrow, I'll show you. And I'll have more questions for you too."

"That's it?"

"Yeah."

"You're not going to—I'm free?"

"So far I haven't found anything to indicate you've broken any laws." He raised one eyebrow, and I imagined he was analyzing me, or profiling me, attempting to discern if he'd missed something.

"Erik told me I hadn't broken any US laws."

He shoved his hands into his pockets and nodded. "I'll see you tomorrow."

I followed him down the stairs and to the front door. The palm trees along the street bent in the wind. As he drove away, in an entourage of golf carts for his investigative team, Poppy approached, her long skirt blowing out in front of her like a sail, her hands planted to her front, holding it down in place over her underwear. She waved her arm, and I stepped down my porch steps to meet her in the yard.

"We're flying out in the morning. Up to New York. Gabe wants to get the plane far away. We just got back from taking our boat in for dry storage. To be safe. Do you want to fly up with us? Get away? I think we have room for your dog."

My dog! Nym. He's at Logan's.

"Cali, are you okay?"

"Yes, yes. Ah, thank you, but no, I'll stay here. I'll be fine."

"They're saying it's gonna hit as a three or a four. You don't want to stay here. Head out with us."

"It's okay. I'll be fine. Really."

"Well, Gabe has a crew that's boarding up our place, and they're almost done. Do you want to have them put some plywood on your windows?"

"No need. I have metal shutters on all the windows. I just need to click a button."

"Are you serious? Gabe is going to be installing those after this storm. I think he's pissed he didn't think about state-of-the-art storm protection already. But it's not the wind that's the worst. It's the flooding. Why don't you come with us? Even if you're fine, you're gonna be without electricity for days. That's no fun. And Gabe said mandatory evacuations have started. You're not going to have a choice."

"This is America. There's always a choice." The wind whipped strands of hair into my eyes, and I struggled to pull it back into a clasp.

"Poppy, get away from her," Gabe shouted from his porch. His alarmed expression stirred nausea. Bile rose in my throat.

"Babe, what the fuck?" Poppy smiled, amused. Not understanding.

"Gabe, I can explain." But his stern expression warned me there would be no explaining. Another friend was about to be ripped from my life.

"No need to explain. News around here travels fast. Come on, Poppy. We have to go."

"Will someone please explain what the bloody Nora is happening here?"

Before I could say another word, Gabe pulled Poppy away, their bickering floating in the wind.

I jogged to Logan's house. The regular beats of my shoes on pavement kept my fraying insides intact. Other than the wind, there were no signs of an impending storm. The sky wasn't bright blue, but no signs indicated a monster storm hurled our way.

Nym greeted me at the unlocked door. "Poor buddy. I completely forgot about you. I'm so sorry. I've had the worst day." I opened the door wide so he could relieve himself. The blanket I'd used this morning remained thrown haphazardly across the sofa. I folded the blanket and picked up my dirty coffee cup. This morning, it was a different world. I'd been sad, mourning my mother, and my family, but by evening, it felt like a month had passed in one day. As sad as I had been in the morning, I'd had Logan, and that had been enough.

An intense, saturated pain pressurized my chest. "I love you, Logan."

Nym trotted up to my side, and I bent down and buried my face in his neck. When I rose, I could barely see through the tears, but I knew what I had to do.

CHAPTER 27

*L*ogan

TAMARA TAPPED LIGHTLY ON MY OFFICE DOOR, INTERRUPTING MY
meeting with Chad, the mayor.

"Last email's gone out. Last ferry is at noon today," Tamara
informed us. We'd been in full preparation mode for three days.
At this point, we'd battened down as much as possible, and few
residents remained.

"You'll be on it? Or are you getting out earlier?" Chad
asked her.

"I'm planning on catching the ten. I'm going to stay at my
sister's in Raleigh. They're saying it may hit as a four."

"Sounds good," Chad told her. "Thanks for all your help. Get
out of here and stay safe."

"When are you both leaving?" she asked.

Chad leaned back in the guest chair, stretching, so relaxed you'd think he was talking about his golf game. "Me and the missus will head out shortly. I'm going to take my boat over to dry storage, and then we're going out to visit my son in Chattanooga. I figure it'll be a mess here for a while. Where are you going?" He directed his question pointedly at me.

"Haven't decided."

"But you're getting out, right?"

I chugged on a bottle of water. I'd been up all night and hadn't made it home yet. I craved a toothbrush and a splash of water on my face. The damn beard itched like hell. When I got home, I couldn't wait to shave the thing off. I'd only been keeping the aggravating thing because a certain someone said she liked the way it felt on her thigh.

"Logan? You're not signing one of those waivers, are you?" Chad's question sounded more like a command.

"No." His question reminded me, though, of the form I needed to deliver to two residents who right now were refusing to leave the island. Butch Buchanan, an old, retired realtor, claimed he'd never evacuated and never would. Called mandatory evacuations bullshit. Then there was Alice Santera, an older woman on the island who fed all the stray cats. I had more concern for the elderly woman than I did for Butch. "But you just reminded me I need to take these forms around. After I make it home."

"Did the Coast Guard finish packing sandbags?"

"They finished about five a.m. We're in a good place. I need to make rounds one last time. Do you think you'd be able to convince Butch or Alice?"

"Those are our last two?"

"They both said they'd sign away rights." Under orders of

mandatory evacuation, if one stayed, they had to waive all rights to emergency assistance and essentially say they knew their lives were in danger. If they received emergency help, they would have to pay for it.

"Did you ask them for their social security numbers so you can ID the bodies? That worked in Virginia."

"No." I scratched my beard. My dry eyes ached. The last couple of days had been filled with boarding up windows, moving deck furniture, and even shoveling sand and building sandbag walls.

"You like you're about dead on your feet." Chad stood and pointed his index finger at Tamara, taking charge. "You, missy, you get out of here. We'll be in touch after it hits." She flashed a smile, waved, and exited the building. "And you," he swung the finger at my chest, "get home. Shower. I'll swing by and talk with Alice and Butch. I'll text you and let you know how it goes. Then you can do whatever you need to do, but I want you on that noon ferry. You got it?"

"Yes, sir."

"Your buddies are already out of here, right?" Chad hung back, watching me close my office. For whatever reason, I locked the door.

"Gabe and Poppy flew out two days ago. Tate and Luna sailed north. I think he plans on docking in Annapolis."

"He's banking on the storm not heading up the coast, huh?"

"Well, aren't they saying it's going to head inland?"

"You're new here. If you'd been around long enough, you'd know those weather people don't know shit."

"Yeah." I'd been hearing that for days, but it certainly seemed to me the monster storm on the radar screen was headed this way.

"You hear from your girlfriend?"

Robert and Samuel entered the building, and I used the opportunity to duck Chad's question.

"Hey, guys. Last ferry at noon."

"We're aware." Of course they were.

"We stopped by your place and boarded up the windows. But now we need to get back on the mainland. We've got our own homes to get prepped."

"You both go. Stay safe. And thanks for everything." They'd worked through the night.

"Did you decide where you're going to hunker down?" Samuel asked me.

"Not yet. I'll probably get in my car and drive west. I want to be close enough that I can come back over after she hits."

Samuel nodded, and I got a whiff of his pungent body odor as he stepped closer.

"Well, don't push it. Traffic reports are bad right now." He held his hand out to shake, and it felt wrong. Final. I wanted to push his hand away but sucked it up and gave his hand a vigorous shake then patted him on his back.

"Any more from the FBI?" Samuel asked. He'd been smart enough to know he walked on tender territory, but he couldn't help but lodge a question every few hours. International crime. Right here. The sort of shit cops lived for. But not me. I felt sick.

"No news." And I didn't want to talk about it. "Let's get out of here. Good work, team. I think we're about as locked down as we can be. Chad, I'll be looking for your text."

Back at my house, my windows were indeed boarded up with plywood. I opened the back door, and the emptiness hit me first. The blanket Cali had been using was folded neatly.

The kitchen counter gleamed white. The coffee pot sat unused.

In my bedroom, I physically flinched at the row of empty hangers on the portion of the closet she'd been using. She'd moved everything out. The empty dog bed mocked me.

I brushed my face. Pulled out my shaving kit, took scissors to my beard. Then I foamed up and shaved off the dark bush. In the mirror, the clean skin shone whiter. I ran the shower hot until the steam fogged the mirror. The scalding water pounded my back, my face, my scalp. Exhaustion helped to mask the deep ache, but even in my sleep-deprived state, I recognized it for what it was—a mask.

When the water lost its heat, I ended the shower. A low-level throbbing emanated from behind my eyes, and my stomach churned, reminding me I'd had nothing but water and coffee. After getting dressed, I opened the refrigerator.

In stacked plastic containers, our leftover meals from the night before I discovered the truth about her rested next to a round wrapped tray of cinnamon buns. A note attached, in her handwriting, included cooking instructions. On the second shelf, a new oversized jar of grape jelly bore a yellow Post-it note. I lifted it.

"Don't forget to eat. Fresh bread and peanut butter are in the cabinet. Stay safe. I never meant to hurt you. I assume you know everything from Matt, but if you have any additional questions, please ask. I love you, always. Cali."

I balled up the note and tossed it in the trash.

Then I picked up the phone. No text from Chad yet. I hoped he could convince that stubborn old woman to get off the island. But if he couldn't, I planned on staying. I'd check on her before the storm hit and after. Same with Butch. Funny how all the people staying on the island and risking their necks were singles.

I pressed Matt's name and held the phone to my ear.

"Hey. Was wondering when I'd hear from you. You all evacuated?"

"Haven Island is cleared."

"You're staying?" I noted the tinge of disapproval.

"Yep."

"Is that safe?"

"We've got a lighthouse that's been here for almost two hundred years. I can hunker down. I'll be fine."

"Okay. Well, call me when it's over. Let me know you survived."

"Will do." Out of habit, I dragged my fingers across my now smooth skin. "So, did you end up pressing charges?" I had no need to ask, but curiosity prevailed.

"No. She's been assisting us."

"Did she ask for immunity?"

"No. Hasn't even asked for a lawyer."

"What?"

"She handed over her phone, computers, servers. Everything. I know you're pissed at her, but from what I can tell, she hasn't done anything wrong. At least, from a legal perspective. And, yeah, she knew some of what her brother was up to, but I think he kept her mostly in the dark. Probably for her own safety. She looked pretty broken when I last saw her. You may want to check up on her."

"She's probably on her way back to Seattle."

"No. She told me she'd be on Haven Island if I needed her."

"Are you tracking her?"

"No. NSA doesn't have authority to monitor US citizens on US soil. You know that. Besides, she gave me her phones."

"Oh, man. She's probably out of the country by now." *How'd they screw this one up so bad?*

"Maybe. But I don't think so."

"You screwed up. You should've filed charges. Kept her in custody."

"For what? We have nothing to charge her with."

My addled brain didn't fully process his statement. Exhaustion smothered logical thought processes. Maybe she had broken no specific outdated US laws, but she'd lied to me.

For the hell of it, I jumped on the department's ATV and roamed the beaches one last time. The waves had grown, and whitecaps dotted the deep blue across the horizon. The wind had stalled, and the horizon held a foreboding dark hue. However, if you looked to the mainland, the sky shone blue. The dichotomy struck me as eerie. There were no birds, seagulls, pelicans, anything, as far as the eye could see. Silence and suffocating humidity prevailed. Under the blanket of heavy, still heat, I found it hard to breathe.

All the ocean homes had either been boarded up or had metal shutters pulled down. Many of the homes had sandbags around the basement level, but they had built the vast majority of these homes with hurricanes in mind. It was why many of these homes were built on pilings and living areas were almost always on the second floor. Some homes had nothing but parking and a stairwell on the ground floor. They prepared these homes for the incoming tide.

My thumb slipped on the accelerator as I passed Cali's home. All the pots of plants that decorated the stairs were gone. They had pulled metal shutters down on all the windows and doors. The place looked secure. Matt had mentioned she had a safe room hidden behind a bookshelf. I stared at the house, searching for signs of life. She'd still have Nym with her, and he'd need to go for a walk, so the fact even the doors were locked up meant she had evacuated. Like I told Matt, he'd probably screwed up by letting her roam free.

My phone rang, and I answered it as I pressed the accelerator.

"We got Butch to come with us. No luck with Alice. She's worried about those cats."

"I'll see what I can do."

"Try the social security number trick on her."

"Will do."

"If you can get her to the marina by eleven, she can ride over with us."

"And then where is she gonna stay? I'm not sure she even has a car on the mainland side."

"That's the problem, isn't it? Butch is riding with us now to Tennessee. Turns out he has a cousin near Chattanooga. And I had to promise him we wouldn't stay more than a week."

"I don't think the prospect of hanging out in the Wilmington Y is going to appeal to Alice."

"It's more appealing than death."

"Maybe to some," I mumbled.

When I arrived at Alice's, I parked in front and scouted her yard. Her home was against the marsh and would be protected by the low-lying trees. But the tide was rising. Chances were her first floor would take in water. Her house was up off the ground, but not a full story up. I pounded on her dark green door. The plantation shutters had been pulled closed, and I couldn't see inside at all.

I called Chad and reported back.

"Really? Well, maybe we talked some sense into her."

I doubted it. My gut told me she was upstairs, settled in with all her felines, and she just didn't feel like fighting with one more person about her decision to stay.

From the seat of the department's ATV, I watched the last ferry leave. The only people on board were the crew, and a handful of realtor management personnel who'd been busy until the last minute taking care of rental properties. I drove away without speaking to anyone, not wanting to deal with the hassle of answering questions about my choosing to stay.

I locked my doors, kicked off my boots, and crashed face first onto my mattress.

Hours later, a loud crash woke me. The pitch-black room unsettled me. I rubbed my face rapidly while listening to the howling wind outside. I made myself a peanut butter and jelly sandwich and ate it in the dark, listening. None of the digital clocks showed the time. We'd lost electricity.

The wind had grown strong, but I didn't hear rain yet. Alice probably sat in her home alone, too. If she and I were the only two on the island, it made sense we should weather the storm together. I pulled on a windbreaker and my boots, grabbed a flashlight and my phone, and headed out the door, back to the ATV.

I cut down the south side of the island, then through the middle. Pitch black enveloped the whole place. Not a star in the sky. The only light source came from my single headlight. The wind had grown to an almost deafening level.

As I cut across the middle of the island, for no reason in particular, it occurred to me I hadn't been down business row. The back alley held the sewage entrance for the island and the trash department. Plus, a few random businesses. I drove down the street, searching for any loose item, any forgotten chair or potted plant that would cause havoc tossed by the wind.

A narrow strip of light emanated from the bottom of a garage door. Curious, I drove to the light. The island lost electricity, so the light meant someone had a generator. The small metal building didn't have a business sign I could see.

I knocked on the door. The wind whipped around the corner of the building. Chances were someone just left a light on. But why would this area of the island still have electricity? The high winds blew sticks and dried leaves around. The crickets and frogs had gone silent. The door with the ray of light bothered me. My gut said something wasn't right.

I pounded on the door. I shone the flashlight over it. Three deadbolts. There would be no breaking this door down. I tugged on the garage door handle. I strained, lifting from my lower core. Light rain struck my face and back. The outer bands of the storm had arrived.

I returned to the door and pounded both fists, releasing all the rage and frustration and pain from the last several days. It was as if a dam had released, and as the skies opened up, so did I.

The door opened as my fist crashed onto it, and I stumbled forward, right into a blinding yellow light.

ali

"LOGAN?" HE SHIELDED HIS EYES WITH HIS HAND. THE WIND whipped. Leaves rustled. On the ground at his feet, sporadic raindrops darkened the concrete lip that extended out from the building to the ground. Nym whimpered.

Logan pushed his way inside, and I closed the door on the storm. The low Jack Johnson melody playing filtered down the stairs.

"What the hell are you doing here?" I blinked, taken aback by his vitriol. A vein protruded from his neck. He scowled.

"Riding out the storm. I figured it would be safer here than in an oceanfront home."

"There's a Cat 4 hurricane barreling down on us. Mandatory evacuations. I'll ask one more time. What the hell are you doing here?"

The yelling struck me as completely uncalled for. But my gaze fell. I waffled on my socked feet. He'd made his feelings clear. Why did he care if I stayed?

"Is it against the law for me to be here?"

"Technically, yes. I could fine you. Have you not been listening to the news?"

"I've had a few other things going on these past few days." As he well knew.

"I thought you'd go to Seattle." *Why? To see family I don't have there?*

"This building is secure. I'll be fine." I placed my hand on the doorknob. His hands rested on his hips. He continued that scowling thing. "Why are you here?"

Logan pinched his nose and closed his eyes. I had the distinct impression he struggled to get his emotions under control—his anger under control. A ghostly pale color shone on his freshly shaved skin, noticeably lighter than the skin on his forehead or his arms.

"You shaved your beard. It looks good."

His fingers shifted up from his nose to his forehead where he massaged. He huffed.

"You said you liked the beard. So I shaved it."

Ah, so that's the way it is. I swung the door open. Nym ventured out into the darkness, tail halfway between his legs.

"Well, you can stop back by later and arrest me. Or fine me. Or whatever you do." Dirt from the bottom of his boots littered the once spotless concrete floor.

"I can't leave you here. Did you hear me? There's a hurricane coming."

"Well, why is it okay for you to be here?"

He scratched his jaw. Exhaustion haunted his face, and the

look he gave me said he just wanted the day to end. He gritted his teeth, stepped into the doorway, and shouted for Nym. The dog trotted back inside, his snout extended, sniffing.

"What is this place?" He circled the downstairs area. "A garage?"

It looked like it. I parked my golf cart on the concrete pad. I didn't use the downstairs area. Upstairs was a fully livable office, bathroom, and where the servers had been housed.

"This is my office. The building is reinforced metal. No windows. I figured it's as safe as anything."

He pointed at the garage door as he scanned the ceiling. "Where's the button to open that?"

I pointed to the large white square directly beside the entrance door he'd come through.

"Why? Is that illegal?"

"Funny." He pressed the button and the heavy door slowly lifted.

"What are you doing?" I called out to his retreating back. He slung a leg over an ATV. The headlight flicked on, lighting up a large swatch of street, and then rolled the vehicle into the spot beside my cart. Wind blew from outside, through the downstairs. A couple of stray leaves flew in. The rain outside had picked up, and the wind cast it indoors. I smashed the button to close the garage door as Logan turned the ignition off.

"What are you doing?" I asked again, although it looked somewhat obvious what he planned on doing.

"To my knowledge, you're the only resident still on the island. I'm doing my job. I'm protecting you."

"From a storm?"

He bent down and scratched behind Nym's ear. The dog's tail wagged. When he spoke, he spoke to my dog.

"I'm not leaving you alone. I can't believe you stayed. Stupid."

"I'm not asking for public services. I'll be fine."

"What do you have upstairs?"

"How did you find me?" Frustration rose. He wouldn't answer my questions. He barged in. He'd made his feelings about me clear. He'd never forgive me for lying. I got that. He'd been lied to before, and he had this black and white view of the world. I now resided in the black quadrant.

"I saw a light. Doing one last tour of the island before locking down for the night. I was about to walk away when you opened the door."

"Is it too late for you to make it over to the mainland?" He owned a small boat. It would be a rough ride across the inlet, but I had to believe he could still make it across.

"How do you have electricity? A generator?"

"Yes."

"Can you get a news station?"

"I have internet here. I've been watching online."

"Can I have a look?" The vein on his throat no longer pulsed. A semblance of the Logan I knew had returned. And, if we were indeed the only two humans left on the island, I supposed I'd rather the two of us ride it out together. Without saying a word, I climbed the stairs.

Nym trotted past me, leading the way. I'd already prepared the place for a long night in. The pullout sofa had pillows and a thick comforter over it, and my old laptop lay open where I'd left it when I'd heard pounding downstairs. The laptop was from my grad school days, a first-generation MacBook Air. I'd given the laptops I used for work over to Matt. He'd promised to return them, but I wasn't holding my breath for a speedy return. He'd also taken my trusted BlackBerry Classic, which had served as my primary communication tool to Erik, and my personal iPhone with my address book. Even if I dug up an old phone, I couldn't remember anyone's phone numbers. With my ancient computer, I had used the iMessage app to text both Poppy and Luna. Poppy hadn't returned my text, but Luna had. Apparently, Tate had yet to tell her to stay away from me. He'd actually texted me separately and told me to stay strong, that he hadn't heard details, but he and Luna would be here for me.

Logan took off his coat and hung it on the back of one of the two chairs at the round table.

"You've got a nice setup here." He stared at the empty wire cages lined against one wall. His sarcasm didn't go over my head.

"They used to hold servers."

"NSA confiscated them?"

"No. I offered them. I'm not sure if the FBI or the NSA took them."

"Why do you sound so sad about that?"

I stared up in the rafters. I knew a camera resided in the corner, and everything I said was most likely being watched and recorded by my brother or someone on his team.

"I love my brother. I may not agree with everything he was doing, but I love him." Logan sat in the chair, much like the NSA and FBI had during my hours of interrogation. I crossed my legs and pulled a pillow onto my lap. The silence between us weighed the air down. I loved Logan too, and I wanted so much to crawl over to him and beg forgiveness. But there was a coldness to his gaze that held me at bay. I'd always known, on some level, that he'd never forgive me if he found out I'd lied to him. I suspected he could forgive me for protecting my brother. But lying to him about my divorce, about something so personal to him, that was where I'd severed our relationship.

"What exactly was your brother doing?"

"Matt didn't tell you?"

"I want to hear it from you. More specifically, I want to hear what you believed he was doing." He leaned forward and rested his forearms on his thighs, waiting.

"Years ago, I suspected he'd gotten in over his head. He became obsessed with pro-democracy, freedom of the Internet kind of movements. When we were kids, he obsessed over games. He then discovered hacking…which is kind of like a game." Most people didn't understand that, but that was what it was. A challenge. Or that was how it started. His harsh exterior softened, and I endeavored to help Logan understand. "You build your skill level. You tackle increasingly complex challenges. He found other like-minded people. It's almost like a club. We grew apart. I really didn't know the extent of what he was involved in."

"But at some point, you did?"

"There had been signs. But I didn't fully get it. Not until one day about a year ago. He showed up. Frantic. He believed I was in danger. I wanted to go to the cops, but he said it wouldn't work. They couldn't do anything. Couldn't be trusted. He promised me he just needed me to be safe. And he and a few others were going to break apart the company. He never told me details. For my safety. And he promised he was close to putting it all behind him."

"Did you plan to ever tell me?" *Seriously?*

"No. Logan, you're a cop. How could I? Even believing Erik

was trying to do the right thing, it didn't mean he didn't break the law at some point. He has no regard for the law."

"Why did he move you out here?"

"I picked the location. Apparently, a former partner discovered he had been undermining some of their plans. He hired an assassin. Killed a colleague's girlfriend. Erik doesn't have a girlfriend. He was convinced I was next."

"And you couldn't go to the police because…?"

"He also said that the US government would arrest him for certain things he'd done. He told me that individuals within the Chinese government were trying to find him. And the Russians. He didn't want me to become a pawn, taken by either side. He promised me he'd be done soon. It would all be behind us soon."

Outside, a sharp wail screeched.

"You didn't hire a lawyer?" He drilled me with his gaze. Anger remained, but something else too.

"I didn't need a lawyer. I didn't do anything wrong." Of course, if they'd charged me with something, I would've hired one. I wouldn't have been like Logan and gone through a divorce without hiring legal assistance. An almost human howl filled the room.

"Wind's picking up." He sat up straight and studied the roofline.

"I have food and water in that closet right there. Nothing fancy, but we should be good for at least a week. If it floods downstairs, we'll be fine. The water's not going to rise to the second floor. But if it does, that ladder leads to a roof access."

"It's better than my plan to climb inside the lighthouse. Although I've heard others have ridden out hurricanes inside it. It can be our backup plan."

"There are a lot of spiderwebs in there." But the walls were incredibly thick. I didn't say anything else about the lighthouse. Logan didn't care about spiders.

The silence between us weighed heavily. We'd had something great, and I destroyed it.

"Do you want some water? Wine?"

"You packed wine?"

"I figured why not."

"I'm good." He scrubbed his face with his hand. "Actually, I'd been on my way to check on Alice. I went by earlier, and it looked like she wasn't home. But I worried she was pulling what you're pulling—hiding out."

"Luna and Jasmine asked me to check on her. She promised me she was leaving on a ferry. She had all of her cats trapped upstairs with a month's supply of dry food."

"Good. I wonder why she didn't tell Chad she was leaving."

"When did Chad go by? I saw her about an hour before the last ferry. I think Jasmine had more to do with convincing her to leave than anyone. It's important to have someone." I trailed off as my words spun through me. If my mom were alive, she would've begged me to get to safety. And I would've done so. I hadn't heard a word from my brother or dad, not since Erik called, warning me they were on the way to pick me up. I wondered...did Erik see me offer everything up willingly? In the course of a couple of weeks, had I lost my entire family?

"Why do you look so sad?" He remained in his interrogation pose, legs wide, a false casual stance.

"Just thinking. I'm going to lie down and rest. Make yourself at home." I lifted the laptop and carried it over to him. "You can get Internet from here. There are pretty good components in the roof. We should have access for a lot of the storm. Maybe."

I lay down on my side. A coldness settled across the room,

and I wrapped myself in a comforter. He remained in his sitting position, hands resting on his thighs. His icy stare weighed on me, even when I closed my eyelids. The weight of his anger prevented rest. Too many things remained unsaid.

"I'm sorry I lied to you. When I said I was divorced, it had nothing to do with you. And I tried my best to never repeat that lie to you. What I felt for you was real. Very real. But I know you can't forgive me. As you said, you've dedicated your life to catching bad guys. And now, in your eyes, I'm a bad guy. So is my brother." The stony gaze remained frigid, to the point I wasn't certain he heard me. The rain on the metal roof above drummed out a constant hammering beat. But I'd developed a habit of talking to my dog, of talking to no one, and I continued.

"I understand why you believe my brother is a criminal. I can see your point of view. He's bad in that he's spreading false information and trying to make our country less stable. And he's broken laws. I believe that someone in his company, or in his group, has become enamored with money. And I suspect they use causes to justify their actions. My brother is not greedy. He's not evil. He's just… Unlike you, I believe in gray. I believe we live in a world with hundreds of shades of gray. No matter how much you want to believe in black and white, right and wrong, there are shades."

"Are you certain you don't live in the dark?"

My first response, *how can you ever be certain*, sounded too hollow and pointless. I raised my gaze and met his cold one head-on.

"I am a good person. I make mistakes, but I do things I believe are good. Good for others, for my family, for our country. I'm a humanist. No matter what you think…" I choked on rising emotion and swallowed. "I've promised to be as helpful as I can to your friend. To our country."

I closed my eyes. I hated his judgement. I wished he'd never found me. I'd prefer to ride out the storm alone with Nym.

"I want to hate you."

"I know." I lied to him. After Bethany, to him, it was an unforgivable sin. As I got to know him, I'd realized that. And I still lied. But I couldn't change what I had done. And if I had to do it over, I couldn't honestly say I'd do anything differently.

A loud thud crashed against the side of the building. Probably a tree limb. I opened my eyes. Logan kneeled on the floor before me, his face inches away, his eyes so dark the pupil blended with the iris.

CHAPTER 29

ogan

I trailed my fingers along the side of her face, over the rim of her cheekbone and down to her lips. My breathing quickened, riled by her proximity. The wind outside hissed as it whipped around the corners of the building.

"Why are you here?"

Her question struck me as odd. From the moment I discovered she was still here, there was no question in my mind about where I would be. Before, I didn't particularly care what happened to me—perhaps one reason I never evacuated. But the moment I discovered her, she became my priority.

"I destroyed us. I get it. Just go."

"I can't." If she pressed, asking why, I'd blame it on the job.

"Do you want to…hurt me?"

She inched away. Fuck. I didn't mean to scare her.

"I could never hurt you. I want to protect you. My anger, my hurt. It doesn't change that I love you." No matter how much I might want to hate her, I couldn't.

"My brother is still a criminal. He's wanted by the FBI. And countless others. You can't be with me. You made that clear."

"Yes. You lied."

"And now you know the truth."

"And I'm angry. Pissed as hell." The trouble with anger was that it sometimes needed a physical release. I'd tried to pound it out hammering wood over windows and heaving sandbags, but it still sat in my chest, as corrosive as the salt air. "We had a good thing."

Silence reigned between us. My thumb brushed her soft skin, outlining her angular cheekbone. All that anger didn't eliminate a much more powerful emotion. "I love you."

"But not enough." Her whisper cracked my chest open. Was she right?

I traced her soft lips, back and forth. My thumb slipped into her mouth, and her lips closed on the end, and her upper teeth scraped.

"You should go." The storm outside howled, covering her quiet words.

"No." I closed my eyes and inhaled. Her familiar shampoo, rosemary and eucalyptus. My heart hammered away, beating away reason. Smashing logic to smithereens.

I wasn't sure if she kissed me first or if I crashed down on her, but I covered her body with mine and captured her mouth with a hungry urgency. The pounding rain and raging storm intensified the chaos in my head and chest.

She tugged on my shirt. I sent hers flying, then her bra,

while she worked on my zipper. Our breathing was ragged and heavy when I paused, taking her in, in white silk panties and nothing else. Her long, lean thighs and her smooth, light olive skin. I fell over her, finding my place between her legs. Her palm flattened on my chest and pressed.

"Lights. Off," she demanded.

I'd gladly give her darkness if it meant I could have her. For now. Total blackness fell over the room.

"This what you want?"

"Yeah. If there are cameras... I'd rather what happens between us remain private."

I stumbled, tripping over the edge of a rug, arm out as I retraced my steps. My knee hit the fold-out bed first, and I felt my way along the rumpled comforter, crawling my way back up to her.

"Cameras. Your brother?"

"Well, I let a swarm of agents up here. We could have teams of people watching, for all I know. Or listening."

I trailed kisses down her neck to her breasts.

"Well, if someone's listening, we should give them a show." I twirled my tongue around her nipple, then clamped my teeth around the bud.

Her fingers scratched my scalp, and I scraped my smooth jaw between her breasts until she squirmed.

"Just so you know, I haven't broken any laws."

I kissed the hollow between her breasts.

"I'm sure you have. Were you the one managing the servers?"

"Yes." Her legs wrapped around me, and I pressed against her. I wanted inside her. My cock throbbed with need.

"I'm sure you broke the law." I nuzzled below her ear.

"Probably many laws." I heard her intake of air, felt her muscles tense. "And your brother is a criminal." I raised up on my arms. "Doesn't mean we can't fuck."

I settled between her legs, the tip of my iron-hard erection inches from her core. And I kissed her. Her fingernails scratched my back, and her thighs wrapped around me, inching me closer.

The pounding of rain on top of the metal roof hit a crescendo, overpowering all other sounds. Inside her compound, need raged. I explored the familiar curves I'd missed. My tongue teased her nipple, and I sucked and bit, lavishing attention on both of her small, perfect breasts. Her fingers reached between us and wrapped around my cock. Her thumb coaxed the tip, smearing the pre-cum. The pressure on the base of my spine intensified.

I tasted my way down her body. Her thighs fell to my shoulders. In the dark, we were shadows. She rested back on her elbows, watching. I dipped my tongue, and she whimpered. Her fingers guided my head, directing, begging. I slipped a finger inside, and her thighs jerked. I worked her with my tongue and fingers until she pushed up, quivering and chanting and shouting.

So fucking sweet. I loved her taste, her feel, her smell, and most of all I loved how good it fucking felt to ease my hips into the cradle of hers. My hardness rubbed against her dripping wet sex, and she shuddered. She gripped my ass and tugged.

"Please. Logan. Please."

My lips found hers as I thrust into her. Our tongues matched the pace of our hips. Slow at first, as she stretched around me, tight, warm, and wet. God, she was heaven. My body craved hers. So arousing, so perfect.

"You feel insanely good. So tight." I lifted her knee higher, raising her ass off the mattress, driving home deeper, taking her harder. The storm outside roared as her sounds became louder, as if she was in a competition with the world outside. Panting. Groaning. "Yes—right there—fuck."

I thrust hard, my rhythm in concert with the hurricane. She shuddered beneath me and whimpered.

I flipped her around on the bed like a rag doll, experimenting with positions, determining what felt best not by her facial expressions, which I couldn't see, but by the strength of her moans, the feel of her muscles and how tight her channel gripped my cock.

I worked her mound with my palm as I slammed into her. Sweat dripped down my temple, my muscles trembled, my lower back tensed. Then she pulsed around me as she shrieked, and my groin tightened, and my thrusts became erratic as ecstasy rolled between us.

I collapsed onto her, incapable of movement. My heartrate slowed as I gasped for breath.

The wind outside had picked up into a freight train chorus. A crash against the side of the building sent Nym to our side. I patted the bed, making room at our feet for the dog to join us, and pulled her naked body to my side, nestling us under the covers.

The battering on the roof had grown so loud it sounded like the roof might crash down or a tree might come through the wall. She caressed my jaw. She might like the beard, but I liked feeling the pads of her fingers against my skin. I loved her naked body against mine. I'd missed her so fucking much. But I didn't love every single thing about her.

"Are we okay?" Her tentative question spelled out our reality.

"I'm still angry." The weight of her head shifted against my chest, and I clamped an arm around her, holding her in place. "But I'm more angry at myself. I didn't listen to my gut. You even switched phones, and I didn't catch it."

"What do you mean?"

"You had a BlackBerry. Then suddenly you had an iPhone."

"Yeah. But I figured you'd think the BlackBerry was for work."

"It was for Erik. Right?"

"He thinks it's the least likely to be hacked. He was the only one who called me on it. Always with a burner."

"He used a burner phone, and you didn't stop to think he wasn't up to no good?" Irritation subtly displaced utter bliss.

"I knew he'd gotten in over his head. But I know him. I trusted he'd dig himself out."

"And you named your dogs after hackers." I scratched my head. I wasn't up on the hacking world, so I refused to beat myself up for missing that one.

"They are?" I chuckled at the surprise in her question.

"Did you not name 'em?"

"No. I figured they were from some action movie. All of Erik's avatars are named after movie characters." I made a mental note to mention this to Matt, but they'd probably already figured that out if his online aliases followed the same naming methodology.

"Can you promise me something?"

"What?"

"No more lies? Moving forward? Or will you have this allegiance to your brother…"

She raised up on her forearms, and the bone of her arm protruded into my chest. It hurt, but not enough for me to shift out from under her. In the dark, I could barely see those eyes, but more than anything, I needed to hear her.

"I promise. No more lies. I can't tell you I won't try to protect him or help him, but I'll tell you if I do."

"That's all I ask." She settled back down onto my chest. I pressed my lips to her temple. I had thought I could walk away. Turn my back on her. Cast my judgement. I buried my nose into her hair, breathing her in, holding on to her as if she were my lifeline. "I'm never letting you go."

"I can't change Erik. I have no influence on him."

"You're right. And given I'm in law enforcement, he's hardly ideal family. But here's the thing. You deserve someone who can give you children. And I can't seem to do that. Yet you didn't bat an eye at being with me. Our future won't be Christmas card perfect, but it's the only future I want."

ali

The storm passed, as storms did.

The quiet woke us from a restless sleep. We ventured downstairs and out the door into an eerie darkness. Hands linked, our vision adapted. The rays of the first light cracked through the trees. A chorus of toads and crickets rose to a staccato. Nym trotted around, tail wagging, exploring the wasteland.

A glimmer of light filtered through the trees. Daybreak transformed the dark to light.

"First light." Logan pointed through the trees. "In the military, it's what we call it. Been a while since I've been up for it."

Murky, brown water skimmed the lower lying paved street in front of the building. Toppled trees littered the pavement and all through the woods. The golf cart wouldn't have been able to make it far, but the department's ATV could successfully ramble over the carnage.

"I've had this song running through my head all through the night."

"Oh, yeah?" We stood outside as, minute by minute, our surrounding grew lighter. I kept an eye out for snakes, knowing many might be displaced. He nudged me, waiting for me to continue.

"Bob Marley's song. My mom used to sing it all the time. She'd belt it out, singing "Every Little Thing's Gonna Be Alright." I tapped his chest to the beat. "This. Is. My. Message. To. You."

A giggle escaped as he lifted me and twirled me around as if I were as light as I felt, completely weightless. I would've been more than content to go back inside and spend a leisurely morning in bed, but Logan was fueled by an internal need to survey Hurricane Melba's damage.

After we completed a loop, in some areas wading through water one to two feet deep, Logan reported back to Chad. The club's swimming pools were now murky brown, fences blown over, some homes had roof and siding damage. Dark water swirled in ponds and lakes where dry land formerly stood. Sand covered much of the asphalt near the ocean.

Logan fielded a flurry of inquiries from homeowners and friends who got word he was on the island and could check on their homes.

I attempted to call my father and my brother. Neither picked up. I considered tapping out our old childhood code, but the reality was, if the NSA monitored my texts, they'd figure it out. Our number coding qualified as extraordinarily basic. Each number represented a letter in the English alphabet, only we'd reversed it, so the letter one equaled Z. We'd done it since we were kids. In retrospect, maybe our affinity for a secret language foreshadowed our future. So, skipping the code, I texted my dad through my iMessage app.

All safe. Storm passed. I love you both.

Logan's house survived relatively unscathed. Random sticks and debris scattered throughout his yard and over parts of the street through his neighborhood. The white clapboard needed a fresh paint job after the wrath of Melba, but other than that, his house stood solid. They had built his home in a section that rose high enough, and remained inland enough, he had no flooding.

We parked the ATV, mindful of preserving gasoline, and walked the short distance to my house. The structure itself remained undamaged, probably because of the high-end metal shutters that covered all windows and doors. But a significant portion of the beach had been washed away, and the bulk of the wooden boardwalk extending from my house out to the ocean had been ripped away. The edge of the boardwalk eerily hung over the sand with about a five-foot drop. A passerby might assume someone had just stopped building the boardwalk halfway out over the dunes.

Logan helped me roll up the metal shutters. The island had no electricity or running water, and we expected it wouldn't for quite some time. Reports from the mainland coming in indicated Southport and other towns along the coast had been hit hard and were also without electricity. Those more populated areas would be higher priority. I packed up my rubber rain boots, lots of old shorts and t-shirts I wouldn't mind ruining, and everything I needed for Nym, and we carried it all back to Logan's.

"It feels surreal, doesn't it?" I asked as we lugged my stuff back to his place, taking breaks along the black asphalt road to rest our hands. "We're the only humans in an evacuated town."

"We should make the most of it." He grinned.

When we arrived back at his place, slightly sweaty from hauling the bags, I asked, "So, where do we start?"

He picked me up, my legs circling his waist, and carried me to his bedroom, where he kicked the door closed and promptly dropped me onto the bed.

"Don't we have things to do?"

"The list is endless. Residents will probably start returning tomorrow. Sure, we can get a head start on clearing the paths, but Chad is sending backhoes that will be far more efficient. And today? It's only us."

CHAPTER 31

$\mathcal{L}$ ogan
    6 weeks later

THE BACKHOE'S ENGINE ROARED OVER THE PEACEFUL HUM OF THE ocean's waves. I waved a sweaty, gloved hand in the air, letting the driver know I'd looped the chain around the tree, so he could reverse and drag it into a more manageable location. Island clean-up had been going on full steam for over two weeks. The streets were clear of debris and fallen trees. Electricity had returned, and with it, sewage. The ferry wouldn't be running for a while yet, but residents with private means of getting across were trickling in.

Only a handful of families had returned when we didn't have electricity. We'd gather most evenings and grill food on a charcoal grill, not too differently than we imagined the generator society had done. Chad had told me about the group in one of our phone calls. He said nineteen families moved out here in 1970. They thought they'd have electricity by 1972. Electricity didn't reach the island until 1980. Whenever someone would get particularly frustrated about the slow restoration of electricity, a frustrated comment would undoubtedly be met with something along the lines of, "If the generator society survived, we can too."

I checked the time and climbed on my ATV to pick up Matt. He'd texted that he needed to visit. Cali and Luna had gone over to the mainland to do a big grocery shop, since none of the stores or restaurants on Haven had reopened. I hadn't mentioned his visit to Cali, more because I hadn't wanted to concern her. But that didn't mean I wasn't concerned. Although, if he needed Cali to be here, he would've told me. The last we talked, the FBI didn't plan to press charges against her. He arrived alone, driving what I assumed was a rented boat.

"Hey. Where'd you get this boat?"

"The marina owner across the way."

"Mac?" I'd driven a few boats that way before the hurricane on behalf of owners seeking dry dock storage.

"Yeah, he didn't have time to drive me over but offered to let me take his boat."

"You flashed him your badge, didn't you?"

He grinned. "That's why we have badges."

I helped him tie up, and he jumped off the boat onto the dock.

"What brings you out here?"

"I have a proposition."

"I'm listening." The sun shone into his eyes, and he held up a hand to combat the glare. "You want to go over to the shade, over there?"

The Wisp, my favorite little hangout overlooking the marina, remained closed and shuttered, but their built-in picnic tables had survived the storm. He pointed at them. I led the way with Matt two steps behind me.

"Should I be nervous?" I asked over my shoulder.

"No."

We sat down across from each other. The low hum of engines sounded in the distance, along with the revving of a chainsaw.

"I want you to come work with us. In DC."

"You couldn't call me and ask?" The only reason he'd insist on seeing me in person, especially when we were in clean-up mode, was if he didn't want to be overheard.

"Well, it's more impactful in person. But, if you agree, I have more to tell you."

I scratched my jaw. I'd grown the beard back. Mainly because we went so long without running water. And, well, she liked it.

"There are several positions within NSA that I think could be a good fit. This out here, it's not a good use of your expertise and skill set. It was only meant to give you a chance to regroup." What he meant was he'd expected this assignment would be temporary while I gathered my emotions, licked my wounds, and learned to control my anger.

"You going to bring me through it all out here?" I slapped a tiny biting insect on my neck.

"No. I want you to come to DC. You'll meet with my boss, several of the groups. Talk with them. But it'll be a chance for us to work together."

"I'm open to it, but I can't give you an affirmative without knowing specifics, and I need to talk to Cali."

"Everything still good with you two?"

"As good as it gets." I looked him directly in the eye. She didn't have a ring on her finger, but he needed to know that while I'd backed away earlier, no matter what he said, I wasn't backing away now.

"There could be positions for her."

"She's happy doing translations." We'd talked enough about plans that I knew she was itching to make progress on some of her projects. And I didn't want him bringing her into anything that might be remotely dangerous. I didn't doubt the CIA would snap her up in a heartbeat.

"Well, that's fine. You're not the only person who wants to keep her out of the line of fire."

I leaned forward across the wooden table, urging him to explain that statement. He glanced left and right and looked over his shoulder. Satisfied no one lurked nearby, he said, "We've recruited Erik."

"Really?"

"He came to me. He's got a team ready and willing. He's serious about taking down Spectre, but he's decided he can't do it on his own."

"He hasn't been in touch with her since you interrogated her. At least, that's what she's told me." And I believed her. "She doesn't think she's going to hear from him. She feels like her dad and Erik have both written her off."

"He's convinced he has to play it this way. He says too many people know who he is now. He thinks she's safest if he remains out of touch. He's wicked good at multiple identities. You'd think he trained with us."

"I'll need to tell her this."

"I know. Be careful. Tell her outside. Before too many people are back on the island."

"She's back at the house now. Do you want to see her?"

"No. I promised Erik I'd stay away from her. He recognizes she'd make an ideal recruit, but he swears too many others are aware of her. I don't know if he's right about that. But I can tell you one thing—he loves his sister. And he's a connected man. Word of advice, treat her right."

When I returned home, the cool air from the now functioning air conditioning wrapped around me the second I opened my door. Nym stood two feet away, alert, tail wagging.

"Cali? You home?" Brown paper bags lined up along the counter, and empty oversized reusable bags scattered across the floor.

"Hey," she called from upstairs. We hardly ever went upstairs, as our living area and bedroom were down on the main floor. Her feet clattered down the wooden steps. "I'm using the guest room upstairs to store the bulky items. Does that work?"

"Sure." She stepped up to give me a hug, and I held an arm out to warn her away. "I need a shower."

My warning didn't stop her. She smacked her lips against mine and squeezed my ass.

"Here, I bought new shampoo and soap. Let me get the bathroom stuff unloaded, and then the shower's yours."

"You're in a good mood."

"I am. We had a great day. Before we went to Costco, we went into Wilmington. Did some shopping. Had lunch. Everything over there is like there was never a hurricane. Everything's open. Decked out in holiday decorations."

"Places will be opening here soon."

She hummed what sounded like disagreement as she carried an armful of products into our bedroom.

"Did you get everything you needed?"

"Yeah, we're set. We can handle Armageddon."

I swung the refrigerator door open and reveled in the blast of cold air. I picked up a bottle of water from the lower shelf. It wasn't cold yet, but it was cooler than room temperature, and I ripped off the top and chugged.

After scanning the contents of the remaining groceries and seeing there were no more bathroom-related items, I headed that way. Cali stood in front of her sink, holding a tampon box. Her eyes squinted, and she had the expression of someone doing math in her head.

"Everything okay?"

"I'm late." I barely heard the words, and my breath caught. Her cheeks held a subtle rose hue, barely discernible against her olive skin.

"How late?" She held a pink jumbo box of tampons, and below in the open cabinet, two additional boxes sat.

"Almost a month?"

My brain slowed. It didn't mean anything, did it? "Are you normally late?"

"Never."

"We were only apart for a few days…"

And we never really broke up, did we? During those days of hurricane prep I hadn't seen her at all…

"You're the only person I've been with in *years*." She emphasized the last word and gave me a look that snapped my brain back to the present. I'd believed something was wrong with my sperm, but I'd never been tested or even talked to a doctor.

"Really?"

She picked up the tampon boxes below the sink and stacked them on top of the others, as if presenting evidence. Her fingers trembled.

"Hey." I wrapped my fingers around her arm. "Come here."

Her dark eyes lifted, heavy with emotion, searching.

"*If* you're pregnant, I mean… I don't want to get hopes up. You could just be late. But if you are… I'm…how are you feeling about this?"

"It would be my fault." She spoke like she hadn't heard me, flustered. "I don't even know how. I was still on the pill, but I forgot a day here and there. It was so crazy—" I tugged on her chin, forcing her to look up.

"Hey. Listen to me. Cali, if you're pregnant…" I searched the ceiling for guidance on what to say so she'd understand. "I'll consider it a miracle."

She reached up to my jaw and ran her nails along the rough growth. I leaned into the welcome sensation.

"Me too." Those dark brown eyes glassed over. I recognized the emotion. It was a lot to take in. I lifted her up onto the bathroom counter and stepped between her legs.

And then I kissed her, long and slow. I didn't want her to have any doubt, not about us, or about the baby. When I broke the kiss, I reached out and ran my hand over her flat, tight stomach, in awe that my little baby might be growing inside. And god, I'd told her I couldn't do this.

"You sure you're okay?"

"I think so. Since you're okay with it, I'm thrilled. I mean, I always assumed I'd have a kid one day, but that day was way off in the future. And, you know, if we'd needed to…or if we end up needing to adopt, I'll be okay with it. I think what Luna and Tate did is amazing." Her hands fell over mine on her belly. "It's early. I haven't taken a test. Sometimes women just skip. And a lot's been going on…"

She lifted my hand, calloused and dirty from a day outside on clean-up duty, and slowly placed her lips on each of my knuckles. I recognized she might not be pregnant, but the sheer enormity of my hope that she was showed me how badly I did want to be a father—how badly I wanted to be a father to her children.

Those dark eyes grounded me, and her melodic words soothed. "Even if I'm not, we'll be all right."

EPILOGUE

9 months later
Logan

"How's he doing?" I tiptoed on the carpet in the nursery. My wife held our baby son, swaddled in her arms. She loved to hold him when he slept. Her gaze reflected all the love I felt. The kind of love that filled your insides to the point of bursting with warmth and everything good in the world.

I sat down on the ottoman in front of her rocking chair and lifted her feet into my lap. My thumb drove into the pad of her foot, and she moaned quietly. Everything we did, we did quietly, as we lived in perpetual fear of waking the baby. When he slept, we wouldn't even dare to turn on the television.

Our house in Virginia came wired for functionality with Siri or Alexa, and we disabled it. Cali wouldn't have anything in the house that might be used as a listening device. She insisted we turn our phones off at night, and our computers, and it was with great reluctance that she even agreed to a television. A TV that remained off almost all the time.

Although her reasons for the TV remaining off didn't have as much to do with fear of being watched as it did with the advice from one of her baby books to limit screen time. I told her she's the one in charge and that I'd do whatever she wanted. I didn't watch much television, anyway. Besides, I couldn't imagine anything better than watching my little newborn son. Every facial expression, every "oh" of the lips, if he crinkled his cheeks—it all floored me. And when he wrapped those tiny, frail fingers around my finger, too small to even wrap all the way around, every part of me became his.

Cali held her precious bundle out for me, and I lifted him from her arms and placed my lips ever so softly against his forehead. With great care, I positioned him in the crib. I held my breath, careful to not move too quickly, watching to see if he remained asleep.

Cali joined me, and I wrapped my arm around her as we both gazed down on our baby. Martin Dylan Callahan weighed in at a solid eighteen pounds now, and over ten pounds at birth. His name honored Cali's mother, as Martin had been her maiden name, and Cali believed Dylan bore a strong resemblance to her first name, Dahlia.

I didn't think I could ever love this much. Every day, it surprised me, the emotions that gushed out of me. Having a son didn't take away my love from my wife, but instead it somehow compounded. I'd die for either one of them, my wife or my son. But when I looked to the future, what I hoped for was decades by Cali's side.

She lifted the monitor from the counter and placed an index

finger over her lips, directing me to be silent. As if I needed the direction. You'd think our child had sonic hearing, the way we tiptoed around the house. When we reached the main floor of our home, she wrapped her arms around me, and I closed my eyes, soaking in all the warmth after having been at work all day.

She led me into the kitchen, and a large basket filled with onesies, blue balloons, and baby paraphernalia caught my eye.

"Who sent us that?"

She smiled her smile that told me she had a secret, and it made her happy. She placed a finger over her lips and led me out the door onto our porch.

"It's another gift from my dad. And he says he's going to come visit soon."

"I thought Erik said that wouldn't be a good idea?"

"I don't think he can keep my dad away from his grandson. Son trumps most things, but apparently grandson trumps more."

"Erik is allowing it?" In my new role within the NSA, I happened to get regular updates on her twin. And I ensured he was kept abreast of his sister, and now his nephew. Given how much I loved my wife and son, I appreciated Erik's hyper-protective stance.

"Kind of." She passed me a scroll. Grease smeared the corners and sections in the center. "This arrived via my DoorDash lunch order today."

"Did you even order lunch today?"

"No. But my dad sent me my favorite, Banh Mi."

Cantonese, an artform, covered the page. "What does it say?"

"He's hoping we'll take a long weekend to upstate New York. There's a cabin in the woods."

"He clearly knows everything your brother is doing." We'd debated how much her father knew over the last several months. "I mean, look at the precautions he's taken."

"He's a smart man. And yes, I think my brother has told him what's going on. Dad is planning on spending some time in the cabin, away from everything. Once Erik feels it's safe, he's planning on moving permanently to Virginia, so he'll be closer." She waffled the paper in the air. "He says Mom would want to be near her grandchildren, and he's uprooted anyway. He doesn't think Erik is going to be providing him any grandchildren in the short term."

"Have the two of you talked about Erik?"

"Not really. At some point, Erik must have come clean to him. Or wouldn't you think he'd be full of questions?"

Being a member of the NSA, I knew plenty. There were several organizations we monitored constantly, along with other countries. The Dark Web enabled a brave new world. One that required constant monitoring in an entirely different crime stratosphere. A world that made the organized crime and mafia syndicates from the seventies and eighties look like child's play.

My wife's connections to that world were too close for my comfort level. But I also knew her brother was now playing a key role in our battle for a safe cyberworld. He'd given us invaluable information over the last nine months. His newly formed covert black ops group also served to foster inter-agency communication amongst the FBI, NSA, CIA, and Homeland.

A neighbor waved from across the backyard fence, and I waved back. He picked up a large red ball and disappeared to the front of the house. Our neighbor's kids were toddlers, but they assured us Martin would be a playmate before we blinked. I couldn't help but hope they were wrong. I loved my little man and didn't want any of this to fly by. Although I did look forward to playing ball with him as he grew older.

"Are you good with us spending more time with Dad?"

"Cal, I don't have anything against your father. Nor your brother, but I'm beyond thankful he's being as cautious as he is. If something happened to you, or…" I trailed off because the idea was too painful. One day, Erik would return to the United States, and I suspected we'd see him when he did. And I braced for that inevitability.

"Nothing is going to happen. And even if it does, what do we always say?"

She smiled at me and hummed her mother's song.

The End

The journey continues in the *Twisted Vines* series. Read on for the beginning of *Crushed*, Erik's story.

CRUSHED PROLOGUE

rik

THE RED BULB IN THE CORNER OF THE ROOM FLARES. LIFE transitions to slow motion. The man on the security camera shatters the glass sliding door eight floors below. Dressed in black, he raises a suppressed semi-automatic pistol and steps over the shards of glass then out of the view of the back door security camera. He enters the view of the first-floor security camera. His stride shows purpose.

I pick up my phone and tap out an urgent text to my team.

UNDER ATTACK. GET OUT.

.   .   .

I SLIDE OPEN A DRAWER AND LIFT THE PISTOL I HOPED TO NEVER have to use. The security camera flashes the intruder on the second floor. I push a button on my phone, and the wall slides, exposing a ladder. With my phone in my mouth and the gun in my hand, I climb the cold metal bars to the room above. *Kill or be killed. The tao of Jiu Jitsu.* The click of the panel informs me my location is now secure.

Through the air vent, I watch the wall of monitors. The assassin continues up the flights of stairs without pause. He knows his destination. I steady my breath, and sweat beads on my brow. I swallow, and the sound reverberates through my head. *Focus. Nothing good comes from divided attention.*

The door to the security room opens. The man in black enters, gun in front and at the ready. One step. Two steps. His back to me as he watches the monitors.

I point my gun. Hold steady, same as at the shooting range. I aim for his chest, the largest area. My best chance. I breathe in. *Steady.* My finger pulls.

The loud gun kicks. The recall throws off my aim. A cloud of dust appears on the far wall. *Dammit.*

The intruder ducks, searching for the source.

Breathe. Steady.

He raises his gun toward my hideout. It's him or me.

Aim.

A cracking sound reverberates through the space. The sound is similar to a strong bullwhip.

The intruder falls back. My finger hovers on the trigger. I never pulled it. Trevor, a member of my team, stands framed in the doorway. His gun points at the man on the floor.

I press my phone, and the wall panel clicks.

I climb down and join Trevor. The intruder wears a

balaclava, the thin black mask preferred by the military and assassins.

"Who do you think he is?" Trevor asks me, or maybe the room. A trickle of blood leaks from the dark hole in the center of the assassin's forehead, darkening the fabric.

I gesture to the body on the floor. "You can do the honors."

He reaches for the mask and unceremoniously tugs hard enough the body half rises. With a sickening thud, the head falls back onto the floor. Trevor closes the eyelids with his thumb.

"You recognize him?" he asks.

"No."

Trevor places two fingers against his neck, I assume out of habit. Then he checks the front pockets and rolls him over. He lifts a single piece of paper from his back pocket and unfolds it. His eyes go wide as he turns it around for me to see.

A candid photo of our team. With addresses.

Fuck.

"He's a professional," Trevor says. "Kane found us."

"We've got to move. Now."

***

Read Erik's story in Crushed… Releasing January 2021!

Read Tate & Luna's story in Rogue Wave.

And Gabe & Poppy are in Adrift.

Thank you for reading!

NOTES & ACKNOWLEDGEMENTS

First Light has gone through massive reiterations. And the more I researched, the more aware I became of all the ransomware attacks in the world, and all the various forms of cybercrime.

Future Crimes by Marc Goodman provides a great overview of our new world, and perhaps more interestingly, the new age crime syndicates. Obviously, there's a tremendous amount of propaganda out there, often spread by fake accounts. A quick Google search shows that in the most recent reporting period, Facebook removed 1.3 BILLION fake accounts. That's with a B, folks. It's a constant purge. The software that I mention, that merges facial features from multiple people into one person— it's real, but not yet widespread.

Have you heard of that phenomenon where you decide you want a particular car, and then suddenly every car you see on the road is THAT kind of car? Well, when I started doing the research for *First Light*, I think that phenomenon occurred. Either that, or suddenly cybercrime began taking up every single news headline. When I started writing this, I felt like I was bordering sci-fi. Not so much. This is very much a contemporary work of fiction. Bottom line—be safe out there, kids.

All those massive iterations I mentioned on *First Light*? Well, the first draft was ROUGH. My developmental editor, Amy Claire Majers, ripped it apart (it needed to be decimated). And then I spent months re-structuring and editing. The story changed. And a heartfelt thank-you goes out to Amy for her honest and direct feedback.

My husband read this one too. He's a programmer, and while he's not a big gamer, technology is his world. And he provided sound insight. He's my rock, and I know he'd love to tell me to stop this crazy, time-intensive, anxiety-provoking little endeavor of mine, but he never fails to support me, and for this, I am eternally grateful.

My editor, Lori Whitwam, the keeper of all the words, refined, word-smithed, and fixed my grammar. Maybe one of these days she can stop correcting my comma usage and I'll finally learn how to correctly type the em-dash, but I'm so grateful for her patience until we arrive at that day. Jessica Meigs went through proofread and caught commas and errant words, because I swear, no matter how many times I read through a manuscript, there always seems to be one more error. Thank you, Jessica!

There were several Hidden Gems beta readers who read this before editing, and to them, thank you for overlooking the flaws, catching issues, and providing great insights.

Last, but most definitely not least, I'd like to thank my ARC readers. You guys rock, and I so much appreciate your volunteering to be on the team and then going out and sharing your reviews. You make all the difference when it releases out in the world.

Most of all, dear readers—THANK YOU! Thank you for picking up this book and giving it a chance. I love to hear from readers. You can contact me through my website at www.isabeljoliebooks.com and also sign up to find out when my next book will be available. Thanks again and again for your support!

ABOUT THE AUTHOR

Isabel Jolie, aka Izzy, lives on a lake, loves dogs of all stripes, and if she's not working, she can be found reading, often with a glass of wine in hand. In prior lives, Izzie worked in marketing and advertising, in a variety of industries, such as financial services, entertainment, and technology. In this life, she loves daydreaming and writing contemporary romances with real, flawed characters and inner strength.

Sign-up for Izzy's newsletter to keep up-to-date on new releases, promotions and giveaways. Or stalk her on your favorite platform. And no, she's not on TikTok. Her teen keeps telling her to stay away…

https://isabeljoliebooks.com/#newsletter